DILYS ROSE was born and brought u
been her home for many years. Previ
collections of short stories, *Lord o*
Pickpockets, Red Tides and *War D*
is a Dangerous Thing, Madame Do
and a novel, *Pest Maiden*. She has also written for stage and
collaborated with musicians and visual artists. Awards include
the first Macallan/Scotland on Sunday Short Story Prize, The RLS
Memorial Award, The Society of Authors' Travel Award, The
Canongate Prize and two Scottish Arts Council Book Awards.
Red Tides was short-listed for both the McVitie's Scottish Writer
of the Year and the Saltire Scottish Book of the Year. *Pest Maiden*
was nominated for the IMPAC Prize. She teaches creative writing
at Edinburgh University. For more information please visit
www.dilysrose.com

Selected Stories

DILYS ROSE

Luath Press Limited
EDINBURGH
www.luath.co.uk

First published 2005

The paper used in this book is recyclable.
It is made from low-chlorine pulps produced in a low-energy,
low-emission manner from renewable forests.

The publisher acknowledges subsidy from the Scottish Arts Council

 Scottish
Arts Council

towards the publication of this volume.

Printed and bound by
Bookmarque Ltd, Croydon

Lazy Sunday
Words and Music by Steve Marriott and Ronnie Lane
© 1968 Avakak Songs and EMI United Partnership Ltd, USA
Worldwide print rights controlled by
Warner Bros Publications Inc/IMP Ltd
Lyrics reproduced by permission of IMP Ltd
All Rights Reserved

Typeset in 10.5 point Sabon
by Jennie Renton

Acknowledgements

Some of these stories have previously been published in *The Glasgow Herald, New Writing Scotland, Original Prints* (Polygon), *Scottish Short Stories, Scotland on Sunday, The Scotsman, Mail on Sunday, End of a Regime, Harpies & Quines, Panurge, A Scottish Feast* (Mariscat), *Telling Stories* (BBC Publications), *Scottish Love Stories* (Polygon), *Edinburgh Review, Cutting Teeth, Flamingo Scottish Short Stories, The Oxford Book of Scottish Short Stories, Chapman 100, Scottish Literature in the Twentieth Century, Macallan Shorts, Tribuna, Brèves, Literature na Swiecie, Szkoci, Det Nye* and *Mai Skot Novellak*. A number of stories have also been broadcast on BBC Radio 3, 4 and Radio Scotland.

With thanks to Robin Robertson,
Geraldine Cooke and Jennie Renton.

Contents

Child's Play

I'M LEARNING MY lesson. I'm not even supposed to be playing with you, Arabella, so sit up like a good girl or I'll have to put you to bed and you'll be in disgrace. That's what I'm in. I know it's dark. I'm not allowed the light on because that's not disgrace. Being in the dark's disgrace. Doing nothing's disgrace. If anybody comes I'll have to hide you under the covers.

You'd cry if you were a crying doll but you don't have the bit inside for crying. Sonya, that's Wendy's doll, cries real tears if you put water in her mouth. She's got a key in her back for the noise. Sonya wets her pants as well. It's the same water. She cries and wets at the same time. That's what Jenny did today, before the lump stuck and the van came and she went away with the fairies. People have a lump in the throat for crying. It grows until the water comes out of your eyes unless you can hold it in. Holding it in is brave but Jenny held it in too long. You've got to swallow it.

I wanted a doll like Sonya but she was too dear so I got you. Wendy's richer. I'm not poor but I'm not rich, I'm comfortable. That's because of sacrifices. My mum says poor people don't know about sacrifices. Jenny Pilly's poor. She's here today and gone tomorrow. Jenny's mum's a fly-by-night. She does the moonlight flit. She doesn't like the scheme so she goes gallivanting. The scheme's at the end of our street but our street's not the scheme. That starts after the witch's house. The witch flies by night too but she doesn't really fly, she sits on her broom. Running up the witch's path and ringing her doorbell is brave. If she catches you, you turn into a dead bird on her fireplace.

I'm not allowed on the scheme. The houses only have numbers, not names as well. Our house is detached. That means it's got a gate and a hedge with a garden right round the house and it's got two doors and it's alone. If a house has a Siamese twin it's a semi. My mum doesn't like semis and houses with numbers.

I don't want to rub shoulders with Tom, Dick and Harry.

My mum says that. I've never seen people rubbing shoulders. Cows do it when they're itchy but people can scratch themselves.

Are you listening, Arabella? I'm going to be strict with you for your own good. You'll thank me when you're older. I'm learning my lesson so you've got to learn yours. I've got the slipper right here, my girl. I'm keeping my eye on you. I don't like it, Arabella, it hurts me more than you. Now give Mummy a kiss, or I'll give you away to the tinks.

Wendy's been my best friend for a whole week. Wendy hates Jenny Pilly so I've got to hate her too.

Jenny Pilly's not just silly
She's a guttersnipe
She's got nits and chappy lips
And all she gets to eat is tripe.

Wendy sang her song in the playground loud, and Jenny's face turned red and she said a swear. Wendy sang it again, louder, and this time Jenny grabbed Wendy's jotter and wrote SNOBBY TITS on it with a red pencil. The teacher's the only one who's allowed to use a red pencil, except in art. Wendy was nearly crying, she had the lump in her throat but not the water in her eyes. Dunkie Begg got the strap for scribbling BUMS on his jotter. TITS is the same as BUMS, it's dirty. So is PISS. And FANNY is worse than dirty, it's disgusting. So don't ever let me hear you saying that word Arabella, if you do learn to talk, or there will be trouble.

Look at you. What a tyke you are. You're as bad as Jenny. I'll have to send you away to live on the scheme if this goes on, or else I'll give you away to the tinks, wait and see. A tink will turn you into brass or she'll take you everywhere in the rag bag or she'll give you to her baby with the runny nose. She doesn't even have a house on the scheme, you know. She's not got a penny to her name, just bits of gold in her teeth.

Tinks are tykes and guttersnipes are common hussies. Hussies are a sort of lady, like starlings are a sort of bird. Hussies paint their toe-nails and paint the town red. When Jenny's mum paints the town red, Jenny gets to stay up really late. My mum has a special voice for hussies, a faraway voice. The lady in the chemist's, the one with the white lipstick, she's a hussy. When my mum buys toothpaste from her, my mum says thank you to the shelf.

Don't roll your eyes like that, Arabella. If the wind changes they'll stick that way – you'll be cross-eyed and see everything back to front. Jenny could only see stars until the man brought the gas mask. That wasn't supposed to be the consequences. But now she can stay off school. Jenny's not good at anything at school. She's nearly always bottom. If I'm not top or nearly top I'm in disgrace but when Jenny was bottom her mum gave her sweets. Sweets are better than a rose from the inkblock. You get the rose for five gold stars but you can't do anything with it.

I told my mum about the sweets for being bottom and she

said that's the sort of thing riff-raff do. And my dad said birds of a feather flock together. That's a saying. It means people are like birds, there's different kinds, like doves and starlings. With people it's riff-raff which are never-never and common which are undesirable and god-fearing which are respectable and comfortable. Poor ones have faces like marbles and rich ones are rough diamonds. You'll be clever like me if you learn all the words.

Jenny lives in a flat on the never-never. Her name's in a book. We got a story once about never-never land where nobody ever grew up but it wasn't about the scheme. There's lots of old people on the scheme and you've got to grow up to be old. Jenny's never-never is having your name ticked off in a book. A man comes to your house with the book and the suitcase. Sometimes he has a dog with him that's nearly a wolf. You've got to give him money. The Clean-Ezy man comes to our house and the Onion Johnny but not the man with the suitcase. He doesn't go to Wendy's house either, the tick man.

My mum likes me to play with Wendy. She's the lesser of two evils. Her dad's a rough diamond. So is Mr de Rollo next door. He's got lot of shiny things in his house and a silver car which sparkles in the dark, like the stars. He's a dark horse. He made himself by climbing out of the gutter. He's got liquid gold in a bottle. It's a drink. My dad loves Mr de Rollo's liquid gold but the man's got no breeding. Mrs de Rollo's really young. She's got blonde hair out of a bottle.

Breeding is what birds do once they've got a nest.
Breeding is how you tell the sheep from the goats.

I told you, Arabella, you'll be cross-eyed. You'll see everything all wonky, like when you look at the magic mirrors at the shows. One blows you up fat like a balloon and one makes you long and thin like a clothes-pole and one makes you turn wavy. It's not like the witch's magic. If they had a mirror that turned you rich if you were poor, that would be real magic. But if you were rich to begin with, you'd have to turn poor. Jenny would turn into Wendy and Wendy would turn into Jenny. I'd have to turn into somebody but I couldn't turn rich or poor from comfortable. I'd be like the wavy mirror. Jenny could be my best friend instead of Wendy.

If Jenny was my best friend, maybe I wouldn't have to write Thank-You letters. She never has to. I have to write if I get a present, always, even if it's horrible, and say it's lovely. My mum says I mustn't look a gift horse in the mouth. Auntie Eunice is a gift horse but I never see her so I can't look her in the mouth. Probably she's got huge teeth like real horses. Anyway she always sends me fawn tights and I hate fawn. One time I asked my mum if I could get a present on the never-never so I could send it back if I didn't like it and she said the day that happens will be over her dead body. She says that about me staying up to watch the grown-up programmes. Jenny's allowed to but I'm not because they're tripe and tripe is common. There's lot of kissing and crying but the kissing is unsuitable. On the television people kiss on the lips. They go on for ages and it's truelove.

Truelove is unsuitable.

The kissing I do isn't truelove because I don't get kissed back. It's a Thank-You kiss or and I'm-Sorry kiss and it's really only half a kiss. Somebody turns their face to the side and I've got to do it to their cheek. Cheek-by-jowl. It's the same when I'm in disgrace, my mum won't kiss back.

They don't have disgrace at Sunday School, just at real school and at home. You don't have to be quiet or good at tests and have breeding. You just have to give away all your clothes to the tinks and the loving shepherd will save you, even if you're bad. That's because of magic. They've got that mirror, see. It's very far away. It's in the kingdom of heaven where you never die. But you've got to be dead to get there maybe. You can even give away fawn tights from Auntie Eunice and it's not ungrateful because it's better to give than to receive. The poor inherit the earth. The rich people turn poor and go to the kingdom of heaven and the poor inherit the world. The world becomes heaven on earth. That's the magic and nobody has to live on the scheme anymore.

It's because of magic I'm in disgrace. See, there's different kinds of magic. There's flying on a broom and magic mirrors and there's the kind Wendy does to people if they don't do the dare. It's called You-Are-Getting-Sleepy and I was holding Jenny's arms behind her back so Wendy could do the magic with her fingers. Wendy must have done too much of the trick because you're not supposed to hit your head and black out. You're just supposed to fall asleep and wake up as Wendy's slave. Jenny didn't wake up at all. Not even when the Jani did the kiss of life, not even when they put the gas mask on her face. Jenny's in the dark now, like me, but she's not in disgrace. She can't even see with her eyes open.

I've got to learn my lesson.

The kingdom of heaven is over my dead body.
Rough diamonds thank their lucky stars.
Guttersnipes are undesirable.
Birds of a feather are elements.
Fly-by-nights are dark horses.
Spare the rod and spoil the consequences.
Breeding makes you comfortable.
Riff-raff rub shoulders.
Never-never land is gone to the dogs.

Have you got that, Arabella?

Our Lady of the Pickpockets

FOR MANY HOURS now no buses have left. It is because of the rains. Everywhere is mud in my town, in Villahermosa. Her name mean 'beautiful' but she is not. Tonight she is a wet black sow and the tourists are stuck in her belly. My people know how to wait. Angél say they are all waiting, for death, or a Greyhound bus to Téjas. It is all the same to them. Many times my people will wait all night in the bus station, without speaking, without moving. They know every way to sleep, up against the wall like sack of beans, piled together on the bench, flat out on the floor. They sleep even with the eyes open. Angél say this is because they live with the eyes closed.

Tonight there is no sleeping on the floor. Sometimes Emilia, the desk-girl, she take her broom and sweep the water to the door. Each time she sweep, Oswaldo check through the peanut shells and cigarette butts for coins. He find no coins. The black water always returns.

Tourists, they don't know how to wait: always they must be speaking or moving. They don't know how to do nothing. Each minute somebody get up and go look into the night. There

7

is nothing to see but two or three streetlights. Each streetlight has a cloud of mosquitoes in its halo. And under the mosquitoes, pariahs, always pariahs, pick-picking their sores. They are waiting, too, to die, or for something to die which they can eat.

In the bus station, nothing. In Brasil Street is a café-bar. It have tequila, beer and coffee but Emilia don't tell tourists a Goddamn thing. She give them a rough deal. It is because they will not speak her language and she cannot speak theirs. Only money she knows. Dollars, cents, nickels, dimes. Is not enough. I know words. I don't have to spit-shine like Oswaldo, day and night and no shoes on the feet.

– Madame, I say, Madame?

This lady have hair like ripe maize. It swing over her face. She is drawing on a map, arrows. The arrows go up the page. They cross from one colour to another. The border is where the colour changes and at the border is a blue line, a river. Angél tell me about this river: American farmers shoot Méxicano wetbacks like rats.

– Madame, I say, Where you go?

She look up at me so I smile. Angél say a smile go a long way with gringos. Téjas is a long way.

Madame sit beside a man who drum his boot heels on the floor. Madame put down her map on the bench. Beside her she has a backpack and a big skin bag. Beside the man is a backpack and a parcel.

– At least we got most of the stuff we wanted, Mister say.

He pat his parcel like pet. Madame has one arm inside the skin bag. She bring out cigarettes, cheap Méxicano cigarettes. Angél smoke only American brands. She say:

– How long can we go on like this? One trip after another, one bus station after another. Can't we even get some wheels?

Mister twist round. He try to see Madame's face but is hidden in the hair.

– We can't have everything, he say in a quiet voice, a voice for a baby. You know that.

8

– Everything! We can't have anything. After all this time we can't have what any peasant here can manage no sweat, she say.

– Please Eleanor, I'm tired, Mister say and turn away.

Madame reach for her matches but they drop on the wet floor. I pick them up.

– Madame, I say. Allow me.

I am always polite. You don't get nowhere but into the street without manners. I strike the match on my thumbnail. Angél he teach me this trick. Madame like me now. It is enough.

Behind Mister's head I can see Angél. He is over in the corner pretending to read the newspaper but he is watching. He can read only photo-romances. Oswaldo spit on Angél's boots. The boots must shine like hubcaps for Angél. Is normal.

– Madame, I say, Téjas?

– San Cristóbal, she say.

Many many tourists go there, and to the ocean. Villahermosa has no ocean like Merída, and no mountains like San Cristóbal, only rivers in the streets when it rains. San Cristóbal I have seen only in posters, since first I began sleeping here the same posters. On my first night, Angél he come up to me, he share my bench and share with me his blanket. He drink mescal and tell me about Texas. He say Villahermosa is a stinking pigsty. He say my eyes will fall out when I see Téjas.

– After San Cristóbal, Madame, Téjas?

She point to the arrows on the map. Her finger with the sparkling rings it stop at every arrow – San Cristóbal, Oaxaca, México city, Chihuahua, El Paso, Téjas. A long way.

– No children, Madame? You, Mister, no children?

– Not yet, she say. But maybe…

Mister make a long face. He go look for the bus again. Madame she follow him with the eyes, the way pariahs follow the trash cart. Her eyes are hungry.

– No mother, Madame, no father. No home. Only the bus station. Only ten years old, Madame.

I am eleven but ten is good number. Madame, she look at me for a long time like she trying to see under my skin. When she stop looking she give me chocolate. She believe. It is enough. I know how to wait.

Mister does not believe.

– What's your game? he say. Here's a dollar. You get yourself off home.

He hold the note between his thumb and finger. His fist is tight.

– A real American dollar.

A dollar is not enough.

– Here kid.

He wave the green paper at me. It is new and crisp. It crackle like pampas grass. I keep my hands behind my back.

– No game, Mister, I say. No home. Take me with you, to San Cristóbal, to Téjas. Please Mister.

Mister turn to Madame.

– This is your doing, Eleanor, he say. All this travelling's made you flip. Can't you even use some Goddamn sense and say no? Jesus Eleanor, can't you do better than *maybe*?

For a long time they talk. I don't know all the words but I know what the voices say behind the words. Mister does not want to say yes to me. But also does not want Madame to be sad. One minute he say: Okay, if that's what you really want. And then: You must be outta your mind. You'll want to take along one of those scabby dogs next.

More talking and then she take his hand and whisper something. He laugh.

Everyone is picking up their bags and running to the door.

– Mister, Madame, the bus is here!

I will ask about Téjas tomorrow. Angél say one foot on the road can take you far. Everybody is happy now: I because I am on the road, Mister because he is holding Madame close, Madame because we are all together. She smile at Mister all the time until he fall asleep. While he sleep, she smoke. The lights in the bus are out and only an old woman is talking, to her chicken. All night I light Madame's cigarettes and watch her face glow in the flame. Like this, in the flame light, her face is like the Madonna in my locket. I wear the locket under my shirt. Angél stole it for me, from the stall of Our Lady, in the market. Our Lady of the Pickpockets. Tonight she bring me luck.

But this town we have come to is so small! There is not even a bus station. And cold! Madame say is cold because we are above the clouds. So many mountains everywhere, nothing but mountains and chapels and low white houses. Is very early. The peasants are running down the mountains to market, bent under their loads. Very poor peasants – no mules. Madame, she think it is beautiful here but there is nothing for me. I don't want to carry bales of maize on my head until I die. Oswaldo's father was peasant. When he die, his back is bent like meat-hook.

    – Tomorrow, Madame, Téjas? I say.

    – Cut it out kid, Mister say to me. Then to her: What about the sleeping arrangements? Have you figured that?

    And she say:

    – We'll work something out.

Mister stop at a hospedaje on a back street. He go in and come back with the señora who is fat and ancient. We must follow her across the courtyard very very slowly, because she must rest on her stick after every step. It is a clean place, with flowers and fruit trees and tiles. A boy is polishing the tiles. Much work for the boy.

    The señora give us a room. A room with two beds. For me alone, one bed! For this I thank Our Lady. Already Mister is taking off his clothes. Everything he take off, so slowly. He groan. He tug at his boots. He sound like he sick but he want only Madame to stop unpacking and go to bed. He want to put his head on her chest and his hands… I know about these things.

    – Sleep, sleep! he call out like it for sale.

Madame close the blinds. The shutters are already shut but still the sun make stripes on the walls, stripes across the big bed.

I take off only my shoes. Everybody is to sleep until noon. I am too hungry for sleep. Instead, I listen. Each sound I can hear, alone – the señora pounding garbanzos, the boy beating out a rug, the cart bumping over holes in the road. In Villahermosa, from first light, always I hear traffic and scraping and hammering from the new railway station. Maybe some day trains will run all the way to Téjas, without stopping.

Inside I can hear the game in the big bed. Is normal. First whispers and bed-springs creaking. Now Mister's on top of Madame. It's begun. He put his head on her chest, he hold her down, hold on tight. It's like rodeo. Mister's a cowboy on a wild mare. Madame she buck but Mister hold on. He work hard not to fall off. He's breaking her in. There. He done it. He's won. Now he snore.

We have eaten a good meal and have been to the market where Mister buy twenty peasant dresses. He is happy because I save him much money. I bargain for him in Spanish. It is almost dark and we are walking through the crowds to the fiesta. Everyone in town must be going because the streets are packed with people. Madame hold my hand. Already she being mother to me. I can hear noise all round – music from the shows and chapel bells and guns and rockets.

– We'll talk about it later, Madame say.

– We gotta take care of it tonight, Mister say.

Madame, she pretend she don't hear. Many times today it is like this.

– Eleanor, he say. Look at me when I'm talking to you. What if we run into trouble? What if someone thinks we're trying to abduct the child?

I do not know this word *abduct*.

We go round the shows. Mostly, I try a game and they watch.

I win many prizes – cigarettes, glasses, toy animals, a key-ring. Madame buy me a bag for my prizes. Now the streets are crazy with noise. Drunk men are singing and dancing and the air smells of sausage, sweat and beer. It's like the smell of Angél's blanket, the one he share with me if I am good. Téjas, Angél say, that's all you need to say.

– Mister, I say. Tomorrow, Téjas?

Mister is watching the man swallow fire. I pull on his sleeve. He bend down so his face is next to mine.

– We've been through this before. Texas is not possible.

– Possible, Mister, possible.

– You like it here, don't you? It's a beautiful town. We're gonna try to fix you up here, with a priest maybe. You'll get a room, maybe, all of your own. Believe me, he say, Texas ain't so great.

Angél is at the market. The rains have finished in Villahermosa and Emilia has washed the floor. Angél is selling my prizes. And Mister's watch and Madame's rings. I take them because they give me no money, not even when I say I go with them in the big bed. Is normal. But Madame cry and Mister yell:

– You see! Even he thinks that's why he's here. Everyone must think so. And you call him a child!

Angél is happy to have the watch to sell and the rings. We will eat well tonight and the next night and the next. Angél say is better to take your skin to the market, better to swallow fire, better to steal than to starve. I can use my eyes and my good smile and I have my Madonna. Now, under my shirt, I also keep Madame's map, with arrows going all the way to Texas. It is enough. I know how to wait.

The Fence

THE TWO BIG girls looked at each other. They were the same age: five-and-three-quarters. Both had greenish, slanty eyes, long fairish hair and missing front tooth. Both were tousled-looking, in spite of their mothers' earlier attempts to tidy them up. They liked each other on sight. The town girl had come dressed for the country, in T-shirt, leggings and wellies, though it was a warm, dry day. The country girl was wearing a crumpled party dress but changed immediately into T-shirt, leggings and wellies, adding a garish rag of a cardigan, embarrassing her mother.

– Not that dreadful old thing. It's fit for the bucket.

– I think it's a beautiful cardigan, said the town girl. I wish I'd brought my cardigan. We could have been like twins!

While the town parents were being shown round what was – even by their own lax standards – a stunningly messy country house, the country girl took the town girl out to play in the filthiest ditch in the vicinity. Both girls had to be scrubbed thoroughly before lunch.

– I hate beetroot.

– No you don't. Last time you had it... no, please, no. The window doesn't like beetroot.

– Neither do I.

– Does anybody like beetroot? Hands up anybody in this room who likes beetroot and I'll give them a prize.

– So. What are you working on these days?

– What kind of prize?

– I want a prize, I want a prize!

– There no need to shout. Nobody's deaf, you know.

– Grandad's deaf.

– Yes but Grandad's not here, is he?

– But I know him. You said Nobody's deaf *you know*...

– I see your name in the papers from time to time.

– Sorry... sorry to interrupt but... could you move that...

– Never mind. No sense in crying over spilt milk.

– I didn't do that, I didn't! She pushed me.

– Did not. You're a bloody fibber.

– What was that?

– What was what? I didn't hear anything. Did you hear anything?

– Do you do a lot for the papers these days?

– What did you *say?*

– Nothing. You said...

– Yes you did, you said *bloody*...

– So? You say bloody. Why shouldn't I?

– Shall I get something to clean up that milk?

– Well, I'm kept fairly busy these days. Lucky really, the way things are going.

Lunch was an altogether fraught affair. Nobody really knew each other. The country father and town mother had bumped into each other a few times, years back, had recently bumped into each other again and – for the sake of the children – agreed to meet up. The food was served – no, neither served nor passed around, dumped on the table and up for grabs – in the conservatory, the only bright and clutter-free area in the house. A massive rambling jasmine draped itself across one wall like a lace curtain, giving off an overpowering odour of smoky Chinese tea.

The tranquil surroundings were completely lost under the prevailing racket which five young children (four girls, one boy) generated from the table. The town parents were slightly hungover from the night before and the noise set their heads thumping. The country parents had an extra child to deal with, a tired boy who kicked, screamed and lunged at every breakable or spillable object within reach of his cross little fists. The mother pleaded politely with this child and that, the father was politely firm but all their pussyfooting was having no effect, unless it was to spur the children on to even more disgusting acts of mutiny. At the table, the big girls sealed their friendship by behaving as badly as possible. They were banished to the garden immediately after pudding, which was exactly what they wanted. The only person to eat a decent meal was the youngest child, who sat stolidly in her highchair, pushing into her mouth whatever she was given.

The big girls ran ahead up the steep path through the woods, whooping and screeching like old friends, though they'd only known each other an hour. The mothers trailed alongside each other, gazing indulgently at their little ones who pattered along, picking up leaves and stones, clambered over fallen logs and, as there were no toys to fight over, ignored each other. For conversation, the women compared notes on their children: whose woke the earliest, went to bed latest, was up most often during the night, was out of nappies first; whose was a picky eater, whose had problems with allergies, rashes, bowels. Then they compared notes on their partner's performance as a father: did he cook, wash up, put the kids to bed, get them dressed in the morning; did he clean the toilet? That was usually a reliable topic, something to agree about.

At the foot of the path, the boy, even more wabbit and grizzly than at lunchtime, clung to his tricycle, demanding that his daddy pull him, on his trike, up the hill, not by hand but by means of the shepherd's crook the country father had brought out with him. The town father ignored the other man's futile attempt to persuade the boy to leave the trike where it was and pick it up on the way back. The town father wasn't impressed by the country father's crook, which struck him as ostentatious. It wasn't as if there were any sheep around which needed to be rescued.

The town father lit a cigarette, took a deep drag of tobacco-laced country air and looked up at the trees, wondering what they were called. Didn't trees have families too? He was relieved that lunch was over. At least in the open, the noise had, to an almost tolerable extent, dissipated. As far as he was concerned, he'd done his bit: contributed to the table talk when called upon to do so, supplied the facts and figures when pressed. At that moment he'd have been happy to sit down, under a tree of any kind, and read the newspaper he'd optimistically brought out with him.

The mothers were comparing notes on the relative merits of staying at home with children and going back to work. They hovered around the area of dense woodland where the big girls had last been seen. They hadn't been seen, or heard – which was more significant – for some time and a mild waver of panic crept into the mothers' conversation. The country father, lugging his load, a harried smile drawn tight across his face, caught up with the town father. Over the persistent girning of his son, he began to explain the difficulties, in the country, of fitting in. There were, he said, the rich and the poor, who didn't, wouldn't talk to each other. At all. For years on end. And themselves, who sat on the fence, who'd talk to anyone, if they were given the chance. The rich owned land, the poor were farmworkers and redundant miners. The country father sympathised with the miners. But couldn't find any personal good reason not to speak to some of the other side, like Major Cunningham and his good-looking daughter. Married to a musician. A successful musician. Interesting people.

– EEEEYYAAHHH!

The big girls burst out of the bushes, bared their bums, stuck out their tongues and cackled like hyenas in at the kill. The mother smiled vaguely, relieved that their daughters had not fallen in a ditch, or had their clothes torn to shreds by the rusty barbed wire which snaked through the undergrowth. The town father laughed. The country father threw down his crook and marched over to them and, in spite of his naked rage, said something very quiet and restrained to them, which nobody else could hear. For the time it took to pull up their knickers, the girls were suitably shamefaced. But one look at each other and they resumed their hideous cackling and ran off up the path. None of the adults, now bunched together and inching forward in the oblique manner of a spider, could be bothered running after them.

– They really seem to be getting on well, don't they?

– Don't they?

– It's amazing how children can just get on like that, become friends straight away.

– You'd think they'd known each other for years.

– Of course it's all black and white with children. Clear cut.

– Hmmm, well, I wouldn't say, I mean sometimes it can be a bit more... complicated.

– Anyway, they've hit it off, which is just as well.

– It wouldn't have been fun for anybody if that pair hadn't got on.

– It would not.

The path joined another and the two forks merged into a broader single track. From the other path, a fluffy golden retriever bounded towards the junction. Screaming in fright, the town girl made a dash for her mother. A leashed dog in the park was one thing, a free-ranging one another. Not that the animal had any interest in the girl. It stopped at the junction and barked idiotically until its owners, the Cunninghams, appeared: a silver-haired grandmother (peony lips, trench coat and sunglasses, though the sky was overcast) a ruddy grandfather (blazer, walking stick, dog lead and whistle), their tall, big-boned daughter (boots and breeches, wax jacket, silk scarf knotted tightly at the neck) and her two girls (mousy pigtails tied with bows, identical Shirley Temple dresses). The country girl yanked the town girl's hand away from her mother's sleeve and clutched it between her own.

– Lovely day.
– Isn't it.
– Mmmmnn, yes. How are you all?
– Oh, just fine, aren't we?
– Jolly good.
– Are you scared of the dog, dear?
– Put it on a lead! Put it on a lead!
– It doesn't chase children, dear. Just birds.
– PLEASE!

The grandmother sighed and smiled.

– James, the dog.
– Jolly good.

The grandfather gave his whistle a couple of blasts and the dog obediently trotted over to be tethered.

– I say, your lot are getting big.
    – Aren't they. And yours. My goodness.
    – Yes they're growing out of everything. Cost a fortune, little girls, don't they?
    – Mmmnnn.
    – And you never get it back with girls, do you? No matter what they say about equality and all that, they never really pay their way. Did you know that in some places people just do away with girl babies, flush them down the river.

– I've read about it.

– India or China. Someplace like that. I say, you two. Come and say hello. Don't be rude.

– Yes, why don't you two go and say hello to the Cunningham girls? I'm sure they'd like to meet you.

– Well, we wouldn't like to meet them.

– Well, I say. That settles that, doesn't it? Horrors, little girls, the lot of them.

– No social graces.

– No. Quite right too. No sense in beating about the bush.

The girls in dresses flounced on ahead, pigtails swinging. The other two took up the rear of the straggling procession. The town parents also lagged a bit, inspecting the greenery with exaggerated interest.

– Well, this is where we leave you.

– Jolly good to see you.

– Yes. Nice to see you too.

– You must come over some time.

– Mmmnn, yes. That would be nice, wouldn't it?

They had stopped in front of a tall house (white walls, sandstone facings, too many windows to count). Major Cunningham pushed open the wrought iron gate and ushered the dog inside. His granddaughters pushed past him and the dogs and positioned themselves on the inside of the sturdy fence, directly in front of the girls in T-shirts, mud-streaked leggings and wellies.

– This is OUR HOUSE.

– So?

– ALL OUR HOUSE. And OUR FENCE.

– So?

The girl inside the fence spoke with a hissing lisp. Outside, the town girl folded her arms and pounded the ground with her boot, the way bulls do before they charge.

– OUR HOUSE, OUR FENCE AND OUR GARDEN.

It was quite a garden: a long sloping lawn; scalloped borders, sculpted bushes, a stone sundial inlaid with brass, an elaborate rockery tumbling down to an oval pond where a bronze mermaid sat and combed her verdigrised locks.

– You can't come in here.

– We don't want to. So there.

– So there.

But the town girl longed to get in and see the mermaid up close and so did the country girl, to show it off to her friend. Both of them liked mermaids. That was why they were friends: they liked the same things; mermaids, princesses, My Little Ponies and all kinds of stuff their parents said were nonsense.

– If you come in here, we'll... KICK YOU!

– OH NO YOU WON'T!

– OH YES WE WILL, WE'LL KICK YOU KICK YOU KICK YOU!

– Girls, girls. Please. Goodness me.

– If you kick us we'll CUT OFF YOUR FEET!

– Well, we'll, we'll... SHOOT YOU! Our daddy's got a gun and we know how to work it, so there.

– SHOOT YOU SHOOT YOU SHOOT YOU!

– Come now, that's enough. Into the house you two. Chop chop. Vicious little monsters aren't they? Terribly nice to see you all. Well, goodbye.

– Yes, nice to see you.

– And nice to meet... your friends.

– Mmmnnn.

– Goodbye.

– Goodbye.

The boy scoots down the hill on his trike, triumphantly. The mothers carry the little ones in their arms. The town father walks with them, carrying the leaves and twigs which have been collected on the walk. The country father, who can't remember where he left his crook, roots about in the bushes. The big girls meander down the hill, arms linked. Looking back at the fence, they promise themselves they'll each have a mermaid one day, but not mottled or mossy, a clean, silky mermaid with a shimmery tail and green eyes like their own and sparkles of water in her hair, like tiny rainbows.

Handholds

SUMMER DUSK. THREE teenage girls, in silhouette, tilt backwards, bracing themselves against the steep slope of the hill. Laughing, they link arms, sway and stagger from side to side, kicking up their legs in a ragged chorus line. Above them, a flicker of late birds or early bats, a spatter of stars. Below, a single pale wave licks the shore. In the hills, the distant waterfall appears to flow upward, to grasp at the cliff like a huge silver hand. The evening smells of sun-dried seaweed, heather.

Where they are is barely a village; a spill of cottages clings to the curving bay, at the bend in the road a red, unvandalised telephone box is waist-deep in thistles and the shoreside campsite holds a solitary, unoccupied caravan. The single-track road whips around the fretted coastline, a wild reel of hairpin bends, rockfalls and sheer, deadly drops. In the distance, the headlights of a car wink and vanish, wink and vanish.

– It's nice here, says Sarah, but...

– But borin, says Dianne.

Dianne sighs loudly and chews a strand of her long, straight hair.

– Ah wish Glen wis drivin that car. Ah wish Glen was beltin roon they bends tae meet me, says Dianne.

– Has Glen got a car?

– Nuh.

– Still. At least you can wish aboot somebody real, says Sarah.

– Ah miss him, says Dianne.

– It's only been four days.

– Ken. Feels like for ever.

– Fuck off, says Sarah. Ye're makin me jealous. Ah've naebody tae miss. God, mibbe ah'll never huv naebody tae miss.

Above their heads the sky is inky. At the horizon, it's pink with thin, mint-green lozenges of cloud.

– See they clouds, says Sarah. Ah fancy jeans that colour.

– God, says Dianne. Make yer arse look massive, a colour like that.

– Ken, says Sarah. But ah'd get noticed.

The third girl, Ciara, breaks the line, waves her arms above her head and jiggles her hips until she stumbles and falls face down on the hill, laughing helplessly.

– Nae mair Hooch for her, says Dianne. You hear me, Ciara. NAE MAIR HOOCH! Ye're pissed awready.

– OOOOHH!

– Ye can hear that awright, can ye no?

Ciara rubs her bluish, moonlit cheeks against the hillside, trying out the feel of grass, moss and heather. Her head feels hot, bubbly and everything is funny, everything; the grass tickling her face, Dianne and Sarah shaking their heads at her, the car bobbing along on the coast road.

– Are we going doon the beach, then? says Dianne.

– Well, we could try the Pizza Hut first, or the chippie. Or one of aw they discos doon the road, says Sarah. Or we could just eye up the talent on the streets.

– Fuck off, says Dianne.

– CAAAA, says Ciara.

– Aye, says Sarah. Car. Dianne wishes Glen was in it.

– GEHHHH?

– Get up ye deef bugger and come oan.

Like a traffic policeman, Sarah beckons to Ciara who stumbles obediently to her feet. The three girls walk, skip and stagger down the hill until they reach the short stretch of road which leads through the caravan site to the beach. A couple of munching sheep scutter in front of the girls, unable to decide what to do next.

– Stupit things, says Dianne.

– Pea brains, said Sarah.

– ShhhhEEEE, says Ciara.

She stretches out a hand to stroke one of their silly, bony noses but the sheep back off nervously; one of them slips into the ditch. Ciara laughs but she's sorry that the sheep don't trust her. She'd never hurt an animal. She loves animals, their warm, comforting smells, their uncomplicated eyes.

As they pass the empty caravan, Ciara stops, presses her face against the window. There's not much to see but the glass is cool against her skin and when she steps back, her mouth leaves a kiss mark. With a finger, she draws two mismatched eyes above the smudged impression of her mouth.

Dianne and Sarah race each other to the shore, trainers thudding softly and throwing up arcs of fine sand. Clownlike, Ciara follows, arms and legs flying out in all directions. When she reaches the water's edge, she birls round and round.

– Get back, says Sarah. Ye'll fa doon daein that. Ye'll get soaked and us two'll get the blame for it.

– Ye're wastin yer breath, says Dianne. She hastae see yer mooth. And ye huvtae say everythin dead slow.

– Ken, says Sarah. Ken. Ah've kent her as long as you, Dianne. But she willnae look at ma mooth, will she? She willnae fuckin stand still.

Dizzy, Ciara veers into the water; Sarah grabs her and pulls her back. Ciara's head jerks backwards and a thin harsh cry, like a gull's, flies from her mouth as she twists free from Sarah's grasp and hits out, a frenzy of elbows, fists, knees. Sarah gasps and groans, doubles up and clutches at her stomach.

– Fucksake, Ciara!

– Ye ken us, Ciara! Sarah roars. Ye've kent us since ye were wee. It's deep the water. And ye cannae swim!

Sarah slowly straightens up, wipes the sand from her jeans.

– Ah'm sair all over.

The small waves make a secretive, whispering sound. Ciara clomps off along the shore, hugging herself. Nothing's funny any more, nothing's a laugh, it's all gone dark and cold. Dianne and Sarah watch as, at the far end of the beach, Ciara disappears behind a jagged stack of rock.

– The rocks here are really really old, says Dianne. Millions and millions of years old. Folk say they're the oldest rocks in the world.

– Huv ye finished yir geography project, then? says Sarah.

– No yet, but there's tons of leaflets in the cottage. Ye widnae think there'd be much tae write aboot a wee place like this but there's stacksa stuff. Aboot rocks and deid folk, ken.

– But nae much need for an entertainments guide. *For visitors to the area, there are nice walks and nice walks. And if ye dinnae go in for walkin, fuck off.*

– That car cannae be far away now. Ah can hear it.

– So can ah.

Dianne and Sarah look up at the road expectantly.

Ciara begins to clamber up the smooth black rocks, still warm from the day's sun, warm as a body. Her hands feel for holds. In the hairline crevices, crisp, salty weed and striped cockles crackle beneath her fingers. She pulls a cockle loose with her nail and lets it roll onto her palm. In her ear, her inner ear, as the doctor explained, pointing to the chart – there's a clever wee cockly thing, the cochlea; inside the cochlea, fluid swishes

28

about like the sea in a shell, and the hearing hairs – all twenty thousand of them – send messages to the brain. Since she was wee and had the fever which made her eyes burn and zapped so many of those hearing hairs, she's seen the doctor's ear chart so many times she could draw it from memory.

With one ear flat against the rock, she can hear the scrape of her fingernails as she feels her way upwards. The sound is very faint, as far away as the stars but she can hear it all the same and that's what matters. She's alone with sea, rock and sky; safe, though she must be careful. Her trainers are wet, her legs long and thin, too thin. Her mum's been worrying about her and since they've been here, she's been baking cakes; every day's been like a birthday. And before the holiday, they went shopping three days in a row and her mum bought her piles of new stuff, just like Dianne and Sarah's, exactly the same.

– Must be dead cosy in a caravan, says Dianne. Wouldn't like it on ma ain, ken, but if Glen wis here... if he had a phone ah could phone him.

   – But he doesnae huv a phone. Or a car. Or a job.

   – Ken.

   – Ye'll just huvtae enjoy missing him. Lie doon in yer bed at night and pretend he's yer pillow or somethin. That's whit ah dae, says Sarah.

   – Eh?

   – Pretend.

Ciara pulls herself on to a ledge where she can dangle her legs over the edge and look down. A clear patch of violet water swarms with flashing green strands, like seaweed but too fast, too muscular; not seaweed but baby eels, pretty now, like little neon ribbons but she imagines all those babies stretching and swelling, filling up the water. Her mouth is dry. It doesn't make sense that drinking loads of Hooch makes you thirsty. Sliding back from the ledge, Ciara looks up at the sky, at the stars. She likes stars, the way they breathe out light and throw their shining rays across millions of miles of nothing. Sometimes they don't seem so far away...

She has climbed higher than she intended to. It's as far back down to the shore now as it is up to the road, where the approaching car dazzles her with its headlights. Ciara blinks and shrinks back onto the ledge, out of sight. The car slows down, turns in through a gap in the dyke and draws up outside the caravan. A man and a woman get out, stretch their dark, bulky bodies and stride around aimlessly, as if they're stiff from being in the car too long, then the woman hooks her arm on to the man's and they stroll to the edge of the grass where they stop and stare in the way people only do at the seaside; feet apart, bodies slack, eyes steady. They stand and stare and do nothing, watching lilac become purple, orange become red. When the woman begins to wave her free arm in front of her face, they turn and make their way back to the caravan. Midges. When the sun goes down, midges blow about the beach in loose, nipping clouds but up on the rocks where Ciara is crouching invisibly, she only has bloated flies and creepy crawlies to contend with.

The man moves from the shoulders; Ciara sees her dad in the thrusting shoulders, the jutting, angry chin. Her dad and Horse. Horse walks just like her dad, though she's never thought about it before. She doesn't ever want to see Horse again but when school starts, he'll be there, day after day, his jutting angry chin, his yellow teeth and scraped-looking skin... She'd like to see her dad, if only he didn't get so cross with her. Last time it was her table manners. She was eating her tea with him and he sat and watched her, his face going dark and stormy, then he wrote in big angry letters:

YOU SOUND LIKE A PIG. IT MAKES ME SICK.

The noise she was making was a noise she couldn't hear.

On the beach, Dianne and Sarah are pretending to talk to each other but they're not really concentrating on what they're saying; they're watching the couple in the caravan. Ciara can tell by the way their heads flick back and forth. Sometimes, too, they look over at the rocks but they can't see her; they're looking at the wrong place, at a route she might have taken, but didn't.

A yellow brick of light glows in the window of the caravan. The man bends into the boot of the car, pulls out bags and boxes and dumps them on the caravan step; the woman takes them inside. They move quickly and smoothly, without looking at each other, as if this fetching and carrying is a natural routine. And when the door of the caravan is closed, the curtain drawn, the man and woman pass back and forth, flat grey shadows, sometimes one at a time, sometimes doubling up, sliding across each other, darkening at the overlap like layers of tissue.

On the far side of the bay, her mum is in the holiday cottage, drinking wine with Dianne and Sarah's mum, enjoying the sunset and the peace and quiet, not wanting to think about what might happen when school starts again. Ciara doesn't want to think about school either. What's here now is fine, just fine. Her best friends are along the beach, stick figures on the dark sand. Maybe they're wondering where she is hiding and whether they should go and look for her. The sea is swallowing the last dregs of sunlight. Ciara is on a narrow ledge halfway up a stack, searching for handholds; in her head she can hear a deep, deep booming.

London

HE LEFT HOME with a suitcase containing two shirts, some underwear and a dozen rock'n'roll records. At six a.m. he arrived at the flat which his sister shared with numerous students. He arrived with no plans and no money. At that time in the morning she wasn't pleased to see him, and told him so, before she crawled over her snoring boyfriend and rolled off the mattress, the only real piece of furniture in the room. He looked out of the curtainless window while she wrapped herself in a bath towel.

– You can't stay here, she said. This is the first place they'll look.

She plucked a couple of cracked mugs from the stack of dishes in the sink and rinsed them under the tap.

– I know, he replied. I'm going to London.

He drank his coffee in gulps, put the address and the five pound note she had given him into his pocket, and left. When he reached the A1 he stuck out his thumb.

He stayed with his big sister's friend – who didn't like rock'n'roll – for a week, listening to the gloomy songs she played incessantly, songs to kill yourself to. He didn't know what to say when his hostess unaccountably crumpled into a weeping heap. This happened several times a day. He made cups of coffee for her, changed the record when she felt too miserable to get out of her chair. He washed a few dishes and slept on the couch.

He stayed until two police officers arrived at the door. They escorted him to the station where they put him and his empty suitcase on a northbound train. He'd sold his records to help pay for his keep. His shirts had gone missing at the launderette.

On his return home, his mother was very upset about the shirts and his father was very upset about his mother being upset. Nobody asked him if he'd had a good time.

Some years later, on the rare occasion of a family gathering – in his big sister's plush new home – he is reminded of that episode in his life. It has never before been mentioned in the presence of his parents but now his sister, snug in a fluffy white armchair, is concentrating on the cockroaches, the suicide songs and the sour milk for breakfast. She is even reproaching herself for not having sent him home immediately. His mother is looking anxiously at his father who is looking irritably at him.

– I had a great time, he tells them. Wouldn't have missed a bit of it.

Rope

THE LEATHER LEASHES are taut as rigged hawsers. The man strains to match the force of their muzzled heads and harnessed shoulders. They're taking him for a walk, these muscle-bound, rock-skulled dogs with boiled red eyes and drooling jaws. These are no pets in the ordinary sense; no cuddly beasts with which an animal lover might share a bit of harmless rough and tumble, no fluffy mutts which lope after sticks and balls and deposit them at the feet of an approving master, begging for claps on warm compliant heads and the game to begin again.

Nothing at all is compliant about this pair, nothing tamed except by force. It's in his every step, the strain of control, of keeping these power-packs in check; these bald brutes pitting their wills against his. His belted mac perfectly matches their own coats, close-cropped, colourless as putty.

To love animals like these takes something other than delight. There is nothing to love in these dogs unless you can count devotion to their transparent savagery, their naked ugliness; every step the man takes is one of restraint, of struggle for control. If the bitch's lead goes slack, if she pauses to sniff the soiled municipal turf or if the dog thrusts thuggishly at a whimsical, parkwise squirrel, it is all the man can do to keep them in check.

Like the dogs, the boy too moves from the shoulders, as if he sees some aggro up ahead, something to square up to, as if he's going to hit something head-on, though there's only his dad's tightly belted back, his dad clenched in the steel grip of his will, his dad's body hard, unyielding, buttoned up against the elements.

The boy doesn't mind the cold. The winter wind scrabbles through his outsize lumberjack shirt. He shivers at the thrill of it nipping his chest, scratching at his belly, his belt buckle. On either side of his dad he sees Cass and Tara's thin, bare tails twitch as they walk, stick up from squat, wagging bums, porking the foggy air like it's flesh.

Flesh: that word. he just has to say the word and he imagines Chantelle trotting ahead of him, Chantelle with her pale lips and arched black eyebrows, her pointy tits and long, long legs. He feels hungry. A burger would hit the spot: meat, melted cheese and a soft, spongy roll; something to put in his mouth. If he had something to put in his mouth he wouldn't have to think about Chantelle's body or dogs' tails porking the fog.

The boy needs a haircut; his thick fringe swings into his puppy eyes as he shoulders forward, shirt-tail flapping, trainer laces trailing. It will be his turn soon, his shot. His dad will wrap the leashes round his gloved palms until the dogs are half-choked, until their tongues go purple and slop out of their mouths. Then his dad will hand the dogs over to him.

He has to go through this stuff with the dogs; it's crap and sometimes he moans about it but there's no point, there's no way around it. It's Friday and he wants money. His dad will hand over a fiver.

– If you've shown some progress with the dogs, son. I want to see some progress.

There was always this progress thing, this way his dad had of measuring him up, even though you never got to see it in his face. You couldn't tell anything from his dad's face about how he felt; it hardly moved. Even when he spoke, his face looked frozen and grey, like his coat.

You've got to have money in your pocket. Chantelle always has loads of money. In the lunch break, she flashes her cash about and treats her pals to cream cakes. One time he was standing right behind her in the baker's, in the queue for filled rolls and pizza. With all the jostling going on, it was easy to rub up against her short tight skirt, accidentally on purpose. He just about came on the spot.

Chantelle hardly knows he exists. And if she knew, if she knew what he did while he chanted her name over and over? Jeer, probably, or pity him and one is as bad as the other. Chantelle doesn't go with schoolboys; she's into men. Men are into Chantelle. Boys are dross to Chantelle but one day he'd show her, one day he'd give her one, ram her right up the crack. She'd be down on the grass, laughing and trying to fight him off with scorn. He'd pin her down so she'd have to kick and bite and scratch but he'd be strong, and rock-hard. Her skirt would ride up her thighs as he pulled down her pants in one easy movement and then he'd be up there, up inside her...

His dad is pushing his biscuit-coloured hair out of his eyes. The boy has forgotten the colour of his dad's eyes. They're just dark gaps, gashes in his face. His dad's eyes are not looking out or in, they're looking away, always looking away, even now when he calls him over, yanks him out of the Chantelle fantasy and back to the sweaty smell of the dogs, to their thonged leashes cutting into his dad's thick gloves, their short strangled pants as they gasp for more rope, his dad's faraway groan, his dad's hands clasping his own, the leather rope between them. There was always this thing between them, this thing handed from father to son.

As soon as his dad lets go, the dogs tear off. They're making for a tree – head-butting's a favourite trick – but instead of charging it together, they split up at the last moment, forking at the tree and dragging him hard against the truck, stretching his legs and arms like the bands of a catapult, scraping his nose, chin, belly against the rough bark. His bare hands burn. Why doesn't he get to wear gloves like his dad? His eyes burn too, prickly with tears but he won't cry out, won't howl in pain, bawl at the dogs or his dad, won't let the shame show.

Folk are looking. Folk are laughing. His dad is laughing. The dogs are bastards, doing this to him when there are folk about. Some have stopped to look and point him out to each other. His dad's a bastard, standing there watching and laughing.

– Need a hand, son?
– Nuh.
– You've scuppered yourself, son.
– I'm OK, right!
– You need a bit more control, another wee lesson in leash management.

He isn't giving in. He's had it with giving in, had it with his dad's wee lessons. He'll just hang on like this, jammed up against the tree like a fucking clown until the dogs stop straining, until there's a bit of slack from one of them.

His dad's lessons took place out the back, in the concrete yard where dandelions and thistles burst through the cracks. It felt like prison, being marched around with the dogs, his dad ordering him about, barred in by windows on all sides. The dogs had their kennel in the yard and the run, well it was a big cage really, with a dirty great padlock on the steel door. His dad built it. He held pliers and hammers and bags of screws. When Tara had her pups – just the one litter – his dad threw in a couple of blankets. The pups were sold and then the vet sorted her. The vet said he could fix Cass too so he wouldn't strain at the leash but his dad didn't want that. His dad thought that was cruel, though he whipped the dog often enough for it.

– Grip it like this son, close to the body, son, grip it like your life depended on it. Let them know who's boss.

He knows fine who's boss right now, who's always bloody boss. His dad just won't accept it, won't see that it's all he can do to stay on his feet, never mind trying to make the bastards walk to heel. But this is what they do; night after night they pretend that one day he'll take over, take his dad's place, put on the gloves and tighten the muzzles, clip on the leads and hit the streets, a team to be reckoned with.

It had to happen when there were all these folk out for the shows, drifting through the fog with their bouncy balloons and puke-pink teddy bears. He can see the lights, their colours milky in the fog, and hear the muffled mess of noise; squealing voices, roaring machinery, thudding music. Some of his pals have been to the shows already. Others will be there tonight. Pug told him about a new ride, the Terminator, which swings up really fast and high and all the girls' skirts fly up. If you stand in the right place, you can see everything. Chantelle might be there. He'd like to watch Chantelle on the Terminator, or anything else. He'd like to watch her being tossed about, squealing.

The rides make him sick and the sideshows are crap but he likes the food smells; burgers, onions, candy floss, popcorn, all the warm, sweet, greasy smells. He likes the crowds, likes being in the thick of people, the closeness. And the noise. Once you're in there, the noise is like a wall, blocking everything else out. But the noise is still too far away to block out the dogs, yapping and panting on either side of the tree and not fucking budging an inch.

– I've better things to do than stay here all night, son.

– Me too.

– Call it a day, son. Just call it a day.

His dad is flexing his fingers in a showy, self-important way. His dad likes people to see the thick black gloves which make his hands look too big for his body, make them slow and clumsy and evil-looking, like the mechanical mitts of a robot.

The only chance to get free of this tug-of-war with the dogs is to go for one at a time. Cass is on his right. The dog is stronger than the bitch but the boy's right arm is stronger than his left, so he wedges his left arm against the tree and tugs on the right with everything he's got and he can see it happening, he can see the bastard turn tail and trot towards him but it's too late to stop the pulling. He wheels round the tree, lands flat on his back on the wet grass and there's a shadow above him, closing in, and the shadow raises a foot and stamps on his open hands. And then his dad's gloved hands reach down and clamp around the leashes before he lifts his foot.

The boy tries to shake the slimy leaves off his clothes but they cling on, like shreds of wet skin and he has to peel them off one by one; they leave behind gouts of greasy, leafy mud. Leaf and grass stains don't come off. He remembers his mother telling him that, years ago. The shirt's gubbed and it's his favourite; a genuine American skateboarding shirt from the best place in town. Weeks, no, months he'd saved up for it, served his time out the back with his dad and the dogs and now it's gubbed. He presses his fingers into his armpits. He's finished with it all, finished. He'll never get to grips with the handling. And doesn't want to. This thumb's rigid. Maybe it's broken. Maybe his dad's broken his thumb. Maybe he should go to hospital. He's surrounded by hospitals. To the left, near the school, is the Royal. To the right, bang up against his old primary, is the Sick Kids. He's been there a few times when he was wee, quite a few. He got to know the nurses and some of them were OK, kind, but he's too old for the Sick Kids now.

His dad and the dogs are plodding on. Their breaths echo, poke holes in the fog. His dad holds his head high and stiff. The dogs, cowed by the whipping they got from his dad, walk to heel, their hurt noses skimming the ground. The team dissolves slowly, melts away. The boy stays where he is. They're not his dogs. It's not his life.

Twilight

THE CHILDREN HAVE many names for me. Twilight is the one I like best. They call me this because, if they see me at all, it is at the time when all the colour goes out of the day, as if it were sucked away by the fierce dragging tide we have on this part of the coast. I say we, but I am not from around here, although I have come to regard it as my home.

At dusk I fetch water from the well at the end of the street, at the time when the flying foxes begin to cross the sky. Just before the streetlights go on – but we do not have so many – these large bats pass over the big banyan tree in the town square. I say town but really it is only a village with a little bit extra, for example the prison. The prison stands on a cliff not far from the house where I live, the house which has become for me both prison and sanctuary.

With little else to do now that the boats have been pulled out of the water, now that the unsold papaya and plantain in the market, the ladies' finger and the chilli have been packed up, now that the crows have stopped arguing in the tree-tops, the street vendors raise their heads to watch the slow heavy procession. I can see only the white of an eye or the glint of a gold tooth as one dark face after another tilts skywards.

The bats fly in a loose, straggling line, like the chain gang which has been laying stones on the road outside my house, the new road which, I've heard say, will bring money and work and visitors. Since I have been here I have had no visitors.

The bats are my timepiece. When I see them, I prepare to go out. There is something sad, something sombre about these unpopular creatures opening and closing their black umbrella wings as if they can't decide on the weather. Small boys like to scare them. Bored from playing around their mothers' heels in the market, they whoop and race onto the new football pitch, armed with pebbles which they hurl into the sky.

Like the bats, I too hunt for food at night. I too have my regular route. I used to take my time, to please myself where I wandered when the day's activities had died down to a murmur, when the marketplace was dark and empty, when only the temple and the toddy-shops were receiving visitors. I do not spend so long on the streets now. Now I am more careful.

There are a few good people who leave out a dish of rice for me. And sometimes chicken scraps, buffalo curd. On good nights I might find more food than I can eat before the ants carry it off. Other times nothing but stones and abuse are flung my way. There is no pattern to generosity. In my home town, though, after everything changed for me, things were much worse. I did not go out at all.

My sister still writes once a week with news, for example my mother's eye trouble, for example my father's work problems. My mother's vision is clouding over. My father's work makes him bad-tempered and give him an excuse to spend too much time drinking arak and feeling sorry for himself. His problems never change. Always it is the glazes. All his life he has tried to perfect a special glaze for his waterpots. When I was little he told me he wanted the glaze to shine like my skin. He does not say this nowadays.

I have not seen my family for several years. Really I don't think I will see any of them again. My mother is now too old to put up with the discomfort of a long bus journey although this year my sister learned to drive and the family could come all together by car. But there is always some excuse, for example a doctor's appointment for my mother – which of course she will not keep, for example a rush order for waterpots. My sister does not like to wound me with the truth that really no one wants to come, really no one wants to remember me. To my family I have become a shameful memory.

When I was a child my parents were so proud of me. I was not too dark – the rich bronze my father tried to conjure from his pastes and powders – not too skinny, and had good teeth in spite of the bad well-water. Really it was not hard for my mother to find me a husband when the time came. I did not like the man she chose for me so much, but I accepted him. It was the right thing to do. And before everything began to go wrong with me, he was no so bad really.

Of all people my mother, I hoped, would have had some sympathy, some understanding. But I was no longer the daughter she knew. I had become an unwelcome stranger in my birthplace. My face she no longer recognised as the one from which she had wiped food and dirt and tears a thousand times. In my new skin she feared me. Even in farewell she could not bring herself to embrace me. I had become untouchable, worse than a leper.

Of course my mother had been again the injection from the start. She had always been wary of new ideas, especially anything to do with doctors. Doctors, she said, worked for the government and only cured what it wanted cured. So why else do they not cure the water we have to drink? And why is the water on Queen Street not bad like ours? I tell you why… and so on. My mother believes what she wants to believe.

According to my sister, my mother could have had her vision cleared years ago. The mist which makes her fall down the temple steps, scald herself on the rice water, it could have been altogether removed. But again and again she has put off the operation. Look what happened to Sumona, she says and stumbles onto the verandah. The doctor tells her – he has to shout from the gate as she will no longer let him into the yard – that she spends too much time in bright light. He tells her it is not the well-water but the midday sun which is destroying her sight. So you want me to sit in the dark, as if I'm already in my grave? she says and continues to sit on the veranda from noon until four.

My eyes do not like the sun anymore. I don't see it much and, when I do, it dazzles me. So my mother and I are becoming alike, she blinding herself with too much sunlight, I with too little. But in the dark I see well. There are so many shades of night. Darkness is soothing. It is kind. Really I don't understand why people are afraid of the dark, why lights must be kept burning through the night as if darkness itself were evil. It hides. It protects. Its coolness comforts. Darkness is a friend.

A friend only to crooks and devils, my mother would say. And maybe she is right. Indeed the prisoners understand about darkness as well as I. From first light until sunset, gangs are sent out to work on the road. All day in the bright light and heat is plenty punishment without hard labour as well. When I hear the axes begin to ring on the stones – I am usually falling asleep at this time – I feel almost lucky to be resting in bed, alone, safe.

My mother was a friend to me before it happened. Like many women her age, she was eager for grandchildren. Two daughters and a son married by then, but being the eldest, I should have led the way. The two lost babies didn't count. I wasn't trying hard enough, she believed, even though I was so sick my aunt had to be called in to nurse me, even though the doctor explained to the whole family – he came at dinner to make sure no one wandered off before he had finished – that it wasn't wise, actually it was dangerous for me, that the injection was a new way to make me well again. My mother turned the doctor out of the house.

Sura, my husband, who turned out to be less decent than my mother imagined – he spent even more time in toddy-shops than my father – didn't like me to be sick all the time. It was expensive and my aunt's cooking gave him bellyache. He agreed with the doctor. Later, though, he denied this. I hear from my sister that he has changed his ways since becoming husband to my old school-friend and father of two boys.

Such a long time I have been here and still I am angry. With my mother. My husband. My doctor. Myself. Each evening I meet my reflection in the water I draw from the well. Once a day I must see myself as others see me. Once a day is too often.

Rage flares in me as I creep about the streets. It is no wonder the villagers think me mad as well as ugly, a creature who lives by night, sun blind. If I were a child, perhaps I too would hide in doorways waiting for the freak to come by, sharpening sticks and practising insults. And if I were a mother – but that will never be – maybe I too would cover my baby's eyes as the madwoman passed. As a man stumbling home, my head fuddled from liquor, I too might find it amusing to taunt an unloved creature with dirty propositions. These people I can forgive. But not my family. No, not my family. Not even my sister who writes with news. Not yet. A long time but still too soon. And myself. Can I ever forgive myself?

I can be no one else but me. Really I am the same as I always was. Only the surface has changed, not I, Sumona, whose skin lost its colour like the sky at twilight. Twilight is the name I like best. It does not hurt like some names, for example Pigmeat, which hurts because it is true and nothing can be done. My skin lost all its colour after the doctor's injection: now it is like pork, greyish-white, dead-looking. It does not belong in the daytime world, my skin. Only in a twilight of shadows, drawn blinds, in a world of crooks and devils, as my mother would say.

Tonight I will not rage and burn myself out like the bat who

47

traps itself on the overhead cables and fries. Tonight in my silent house, I will no longer be alone. I am to receive a visitor. This morning, as I was about to sleep, I was sent a message. The message was in code – but I could understand it: it was meant for me. Tapped out by an axe, a regular beat, like temple music, ringing against the stone. I got up from my bed and looked out. A line of men, chained at the ankles, bent into their work.

He was looking up so I knew it was he. He could not speak, of course, he could not even show that he had seen me. A prisoner must be humble or he will be beaten to make him so. My father taught me that. Lower your eyes and avoid a beating.

All day I have lain awake, listening to his message as the gang moves inch by inch along the road. I have spied on him through the blind from time to time. A tall man, strong, dark. He hits the rocks hard. Tonight I know he is going to escape. He has told me, in his way, what is going to happen. I will be ready for him. I will shelter him in my unlit house and in the darkness he and I will be like any other lovers. I do not know anything about this man. Perhaps he is a killer. But I will welcome him.

Wing

– WHAT I WANT to know is, what is wind? the woman barked into the stale air of the bus station waiting-room. She waved her magazine about. The pages fanned out and fluttered sluggishly.

– I mean, everybody knows what rain, is, for heaven's sake, and snow, clouds, hailstones, volcanoes for that matter, but wind? Personally, I don't have the foggiest and when I think about it, it seems quite remarkable that I've lived so long in utter ignorance of wind.

Wing looked up from the floor, where his eyes had been tracing the interlocking loops of a length of dirty string. Apart from the old woman and himself, the waiting-room was empty. He smiled briefly, shyly, leaned across the table between them and picked up a motor magazine, which someone had left behind. In response to his smile, the woman coughed noisily, pushed back flyaway strands of hair from her wide, spluttering mouth and craned her neck in the direction of the door.

Wing turned pages filled with cars, campers, spare parts and accessories. He was not a driver. Never would be, if he could help it. Cars were dirty, noisy machines with no soul. So were buses, but his pushbike was broken, the pushbike which, by day, got him to college and, by night, to his mother's cousin's sushi bar, where he put on a gold waistcoat, black pants and a smile six shifts a week, while most of his classmates were studying, drinking or driving the streets, looking for action. If he ever became rich, he'd buy a sailboat. If he became unimaginably wealthy, he'd buy a glider plane. If the winds of change blew him some unexpected fortune.

The woman took off her glasses and let them swing between a bony finger and thumb. She peered at the window where a maple battered its branches against the glass.

– There has been rather a lot of it about lately, wouldn't you say? Wind, I mean. Keeps me awake at night. Unsettling. Makes me think my apartment building's going to fall down, though between you and me, that might be a blessing in disguise. Not what it used to be, not at all. Tatty. And noise! I don't sleep well, as a rule. Age has something to do with it, I expect. Young people should sleep while they can, instead of staying up all night having wild parties.

– But what I say is, there's too much change in the air nowadays, too much upset. Nobody's happy. Nobody takes what they get these days and makes do. It's trouble trouble everywhere. Blowing the whole place away might not be a bad thing. Blow it away and start again… I don't suppose you could tell me what wind is, could you?

Wing smiled and shook his head. Whenever possible, he avoided speaking the language of Canada. He disliked the sound of it, flat and bland as the prairies, though the woman's voice held a trace of hills. Still, he wasn't exactly sure what wind was, though he knew its ways.

Since he was small, Wing had make kites. He'd made his first when he was six, with the help of his father who was home for the weekend – a rare occurrence – and not too tired or busy with work or drinking. Spring, and above Friendship Hill the Nagasaki sky was dark with fighter kites, dipping and swooping all day long, smashing each other to pieces. But it wasn't the destruction of a kite which decided the winner: it was cutting the cord, setting it free which mattered and even though the loser usually fell to the ground, ripped to shreds, Wing had always thought of this as a kind of victory.

He'd begged his father to help him build a kite, not a fighter, not yet, just a simple flier. At first his father refused, as usual grumbling about things he had to do. Then he suggested buying one, out of laziness rather than respect for the traditional skill. They argued for most of the morning but eventually Wing won and, through hot, hectic streets, happily clutched his father's hands, as they went looking for materials.

The workshop was hidden away at the end of a blind alley and looked like nothing at all from the outside. Inside, though, it was like a magic grotto: finished kites dangled from the ceiling in rows, their tassels twirling at the slightest turn of the air. It was like being underwater, looking up at shoals of paper fish swimming in the draught. On a floor spread with unfinished designs the kitemaker sat, dipping his brush into a big bottle of ink while his wife calmly wound silk thread around bamboo kite bones. A tiny tranquil old couple, doing what they'd always done, in harmony, with no thought of change. In front of them, Wing's father was unusually calm; mostly he was in too much of a hurry, impatient for change.

As the kitemaker wrapped up a package of paper, bamboo, twine and a small pot of glue, Wing asked about the designs, what they meant, where they came from, how many kites the man had made in his long life.

– A boy like yours would have been a blessing to us, he said, and explained how he had no son of his own, how he and his wife would one day be too old, how if the business were to continue, they'd need to find a boy to train.

– When I first opened this place, he said, boys would come

in all the time, asking to be taken on. We didn't need help then and, anyway, couldn't afford it. Now nobody wants to make kites. They want new, they want change, want to work in a big factory, to make cars and computers.

Wing could sense his father's impatience begin to return. He was smiling and bowing, tugging his son's arm, no longer listening to the old man, thinking about the time, thinking that it was time to go and get on with making the kite, to get on with what he'd promised to do, not to take pleasure from it but so that it would be done, so that he could have done his fatherly duty.

They walked home through the Sunrise Gardens. His father agreed to stop for five minutes, to watch the fish. Five minutes. It was always five minutes with his father and though Wing couldn't yet tell the time, he knew there wasn't much in it. He climbed on to the wall round the pond and peered at the water. The surface was starred with lilies. Below, the fish moved, swift and slim, their whiskery mouths gulping the muddy water. Wing decided he wanted a fish on his kite, a flying fish on a background of swirls that could be sea or cloud.

It had felt so rare, so special, that day, his father cutting rods and fashioning a frame while Wing cut and pasted paper triangles, the two of them sitting close, silent and occupied. Since the first simple kite – which had taken a good deal more time than his father had bargained for and, in the end, barely got off the ground – Wing had made countless kites.

When he was old enough to go downtown on his own, he'd returned often to the kitemaker's workshop and helped out, learning what he could. His visits were welcomed by the old couple, who were becoming frail and began to rely on the assistance of his young eyes and steady hand. By the time his mother had given up on his too busy, too absent father and, with Wing, left Japan to join cousins in Canada, he'd learnt a lot about the ways of the wind.

– You see, the trouble is, there are too many people. All the good things about this place had to do with space, being able to spread out, put a bit of distance between you and your neighbour. That's what everybody was after, in my time. But too many people jumped on the bandwagon and spoiled it all here and now we're packed like sardines again. Bloody nuisance, that's what I say, not that anybody cares what I say. And that's another thing. When I was young we listened to the old. Now I'm old, nobody gives a damn what I say. When I tell the caretaker of the complex that if he doesn't do something about the loose windows there's going to be trouble, all I get is dumb glares or empty promises.

Before sleep, Wing liked to look at comic books, the kind in which heroes and villains battled for control of the world with ancient magic and space-age weapons. The men wore bodysuits and exotic armour. The women wore bikinis and thigh-high boots. Monsters came in all shapes and sizes: the steely and muscular, the shapeless hulks, the hideously mutant. The comics gave him ideas for kite designs. As well as waiting tables, he made a bit of money from his kites. Students bought them to hang in their rooms. Relatives bought them for their kids. Sometimes kids were rough with the delicate things, and broke them. Their parents would complain about money wasted.

– Why don't you use tougher materials? they'd say. People use PVC these days. Paper stuff is history.

Lately Wing had been bothered at night, not by the gales which blew cabbage and bakchoy off the street stalls, tore holes in store awnings and upturned trash cans. It was in quiet moments during the night, when even Chinatown was asleep, that he heard another sound, a cold hollow roar. He imagined an illustration: a writhing tormented beast being dragged into the glittering depths of an iceberg. He knew it must be a truck passing the narrow alley-mouth, displacing air, causing an updraught and an echo which bounded along the wall. He knew it must be that but still the sound chilled him.

The woman was staring at him.

– Very quiet today, don't you think? Normally you get all sorts hanging around here, loitering their lives away, pouring out their troubles, spilling their beer and blowing smoke into your face. Why they don't take a bit more care of themselves I don't know. I'm no health fanatic but I do use the pool in the complex every morning. It makes sense, doesn't it? But some of them who hang around here, you'd think they'd no homes to go to, which is probably the case, judging by the state of them. Makes me wonder just how long this country can go on opening its doors to all and sundry. In my day, my day... but I expect I'll never know why a country chooses to set up something sensible and then mess it around. When I think about it, I've a mind to go back to England. But I'd miss the weather. Hah! What am I saying? It's wild out there. Can you see that tree, that red maple, the one they put on their bloody flag? Flailing about like a demented dervish, wouldn't you say? A wild wild wind. I expect that's something else I'll die in ignorance of.

The sun was out, the park busy. A faint but steady breeze stirred the leaves on the trees. Wing passed the animal houses and the popcorn stall, taking the path for the miniature garden. At the pagoda-shaped gate he stopped to read the eroded plaque:

THIS G RD N IS A G FT TO TH CITY
FR M THE PEOP OF JAPAN
WHO S TTL D H RE N 191

Saltwater City, they'd called it when they first arrived by boat, as indentured labour, to work the shipyards, railroads, mills, mines, to cook for prospectors and wash their filthy linen.

Facing east, where a small statue of Lord Buddha smiled down on a mass of chrysanthemums, a slight, pig-tailed woman prayed. Lilies smothered the surface of the pond. The fish below were like those he remembered from the Sunrise Gardens – gold, silver and black with shiny round scales like coins – but bigger; fat, sleek, sluggish. Kids fed them popcorn. On the trellised wall a drab, dusty heron surveyed the pondwater without interest.

From the top of the hill, Wing could taste the salt in the air. A wave of white hotels swept round the sparkling city waterfront, tailing off at the bridge out of town. Under the bridge, on the far side, lay the logging and pyramids of foul yellow sulphur. Nobody liked to live downwind of the mine, though plenty did. Like Chinatown, it was cheap. But the smell of sulphur got under your skin. He'd heard a girl at college say that before class, she'd sneak into a department story perfumery and spray herself with the most expensive scent they had on trial. He hadn't got close enough yet to tell whether she smelled good or bad.

Container ships slid imperceptibly across the horizon: cars to Canada, wood to Japan. Wing unzipped his carrypack, spread the kite on the ground, ironing out the creases with a flat palm. One of his best, at least, his favourite. He listened to the wind sifting through the grass then stood up, turned, threw the kite into the air, jerking it back briskly, for lift. The cord unravelled through his fingers, stinging as the kite leaped and dived, tugging on the line like an angry black fish. He played it through a single loop then cut the cord.

Beyond Vigilance

HIS HAND WAS hot, dry and covered in curly black hairs. He wore a chunky silver ring on his middle finger. His teeth were white and even, eyes shadowy behind tinted glasses. His black jacket was shot through with silver threads. He smelled of garlic and a recently applied sour-sweet cologne. Susie snuffled up to him like a puppy, pawing at his free hand, gazing at him in adoration, yapping non-stop.

– Sam, Sam, I know a joke. Let me tell you a joke...

You could still feel the heat in your palm when you removed your hand. He had one of those handshakes, that reassuring squeeze you'd never quite trusted. Too keen somehow to evince trustworthiness. You wanted rid of him before Billy got back to the bar.

The bar was busy. A crowd of flax-haired Icelandic tourists were listening, with boozy tolerance, to an interminable speech by a fat man in a hat. The PA was playing up; the mike swallowed the speaker's voice, chewed it and spat it out as garble and feedback. There were kids everywhere.

You'd met Sam that morning, in the lift, on your way to the

pool. Susie had been wearing her swimsuit – dayglo pink – which gave her pale skin a greenish tinge. Under the lift's harsh light she looked luminous, spritish. Sam and another man were already in the lift when the two of you squeezed in. They were speaking Spanish, a language barely heard in the hotel. It was better to listen to, easier on the ear than the usual rattling French, measured German and whining English. As the lift descended, the men's conversation switched to Susie, who giggled and squirmed under their appraising eyes. They liked what they saw; Susie knew it and loved it. When the word 'sexy' jumped out from their stream of Spanish, you pulled her close, tried to hide her behind you. But Susie didn't want to be hidden from admirers; at least not youngish, dapper, smiling ones.

– Your little girl is very... pretty, said Sam. When she grow up, she will break the hearts.

– Sam, Sam!

– Yes, my honey?

– Why do bees have sticky hair?

– You have sticky hair? You have some ice cream in it?

– No, it's a joke. You've got to say: *I don't know. Why do bees have sticky hair?*

– Why do bees have sticky hair?

– Because they comb it with a honeycomb!

Susie screeched at her own joke. Sam flashed his teeth and patted her head. He didn't get it.

– Don't bother the man, Susie, you said. He's got work to do.

– It is no bother, Madame. I *love* children. And your little girl, I think she *love* me, yes?

– Susie, why don't you go and play with that wee girl you saw at the pool this morning.

– I don't want to play. I want to be with Sam.

– Okay, my honey, said Sam. You want to see me make disco?

Susie clapped her hands, blinked like a stunned rabbit and skipped after him before you could think of a reason why she shouldn't.

– Stay where I can see you.

Spain loves kids, Billy had said, which is why you'd decided on a week in Majorca. The resort was certainly geared up to kids as consumers. On the main drag – an endless narrow street permanently choked with anarchic traffic – every other shop sold ice cream and trashy plastic toys twirled beneath striped awnings. But apart from the poolside and a shabby, weed-strewn beach at the other end of town, there was nowhere much for kids to play.

Today, though, you'd finally found a little swingpark at the end of a backstreet of low white houses and broad-leaved trees. Late afternoon and the bleached colours of the day were deepening, local life was beginning to resume slowly after siesta. There were no other parents in the park, just a few Spanish kids noisily clambering over each other on the climbing frame and chucking rocks down the chute. Susie ran towards them, fell and grazed her knee. After a thorough inspection of her injury – which was slight – she took a turn on everything but in a wary, joyless way. There were no safety surfaces here, just rubble laced with broken glass and her usual confidence had taken a knock. The Spanish kids had no interest in her which made her embarrassed and self-conscious and keen to get back to the pool.

It was when you were leaving the park that you came across the wee lost boy, hunkered down in the dirt, bawling. His face was blotched with tears, mud and rage. A damp nappy sagged below his shorts. Susie knelt down beside him, asked him where his mummy was and tried to give him a cuddle but the boy pushed her away and kept on roaring.

Susie had wanted to take him to the police station but neither you nor Billy knew where it was and, anyway, trying to shift the child didn't seem like a good idea. He was upset enough as it was without some foreign strangers trying to lift him up. These days, at home, people thought twice about approaching any child, even a lost one. Billy did go back over to the swings and tried, with the few Spanish words he knew, to ask the other kids whether the child was with them. They gawped at him in bewilderment, leaped down from the climbing frame and ran off.

Who knows how long you'd have dithered, had an old woman not made it her business to leave the doorstep she had been mopping and scuff across the street, in her slippers. All three of you began babbling at once, trying to explain, to ask for help. Her eyes quizzed each of you in turn then, laughing at your hopeless Spanish, your worried faces, she swept the lost boy up from the dirt and clamped him on to a broad hip.

– *Llamo a mama. OK, OK.*

You watched as she padded sturdily across the road – causing the traffic to jolt to a halt – talking non-stop to the boy and fending off his hysterical fists with smiles. When she reached her doorstep, she turned and waved.

– *Adiós.*

You walked to the hotel, glancing back from time to time.

– All the kids in that swingpark were too young to be out without a grown-up, said Susie, echoing the fearful arrangements of home.

– It's a bit different here, said Billy.

– How?

– Because Spain likes kids.

– Why was nobody watching that tiny wee boy, then?

You and Billy sat on stools, facing the stage.

– Where's Susie? said Billy.

– She's fine.

– But where is she?

– With the DJ.

You pointed to the back of the stage where Sam was trailing an extension cable behind a heavy curtain. Without hesitation, Susie followed him.

– She's OK.

– How can you tell? said Billy. You can't even see her!

Susie darted in and out of the stage curtain. Sam patted her head indulgently as he went about his preparations but he was clearly more interested in shaking the hands and kissing the cheeks of the tall Icelandic women who, now that their speechmaker had finished, were free to circulate.

– I don't want her hanging around that smoothie, said Billy.

– Susie's pestering him, not the other way round.

– Just look at him. Bloody gigolo if you ask me.

– He's OK. He came up and said hello.

– Did he now. How very nice of him.

The disco music was too loud and awful. A handful of teenage girls sloped on to the floor and jerked about half-heartedly. A wee boy in shirt and bow tie waltzed with his granny. While Sam was busy spinning discs which appealed to no one, Susie and some other kids ran out to the poolside to hunt for snails.

It was not one of those sunken kidney bowls but an old-fashioned rectangular pool with a high stone wall. Flowering shrubs sprouted through the pointing, home to colonies of ants, beetles and snails. The wee kids, like Susie, contented themselves with poking around the walls. The bigger ones clambered on to the wall, daring each other to teeter along it a few screeching steps.

You were usually the one who couldn't relax but tonight it was Billy who was on and off his bar stool, checking on Susie, telling her off for fooling around – though all the kids were running wild – and grumbling about the time when nobody else seemed the least bit ready for bed. Earlier in the holiday, you'd made a point of not keeping her up till all hours because the sun tired her out, the sun and the little differences in everything. And when she reached a certain point she didn't give in; she fought against tiredness, sense and the will of grownups.

But you'd promised, promised her a bit of freedom. It wasn't something kids had much anymore, at home. And if they did, it was called neglect. You couldn't take the risk anymore. If you read the papers, watched the news, you couldn't trust anybody – neighbours, friends, family even. That wee lost boy in the park. Had you done the right thing to hand him over to a stranger, even a local stranger who seemed kind and capable?

Sam had taken a break from the disco, which made it possible to talk without yelling in Billy's ear. It also meant that Susie deserted her pals and trailed after her idol. She was worn out. Her eyelids drooped, she was tripping over her own feet and talking drivel.

– Let's go, said Billy. She's had her bit of disco – didn't even dance. I'm not sitting through another session of that crap.

– It's not fair! Susie wailed. You promised I could stay up. And Sam promised he'd walk me round the pool!

– We can do it another time, my honey, said Sam.

– No, no! I'm going home tomorrow and I'll never see you again, ever.

You wait by the shallow end, in shadow. At the deep end, Billy stands guard. It's quiet outside now and the bay, spanned by paths of rosy light from distant hotels, bars and discos, looks prettier than it does by day. The pool is glassy. On the far side, beyond its black sheen, you can see Susie and the man in silhouette, hand in hand, edging along the high narrow wall.

Verge

HE COULD ALMOST touch the hedgerows on either side of the road. His eyes prickled. There was too much to see, the space insufficient, scale minute. All that sizzling crawling and spawning; it was too close, too vivid and exhausting, like the flutters, twitches and scrabbles of a bad hangover. He wanted to push the hedgerows back to a safe, impressionistic blur.

The car was long out of sight, back down the vermicular road, clapped-out on a narrow heel of gravel which called itself a passing place. The next vehicle to scoot round the bend would probably prang it. If there was one. He'd seen nothing on the road since he'd left the village but parallel curves of hedgerow and, overhead, a narrow ribbon of sky. There was a lack of air, as if the teeming hawthorn and briar had sucked it all up, leaving only a sour-sweet odour, a sickly mix of the blossoming and decomposing. The turgid heat pressed at his temples. He was burning up with thirst. There was always the sherry. Not wanting to return empty-handed – and subject himself to Margot's scorn – he'd brought along a bottle of Fino. The rest of the booze he'd bought in the village was locked in the car boot. A slug of sherry was better than nothing; it might at least take the edge off what promised to be a long walk. He hardly ever walked these days, other than a brief digestive stroll after one of Margot's healthy meals or a meandering toddle with wee Gayle.

They'd come to be near the sea but here he might as well be worlds away from the cheering breeze and the languid contours of coastline from which, on a clear day, you could see Land's End. The cliffs must be somewhere nearby, but where? He hadn't bargained for roads like this at all, expected a bit more from this part of the world. What was the point of going somewhere different if you couldn't see the scenery?

Margot's heart had been set on somewhere foreign, a French château, Italian palazzo – Margot's imagination inclined to the grand cliché – but he'd put his foot down; nothing difficult. No use making a holiday harder work than everyday life. Not going along with Margot's daydream had meant being lumbered with brochures to study at breakfast and dinner conversation – the only time he and Margot had what might pass for conversation – was confined to locations and facilities. Still, talking about holiday homes was better than talking about Iris.

The children were needing to eat. No matter how often Margot asked them nicely not to shout all at once and told them that crying couldn't cure anything, it made no difference. Running about all day in such relentless heat, it was no wonder they were fractious but they wouldn't be told, wouldn't just stay indoors and settle to some restful activity. She would have happily accommodated them at the kitchen table if only they'd let her get on with the food. Her sisters' children seemed totally committed to tormenting each other and Gayle was fretting for Finlay's return.

Since they'd arrived, Gayle hadn't let Grandad out of her sight without a protracted, dramatic farewell. Today she'd pleaded and whined for Finlay to take her along to the village, five slow miles away. The child was entranced by the place. Straight out of a picture book – thatched cottages with blowsy pink roses all but concealing doorways – it hung over a tidal inlet where fat ducks bobbed on the swell and the water sparkled like a fairy tale.

Grandad had got to go on his own for once but God knows what promises the child had extracted from him; a trip to see the pig, the pony, yet another swim in the slimy, disappointing pool. For a man accustomed to calling the shots, Finlay was indulgent to the point of idiocy with Gayle when she so clearly required a firm hand. Never never never would Margot wish any harshness to be inflicted on her darling granddaughter but there had to be limits, guidelines, something to fall back on. If she and Finlay didn't provide them, the child was bound to grow up reckless and adrift. It would only be a matter of time before she was drawn into a swamp of deviant sex, drugs and the inevitable despair of any motherless child.

Guidelines, security, these were things that she and Finlay could take care of with their eyes shut. They couldn't, even under present circumstances, create an impression of a loving couple – that was a long way back down the road. Yet, though their mutual contempt was public and energetic, there was still a private place in each of them where another kind of love struggled to survive.

It was hard to believe; only a few hours down the M8 then off west but even his basic idea of landscape had gone by the board. There was just nothing to see except the dense, bristling hedgerows which rose high above his head. Beyond them there must be fields of peas and wheat, rolling, springy downs, wiry sheep. It was getting dark. He would be late back, no question. Instead of swigging warm sherry from a bottle, he should be on the patio by now, a scotch on ice cool in his hand, working up an appetite as the stunning heat of the day gave way to a mellow evening glow. They had been bloody lucky with the weather;

not a wisp of cloud since they arrived, which was just as well with the screaming kids to contend with. A tonic in their way, the wee ones – and welcome company for Gayle – but there's only so much you can take of what's good for you, a lesson he'd learned from a lifetime with Margot.

He would miss his few minutes' peace, lounging under the rampant clematis while Margot worked wonders in the kitchen, wonders of which, at fifty-nine, he was still ignorant. How long would it be before somebody noticed that he had been gone too long? And who would it be: Gayle, Margot, or one of the in-laws Margot had invited to share their holiday because the two of them were precious little company for each other?

Through the open French windows, she could hear ice crack in glasses and wasps fizz around windfalls from the peach trees. Her sisters and their men were outside, enjoying the sunset. Dorothy, Hannah, Pete, Danny: they were all so casual, so laid-back. Younger than Finlay and herself, closer to Iris in years and attitude. Dorothy's lack of concern about her boys – Margot could barely get them to eat anything but sugar-rich cereal and ice cream – came close to neglect. And Hannah didn't seem to realise that children needed more sleep than adults: those girls of hers stayed up till all hours watching dreadful stuff on the TV. Margot's sisters just didn't seem to worry the way she and Finlay had done, first with Iris and now with Gayle.

The plans, time, energy – the money too, though they'd never grudged the money – what was the point? With Iris they'd tried to shape their daughter's future just a little, just enough to see her on her way in the world, to help her avoid making the same mistakes she and Finlay had made. But Iris, now they were left holding her baby, while she was God knows where, doing God knows what.

As the last light drained from the sky, the hedgerow chorus swelled. It reminded him of some of the stuff Margot listened to on Radio 3: *Our next piece represents the chaos and disintegration of the twentieth century.* Now playing live in the Devon hedgerows. And on top of all that, from the other side of the seething barricade he could hear a heavy, hollow tread which seemed to keep in time with his own faltering steps. Something was accompanying him, something big. When he stopped, it stopped. Probably a cow or a pony but this closeness, this sweaty intimacy with nature wasn't his cup of tea at all. The sherry was giving him a headache but a headache was preferable to the fingers of panic tightening around his throat.

The darkness was total. He couldn't see the road, was aware of it only through his feet which registered every chip of gravel as a potential danger. He continued, his free hand tapping the air. His invisible companion – which he sincerely hoped was animal rather than human – was clumping along again on the other side of the hedge. Was he walking straight? He had to walk straight or he'd end up in a ditch, scratched to hell. He had to get back, soon, but couldn't hurry; he could only creep, one hesitant step at a time. His sandals made contact with the grass verge. That was it. The verge. He had to stay close to the verge. It was his only way of navigating the suffocating, scented path.

The pain was sudden and appalling, as if he'd pushed his finger into an electric socket. It jolted up and down his arm repeatedly as the culprit buzzed angrily around him. He bit his throbbing hand, to prevent himself from screaming into the darkness. A wasp, Christ. He flailed forward, for all he knew reeling across the road, intent only on shaking off the bloody thing.

It was only the second time in his life that he'd been stung by a wasp. The first time, oh the first time; at the very end of a very long afternoon picking rosehips to raise money for black babies in Africa. He'd not been at all keen to spend his entire Saturday on the dusty lane which ran round the back of the cemetery. For hours on end he'd dropped bristly hips into a bucket and, to help pass the time, tried to imagine Margot's breasts beneath her sleeveless blouse. Instead of getting his hands on them as reward for his unstinting labour, or any other tangible sign of her interest – a kiss at the very least – a wasp got him on the mouth. Instantly, his lips had ballooned and blistered, turning him into the least desirable boy in 5B.

He'd not been keen but in those early days he'd go out of his way to keep Margot sweet. Ish. Margot was never sweet. Tongue like a lash and a dab hand at slapping and scratching according to all the Duncans, Alecs and Billys she'd knocked back. Good-looking with it, of course, best-looking bird in 4B. Persuading Margot to even consider a date had been a real achievement. And the competition had been part of the attraction.

Now, God help them both, they were so far away from desire. The very word sounded suspect. Margot, of course, had her needs, he did understand that; they'd both been through the mill with Iris and now there was Gayle. Even if they didn't give a toss for each other any more, somebody had to be there to wait until Margot had stopped weeping, blotted her eyes with the heels of her hands and shaken herself back into Capability Jane.

He'd lost all sense of time and direction. Inching his way forward like a blind man, listening hard, all he could hear now was the buzzing hedgerow and his own rasping breath. What had happened to his invisible companion? Why had it deserted him how, left him with nothing to go by but the strip of grass beneath his feet? He'd never wear sandals again; twigs and bits of grit had worked their way between his toes and God knows what nocturnal wildlife might decide to scrabble over his unprotected feet.

The car appeared without any warning. A flood of light pinned him, blinking, in its beam. Before he thought to shout or wave, it was rounding the next corner, the red eyes of the tailplate disappearing. His feet were covered with gravel thrown up by the car as it passed. As he started to walk on, his legs buckled beneath him. If he hadn't been on the verge, that car would have mowed him down.

Dorothy was rubbing aftersun into Pete's shoulders, Hannah and Danny were canoodling on the lounger. Margot didn't mind that everybody else was lazing about, not at all. She wanted everyone to relax, take it easy. It was meant to be a restful family holiday, and she could manage the food perfectly well by herself, in fact preferred total control of the kitchen. If only Gayle would give up whingeing for Finlay. What in God's name was keeping him? He'd just nipped out to replenish the booze – and so he should, he drank enough of it. Had he stopped in the pub again? She'd told him before they came down here that she wasn't going to spend every night as a grass widow, or a pub widow, or any other kind of widow when she had a perfectly capable husband.

She didn't want to think about the other thing but not wanting to think about something was like shining a light on it. Her perfectly capable husband worked too hard, drank too much, only paid attention to his diet when she shoved advice down his throat. Coronary, stroke, ulcer, brain tumour, liver failure, blood clot, the sudden onset of diabetes, epilepsy, catatonia, the names followed each other like a slow cortege from a never-ending war of attrition, the names and their symptoms printed in solid, gloomy type alongside illustrations in her *Family Guide to Health*.

The dinner wouldn't keep much longer. The adults were half-cut and hungry. The children had been fed and left to their own devices but she'd have to try to put Gayle to bed soon. It wouldn't be easy; the child was holding out for Finlay as if her life depended on it. And maybe it did.

He comes upon the driveway without warning and the relief

he feels in seeing Margot standing on the lit patio, looking out into the dark, is overwhelming. She's holding the child in her arms – and Gayle is no featherweight – rocking her and looking out, for him maybe, maybe just looking out at the stars. He hurries towards them, walking as straight as he can manage, which isn't very straight at all. Now that he's safe, and can see what he's doing, he's aware that the sherry has taken effect, that he's staggering; but it doesn't matter, nor does his throbbing finger, the main thing is that he's back and Margot is here, with his granddaughter, waiting for him. When he reaches the patio, he raises his empty bottle in greeting. It is the wrong gesture.

All the Little Loved Ones

I LOVE MY kids. My husband too, though sometimes he asks me whether I do; asks the question, Do you still love me? He asks it while I am in the middle of rinsing spinach or loading washing into the machine, or chasing a trail of toys across the kitchen floor. When he asks the question at a time like this it's as if he's speaking an ancient, forgotten language. I can remember a few isolated words but can't connect them, can't get the gist, don't know how to answer. Of course I could say, Yes I love you, still love you, of course I still love you. If I didn't still love you I wouldn't be here, would I, wouldn't have hung around just to go through the motions of companionship and sex. Being alone never bothered me. It was something I chose. Before I chose you. But of course that is not accurate. Once you become a parent there is no longer a simple equation. We have three children. All our own. Blood of our blood, flesh of our flesh etc, delivered into our hands in the usual way, a slithering mess of blood and slime and wonder, another tiny miracle.

In reply to the question my husband doesn't want to hear any of my irritating justifications for sticking around, my caustic logic. He doesn't really want to hear anything at all. The response he wants is a visual and tactile one. He wants me to drop the spinach, the laundry, the toys, sweep my hair out of my eyes, turn round, away from what I'm doing and look at him, look lovingly into his dark, demanding eyes, walk across the kitchen floor – which needs to be swept again – stand over him as he sits at the table fingering a daffodil, still bright in its fluted centre but crisp and brown at the edges, as if it's been singed. My husband wants me to cuddle up close.

Sometimes I can do it, the right thing, what's needed. Other times, when I hear those words it's as if I've been turned to marble or ice, to something cold and hard and unyielding. I can't even turn my head away from the sink, far less walk those few steps across the floor. I can't even think about it. And when he asks: What are you thinking? I'm stuck again. Does it count as thinking to be considering whether there is time to bring down the laundry from the pulley to make room for the next load before I shake off the rinsing water, pat the leaves dry, chop off the stalks and spin the green stuff around the magimix? That's usually what my mind is doing, that is its activity and if it can be called thinking, then that's what I'm doing. Thinking about something not worth relating.

– What are you thinking?
– Nothing. I'm not thinking about anything.

Which isn't the same thing. Thinking about nothing means mental activity, a focusing of the mind on the fact or idea of nothing and that's not what I'm doing. I've no interest in that kind of activity, no time for it, no time to ponder the true meaning of life, the essential nature of the universe and so on. Such speculation is beyond me. Usually when I'm asked what I'm thinking my mind is simply vacant and so my reply is made with a clear, vacant conscience.

I'm approaching a precipice. Each day I'm drawn nearer to the edge. I look only at the view. I avoid looking at the drop but I know what's there. At least, I can imagine it. I don't want to be asked either question, the conversation must be kept moving, hopping across the surface of our lives like a smooth flat stone.

Thought is not the point. I am feeling it, the flush, the rush of blood, the sensation of, yes, swooning. It comes in waves. Does it show? I'm sure it must show on my face the way pain might, the way pain would show on my husband's face...

– Do you still love me? What are you thinking?

Tonight I can't even manage my usual 'Nothing'. It wouldn't come out right. I try it in my head, practise it, imagine the word as it would come out. It would sound unnatural, false, a strangled, evasive mumble or else a spat denial. Either way it wouldn't pass. It would lead to probing. A strained, suspicious little duet would begin in the midst of preparing the dinner and I know where this edgy, halting tune leads, I know the notes by heart.

(Practice makes perfect. Up and down the same old scales until you can do them without tripping up, twisting fingers or breaking resolutions, without swearing, yelling, failing or resentment at the necessity of repetition. Without scales the fingers are insufficiently developed to be capable of... Until you can do it in your sleep, until you *do* do it in your sleep, up and down as fast as dexterity permits. Without practice, life skills also atrophy.)

For years we've shared everything we have to share, which wasn't much at first and now is way too much. In the way of possessions at least. We started simply: one room, a bed we nailed together from pine planks and lasted a decade, a few lingering relics from previous couplings (and still I long to ditch that nasty little bronze figurine made by the woman before me. Trollish, with gouged-out eyes. Scary at night, glowering from a corner of the bedroom.) Money was scarce but new love has no need of money. Somewhere to go, to be together is all and we were lucky. We had that. Hell is love with no place to go.

While around us couples were splitting at the seams, we remained intact. In the midst of break-ups and break-outs, we tootled on, sympathetic listeners, providers of impromptu pasta, a pull-out bed for the night, the occasional alibi. We listened to the personal disasters of our friends but wondered, in private, in bed, alone together at the end of another too-late night, what all the fuss was about. Beyond our ken, all that heartbreak, all that angst. What did it have to do with us, our lives, our kids?

An example to us all, we've been told. You two are an example to us all. Of course it was meant to be taken with a pinch of salt, a knowing smile, but it was said frequently enough for the phrase to stick, as if our friends in their cracked, snapped, torn-to-shreds state, our friends who had just said goodbye to someone they loved, or someone they didn't love after all or anymore, as if all of them were suddenly united in a wilderness of unrequited love. While we, in our dusty, cluttered home had achieved something other than an accumulation of consecutive time together.

This is true, of course, and we can be relied upon to provide some display of the example that we are. My husband is likely to take advantage of the opportunity and engage in a bit of public necking. Me, I sling mud, with affection. Either way, between us we manage to steer the chat away from our domestic compatibility, top up our friends' drinks, turn up the volume

74

on the sound system, stir up a bit of jollity until it's time to be left alone together again with our example. Our differences remain.

– Do you still love me? What are you thinking?

Saturday night. The children are asleep. Three little dark heads are thrown back on pillows printed with characters from Lewis Carroll, Disney and Masters of the Universe. Three little mouths blow snores into the intimate bedroom air. Upstairs, the neighbours hammer tacks into a carpet, their dogs romp and bark, their antique plumbing gurgles down the wall but the children sleep on, their sweet breath rising and falling in unison.

We are able to eat in peace, take time to taste the food which my husband has gone to impressive lengths to prepare. The dinner turns out to be an unqualified success: the curry is smooth, spicy, aromatic, the rice dry, each grain distinct, each firm little ellipse brushing against the tongue. The dinner is a joy and a relief. My husband is touchy about his cooking and requires almost as much in the way of reassurance and compliments in this as he does about whether I still love him or not. A bad meal dampens the spirits, is distressing both to the book and the cooked-for. A bad meal can be passed over, unmentioned but not ignored. The stomach, too, longs for more than simply to be filled. A bad meal can be worse than no meal at all.

But it was an excellent meal and I was wholehearted and voluble in my appreciation. Everything was going well. We drank more wine, turned off the overhead light, lit a candle and put on some old favourites: smoochy, emotive stuff, tunes we knew so well we didn't have to listen, just let them fill the gaps in our conversation. So far so good.

Saturdays have to be good. It's pretty much all we have. Of us, the two of us just. One night a week, tiptoeing through the hall so as not to disturb the kids, lingering in the kitchen because it's further away from their bedroom than the living room, we can speak more freely, don't need to keep the talk turned down to a whisper. We drink wine and catch up. It is necessary to catch up, to keep track of each other.

Across the country, while all the little loved ones are asleep, wives and husbands, single parents and surrogates are sitting down together or alone, working out what has to be done. There are always things to be done, to make tomorrow pass smoothly, to make tomorrow work. I look through the glasses and bottles and the shivering candle flames at my husband. The sleeves of his favourite shirt – washed-out blue with pearly buttons, last year's Christmas present from me – are rolled up. His elbows rest on the table which he recently sanded and polished by hand. It took forever. We camped out in the living room while coat after coat of asphyxiating varnish was applied. It looks good now, better than before. But was the effort worth the effect?

My husband's pale fingers are pushed deep into his hair. I look past him out of the kitchen window up the dark sloping street at parked cars and sodium lights, lit windows and smoking chimneys, the blinking red eye of a plane crossing a small trough of blue-black sky. My house is where my life happens. In it there is love, work, a roof, a floor, solidity, houseplants, toys, pots and pans, achievements and failures, inspirations and mistakes, recipes and instruction booklets, guarantees and spare parts, plans, dreams, memories. And there was no need, nothing here pushing me. It is nobody's fault.

I go to playparks a lot, for air, for less mess in the house, and of course because the kids like to get out. Pushing a swing, watching a little one arcing away and rushing back to your hands, it's natural to talk to another parent. It passes the time. You don't get so bored pushing, the child is lulled and amenable. There's no way of reckoning up fault or blame or responsibility, nothing is stable enough, specific enough to be held to account and that's not the point. The swing swung back, I swept my hair out of my eyes and glanced up at a complete stranger, a father. The father smiled.

We know each other's name, the names of children and spouses. That's about all. We ask few questions. No need for questions. We meet and push our children on swings and sometimes we stand just close enough for our shoulders to touch, just close enough to feel that fluttering hollowness, like hunger. We visit the park – even in the rain, to watch the wind shaking the trees and tossing cherry blossoms on to the grass – to be near each other.

Millions have stood on this very same ledge, in the privacy of their own homes, the unweeded gardens of their minds. Millions have stood on the edge, and tested their balance, their common sense, strength of will, they have reckoned up the cost, in mess and misery, have wondered whether below the netless drop a large tree with spread branches awaits to cushion their fall. So simple, so easy. All we have to do is rock on our heels, rock just a shade too far and we will all fall down. Two husbands, two wives and all the little loved ones.

Princess

– LOOK AT ME, look at me, look at me!

Sharon rolled into the room, arms outstretched and a huge grin on her face. Apart from the rollerskates and a Disney tiara, she was wearing nothing at all. Robert picked up his camera and looked through the lens. His six-year-old daughter wobbled towards him, modelling the birthday presents he'd bought her and displaying, in her disregard for clothing, a delight which grabbed his heart and twisted it. He wanted a picture, a whole reel, wanted to preserve this moment as insurance against the future, a souvenir of this day together. He'd been needing something fresh and candid, he'd become too caught up in planned compositions, in thinking more than seeing. His students were learning to use their eyes first and their brains later while he'd been forgetting his own advice and thinking too much about the effects he wanted to achieve. He had lost his innocent attachment to the moment but here was his daughter, dazzling him with her smile and her happy absence of clothes, saying all there was to say about innocence.

He shut the lens and put down the camera.

– Go and put your clothes on, princess.

– I'm not cold, Dad. Why didn't you take any pictures of me?

– The film's finished, he lied. Put your clothes on and we'll go out to the park. Rollerskates are really for outdoors.

– Aw Dad. You could send a picture to Mum to let her see what you gave me.

– Mum doesn't need one of my pictures. She can see the rollerskates whenever she wants. You'll be taking them... *home*... with you.

It burnt his mouth to say the word and mean a place where he didn't live any more.

– But I want you to take some pictures.

– We'll buy a film when we go out. I could take some pictures in the park.

– Call me princess again. I like it when you call me princess.

– We could stop at the ice cream shop, too. Get you a double scoop seeing it's your birthday.

– Okay, Dad.

Lies and bribery. The kind of things Robert didn't want his daughter to encounter but here he was, resorting to them himself. But he couldn't explain to her, he wouldn't tell the stupid truth about why he stopped himself taking any pictures. She wouldn't understand, couldn't. She had not yet been corrupted by the adult world – at least he hoped this much was true – and corruption can only be understood by those who've had acquaintance with it.

As Sharon rumbled down the hall, Robert closed his eyes and imagined the photo of his daughter that he couldn't take. It would have to be a memory, her pink translucent skin, her chubby knees, rounded tummy... even in his mind he was censoring himself, avoiding certain body parts, picturing her without sexual characteristics, the way dolls used to be made, though nowadays many came complete with anatomically accurate genitals. But even this neutered, censored image felt questionable now. With the custody battle turning sourer by the day, could every gesture of affection between himself and his daughter now come under scrutiny, every touch be open to misinterpretation, to distortion?

– Dad, Dad… can you help me?

Sharon was wearing a dress which buttoned down the back, but no underwear. He did up the buttons and awkwardly tied the bow at her waist.

– Go and find some pants, Sharon.

– Nobody's going to see my bum under a dress are they?

– Put some on anyway. You'll catch a chill.

– Daaaad! It's hot. I'm sweating.

– Put some pants on or we're not going for ice cream.

Sharon's lip wobbled.

– It's my birthday, she wailed. Why are you being so horrible?

– Please, Sharon. Just do it and then we'll go out. We'll have a nice time. I've been looking forward to seeing you so much.

– Will you do my hair in plaits, then, like Mum does?

– I'm no good at that, princess. I'll make a mess of it.

That was true enough. But he'd learn.

– I like your flat, Daddy.

– That's good. You can come whenever you want.

– Can I? Can I really? Yeaaaahhh!

Sharon's explosions of enthusiasm startled him these days. He'd expected the break-up to sully her, to turn an exuberant child into a glum, taciturn one but it hadn't happened. Not yet, at any rate. She was still brimful of life and he loved her more than ever for it. There had been tears of course, plenty, of sadness, incomprehension, rage but in between the tears, her eyes were still radiant.

– You'll have to ask Mum, of course. But I don't mind how often you come or how long you stay. Remember that, Sharon. My flat is your home too.

– Why would Mum mind?

– I don't know. She might have other plans. Some days it

might be difficult for her to bring you over.

– If I put on some pants, will you try to do my hair in plaits?

Robert's attempts at fixing Sharon's hair turned into the disaster he'd expected it to be. Sharon screeched and yowled as he tried to brush out tangles and was disgusted by her father's loose, lumpy plaits. After several attempts to improve them he lost patience and told her she'd have to learn to do her hair by herself or choose something easier. In the naked scorn blazing from her eyes, he saw the best and the worst of her mother: Avril's invincible will, a will which had carried them all through hard times together and now, he was sure, would keep her going without him.

The park was mobbed. He'd forgotten to bring his camera but it was probably just as well. As he held Sharon's arm to steady her as she skated, Robert kept a look out for stones, glass, dogs, cyclists; dangers. Now he worried more about her than when they'd been all together as a family, now it was vital that he return Sharon to Avril exactly as she'd arrived; even a grazed knee or the beginnings of a cold could suggest lack of attention, of care. No, his daughter must be returned to her mother in perfect condition, like a gift.

Sharon tugged at Robert's arms.

– Look Dad, look Dad.

A ring of ragged youngsters sprawled on the grass, drinking wine, playing guitars and decorating each other's hair with beads and rows of tiny plaits.

– Janie's got a wee plait just like that in her hair, it's got five blue beads in it, Dad. She got it done at the craft market. D'you think that lady would do one for me, if I asked? We could give her money. Janie said it cost two pounds something. Will you ask, Dad, please? If you haven't enough money I could pay you back. I've got seven pounds sixty-seven pence. Please, Dad.

– You can't just go up to somebody and ask them to do your hair. And it would take ages...

– Will you give me a piggy-back then? I'm tired.

– You're getting a bit big for piggy-backs. And heavy with those skates on.

– I've been skating for ages, Dad. Why won't you do anything I want?

Robert sat down on a bench and eased her onto his back. He should have been more organised and got out of town for the afternoon, even if Avril had shown up two hours later than agreed. The grime of the city and the smell of picnics hung over the park. By the time everyone went away that night, the grass would be barely visible beneath the rubbish people left behind them. It was always the same after a good day. He should know. Sleeping at night had become impossible. Night after night he'd lain awake, listening to unfamiliar noises in the flat; creaks, groans, clicks and drips and an unsettling powdery sound in the wall behind his bed, like crumbling masonry. He imagined the tenement disintegrating little by little so that nobody noticed until it was too late to stop the erosion, too late to do anything other than stare open-mouthed at a pile of debris, the remains of homes, lives. At night, too, it was always harsh, pain-laden human sounds which carried the most: drunks roaring at real or imaginary assailants, bawling babies, couples fighting outside or in. When he heard a couple going for each other he found himself listening intently, greedily almost, trying to picture their faces, the inside of their flats, their beds, trying to work out what had turned lovers into enemies.

He'd been lying awake at night, getting up at dawn and going to the park with his camera to catch the gulls doing their dawn raids on the rubbish left on the grass. There was something intimidating about the big birds striding around in the first light, clean, cruel and faintly amused, like thugs or generals. On the third morning he'd almost got himself arrested. Crouched down behind a tree he'd been waiting for them to land on the grass when a young woman jogger had rounded the bend in the circuit. At the same moment he'd sprung forward, aiming his lens at the gulls. The woman screamed and broke into a sprint, blowing a whistle as she ran. Knowing how quickly the birds would leave again, he continued taking photographs. A park patrol van drew up beside him. The dour, putty-faced warden wasn't at all convinced by his interest in gulls and rubbish; apparently the jogger had claimed that Robert had been photographing her.

– As you'll no doubt have noticed, sir, the young lady was wearing brief, shiny shorts.

Robert laughed out loud. He hadn't noticed the jogger's clothing; he'd been too jarred by her fear to notice anything much. Besides, he was trying to photograph the gulls and rubbish. Brief, shiny shorts, Christ. The warden had certainly been paying close attention.

– If I find you and your camera here again at this time of the morning, sir, you'll be paying a visit to the station.

Sharon's skates banged against his ribs as he lumbered past a cricket game, a football game, a picnicking family; father, mother, a granny, a couple of toddlers trying to turn cartwheels on the grass, and a baby crashed out in a pushchair, its cheeks like tomato skins. Granny was reading the newspaper, the mother peeling boiled eggs, the father pouring juice into coloured plastic beakers. Sharon dragged heavily on his shoulders.

– I wish I had a brother or sister. Look at the baby, Dad. It's so cute!

– It's got sunburn. It should be taken home.

Home home home.

– Choose, Sharon. Two scoops and then we can get going, okay?

Sharon, mesmerised by the tubs of ice cream, had her face pressed against the glass counter; lemon, pistachio, caramel, chocolate, mint, tangerine and some violent pink stuff gleamed frostily. A queue was gathering behind them.

They made their way home even more awkwardly than

before, Sharon trying to lick her scoops of chocolate and tangerine alternately, Robert clutching her arm. Rollerskates and ice cream at the same time, he realised too late, were not a good idea. In the heat the ice cream was melting quickly and he'd forgotten to bring any tissues with him. He seemed to be having to learn things all over again, things he thought he already knew.

– Try and lick the drips, Sharon, he said but it wasn't easy for the child to turn the cone round with one hand. She lost her balance and lurched off to the side.

– Careful!

– I can't help it, Dad!

Her hands and face were already smeared with ice cream and it was only a matter of time until some brown or orange sludge would find its way onto her dress – a birthday present from Avril – buttercup yellow and white, flimsy stuff which would stain in a minute. He knew enough about laundry problems. Working from home, he'd done most of the laundry. He had plenty experience of ruined children's clothes – food, paint, glue, grass, mud, blood, vomit, all contributed indelible stains. It had occurred to him once or twice while he was sorting out the whites from the coloureds that there was maybe some kind of record in stained clothing, some kind of statement about the world he lived in, that it might be have been worth trying a series of photos before he threw the clothes into the washing machine but he'd never got around to it. Now he used the launderette once a week; yes, some things were easier.

Sharon's ice cream was barely half-eaten when it fell out of its cone, slithered down her dress and plopped on to the pavement. An empty soggy cone, the dress a god-awful mess. Tears and more tears. Rollerskates and ice cream, why was he so stupid? Sharon wanted to go back for another but Robert knew he had to get the dress in water as soon as possible.

– Next time you come over we'll go without the rollerskates. We could sit in and order one of the fancy sundaes.

– With a sparkler in it?

– Whatever you want, princess.

Robert washed out Sharon's dress, scrubbing and scrubbing at the sticky stains, holding the cloth up to the light every so often, going at the marks again and again.

Laying out the birthday tea, it already felt like a long day. Sharon had unwillingly agreed to put on the dress meant for the next day, her going home dress. He should have tried to invite some of her friends round, done something more to celebrate the occasion. He'd been lucky enough to have his daughter over for her birthday and – selfishly perhaps – didn't want to share her with anyone. Though a party would have been more cheerful for the child than his own tense company, the breakup had been so recent and bitter he couldn't contemplate other parents arriving in his thrown-together shoebox of a flat, looking around, checking the place out, checking him out. Could he cope, was he safe to leave their precious children with? He wasn't ready for that kind of scrutiny, not now, not yet. Next year, maybe. Maybe by this time next year he and Avril would be able to stand in the same room together, smiling and offering round trays of sandwiches and cakes.

– Mum says I've to have a bath if you've got any clean towels.

– Of course I've got clean towels. What's she talking about?

– I don't know, Dad. She just said it and I'm just telling you because it's what she said. Can I have a party next year and you and Mum both come?

– We'll see.

– That's what grownups say when they mean no.

– It's too far away to think about.

They had played draughts and pick-up sticks, built several castles from bricks and painted a picture together. Sharon had splashed in the bath, the wet dress hanging on the pulley above her and dripping coldly on to her hair. Then they'd watched too many cartoons. Sharon hadn't wanted to go to bed and Robert had let her stay up much later than Avril had suggested – as if he didn't know her bedtime – so late that she had fallen asleep on the couch, thumb in her mouth, a habit she'd given up before she learned to walk. He carried her, heavy with sleep, through to the flimsy camp-bed in the study. She seemed to have grown since he last saw her, only a week ago. Soon he'd need to get her a better bed and turn his darkroom into a proper bedroom. Or give her his room and get a fold-out couch for the living room. Whatever.

Robert was woken in the night by Sharon running down the hall and into his room.

– Had a bad dream, Mummy.

– Dad, Sharon, it's Dad here.

– Had a bad dream, Dad.

She climbed into the bed beside him and lay rigid, staring up into the darkness. He reached out and held her hand while she calmed down.

– I'll take you back to bed now, come on. The bad dream's finished now.

– I want to sleep in your bed.

– I don't think so.

– Mummy lets me sleep in her bed.

– Please, Sharon, it's late. Let me take you through. I'll stay with you for a bit.

– NO, NO, NO!

Robert lay beside his daughter, stroking her cheek, lifting a lock of hair away from her eyes, inhaling her warm breath, humming a tune he'd sung to her as a baby, hearing his voice trembling, hearing it crack like a reed, a thin, lost sound, his own voice in the dark.

Why do the Hands not Weep?

THE COFFEE WAS tepid, tarry, and had probably been sitting on the hotplate since lunchtime but judging by the barmaid's blatant lack of interest in what little custom she had, the visitor reckoned that the odds on a fresh pot of coffee being brewed specially for her were about the same as being mistaken for a local. The barmaid wore the hotel uniform – tummy-hugging tartan skirt, matching waistcoat, white blouse with a flounce at the throat – emphasising the bossy chest and broad, child-bearing hips which appeared to be native to the area. Had there been any other local women in the hotel bar of this small coastal town, other similarities might have been observed. No woman over thirty, for example, wore her hair past her shoulders and the repertoire of the town hairdresser ran to three styles: short bob, short perm and unisex crop. In clothing, lack of choice was also apparent: chunky, bum-concealing pink and peach jerkins had clearly been this season's job lot. Even lipstick shades remained smudged within the pink-to-peachy range.

Apart from the barmaid and herself, there were no women present. These were details which had caught the visitor's attention earlier in the day, as she'd walked back and forward along the curving promenade of the sturdy wee place, pausing at the playing fields like everybody else, to watch marquees being erected and Portaloos hoisted off a massive, articulated lorry and deposited behind a row of copper-berried rowans.

It was six o'clock and the townswomen would be at home, dishing out dinner to their families and discussing whether the weather would settle down and behave itself for the next day. A sudden downpour had made the visitor take shelter in the hotel bar – there was nowhere else nearby except the Seaman's Mission which was closed in preparation for the event of the summer, The Games. Nobody called them Highland Games except outsiders, like herself, who came up from the south to watch the quaint but unsettling spectacle of burly men in kilts whirling like pumped-up dervishes and tossing large heavy objects as far as momentum and meaty shoulders permitted.

The bar was a wilderness of floral carpeting and forlorn clusters of empty tables and chairs. One wall was given over to a plaster relief mural, a Scotch broth of things marine. A handsome, jolly fisherman, the centrepiece of the composition, was as close to the real thing as a battered haddock is to what swims in the sea. A sample of the real thing sat round the only other occupied table. Three men, straight from work, an old boy, a middle-aged one and a chubby-cheeked lad, were putting away a few pints before wending their way home. Their clothes were larded with oil, fish scales, blood and other unidentifiable clart. From where the visitor was sitting, she could smell fishguts and sweat. A pale haze of cigarette smoke rose from the centre of the table and curled round the men, containing and defining them, binding them together in their common purpose.

The old boy with the raw cheeks, watery eyes and chewed-looking woolly hat was grinning at her, his mouth forming an inaudible invitation. He held up his whisky, as if he were proposing a toast and, with his free hand, beckoned her over. She smiled and shook her head.

– D'you do reflexology? the young one asked her.

– No. Why?

– You look like you'd do reflexology. The hippy gear and that. I've done ma back in.

– Well, bed's the best place for you.

She realised her gaff too late; nudges and sniggers rippled round the table.

– Come on over, Blondie. Ye look that lonely there.

– I'm fine.

– We'll no bite.

– Unless ye ask nicely.

The barmaid, who'd heard every word though her gaze had been trained on the door, had a weak chin, a shelving mouth and the cold fathomless glare of a shark. She served her customers because that was her job. She was under no obligation to be pleasant to them and the idea of encouraging custom by hospitable chit-chat was clearly a foreign and therefore dubious notion. Even her regulars were there on sufferance.

The visitor sipped her disgusting coffee and looked out of the window. The rain had stopped as suddenly as it had started. Grey sky had given way to a thin, watery yellow. Clouds, in glittering shades of pewter and lilac, floated above the bay like big slow fish. The sun came out from behind a shoal of herring-coloured chevrons and dazzled her. It didn't surprise her that a lone woman – and a visitor at that – was still considered fair game, but she wasn't in the mood for drunks. She'd leave shortly and drive the hellish but spectacular road back to the B&B, to her small pink room with its brushed nylon bed sheets and a box of bibles in the wardrobe.

– I've come to talk to you.

The middle-aged one dumped his pint glass on the table and sat down. He must have been in his early fifties, though his peat-brown hair was thick and springy with no trace of grey. His crumpled shirt, open at the neck, revealed a small St Christopher on a thick, gold chain.

– I'm a rich man, he said. I don't want for anything. See that, he said, pointing to the fish-packing warehouse on the dock, that's mine. See that car – the silver Merc – that's mine too. I've done fine for myself.

He belched, apologised and downed a couple more inches of his pint.

– D'you mind me talking to you? I'm no wanting to be a bother.

Not feeling up to brutal honesty, she smiled and said nothing.

– Are you here for The Games?

– Not specially but as they're on…

– I'll not be going. The whole town will be there but not me.

His name, he told her, was Andy. Handy Andy his mates called him. He'd worked his way round the ports of Britain and settled in this quiet wee place with its glorious light, grand mountains and sheltered bays.

– Are ye no bringin Blondie over here? said the young one with the bad back. You're no the only one who likes a bit fresh company, man.

– Wheesht, the old boy slurred. Let him be.

– Nae much crack in Andy, Blondie. Ah could entertain ye better'n that auld misery.

The old boy grasped the young one's drinking arm and leaned forward until their faces were almost touching.

– You'd be doing everybody a good turn, laddie, including yourself, if you'd keep that big stupid gob of yours shut.

Unaware of the conversation at the other table, or choosing to ignore it, Andy gripped the edge of the table, rocking forward and breathing his beery breath into her face.

– I won't go to The Games.

– Yes, you said that.

– Did I? Aye, Blondie. I say things over and over. The lads there, they're sick of listening to me.

– Everybody repeats themselves when they're drunk.

– Drunk? I'm not drunk... yet. Can I talk to you?

– You are talking to me.

– Ach...

Andy turned away and cast his eyes over the empty bar. The shark-faced barmaid was leaning against the till, worrying the flounce on her blouse.

– See her there? said Andy. My sister-in-law. A yak yak. She'll tell my wife I was talking to you. Troublemaker. Fuckin yak yak.

His hands were flattened against the varnished wood. A gleaming wedding band hooped a chapped finger.

– I'll buy you a drink.

– I don't want a drink.

– I've plenty money. I'm a rich man. I want for nothing.

– A Coke then. I'm driving.

– Hah! Driving! Me too.

– You know the roads.

– Aye, Blondie, I know the roads, like the back of my hands.

Andy splayed his fingers as wide as they would go, till the veins stood out like a network of converging paths or streams. Through the thin, almost transparent skin, the blue-green tributaries jumped and throbbed. She could almost see the blood pulsing through them. At the knuckles, the slack rucked into little wrinkled mouths but Andy wasn't seeing his hands, the table they pressed against, the floral carpet.

– I've put new brake pads in my car, he said.

He stood up abruptly and went to the bar. His sister-in-law unfolded her arms and, without a word to him, pulled three pints and lined them up.

– And a Coke was it, for your... friend?

– Aye.

– Would she be wanting ice with that?

– Aye. And a slice of lemon and all, if it's not too much trouble for you.

Andy and his sister-in-law exchanged cash for goods without the aid of any social pleasantries.

The visitor realised too late that she should have gone after her coffee and avoided being drawn into this inbred, insular animosity. She'd come for the light, the space, for the absence of noise, dirt, too many people and too much to do. She'd come to watch the changing colours of sea, sky and land. Seven hours driving it had taken to get here, to get away from her own insular domestic bickering. Why waste precious time on somebody else's?

– I don't believe in life after death, says Andy. Do you?

– No.

– When you're dead you're dead. And that's it.

– That's what I think. But nobody can know for certain.

– So I'm never going to see my boy again, am I, Blondie?

That was when he began to talk, the man with the lucrative fish business and the silver Mercedes, when he began to tell the visitor his story of last year's games, the big turnout, the disappointing weather, the beer tent awash with drenched bodies, the humiliation of incomers scooping the lion's share of the prizes. But in spite of the weather and cultural pride being undermined, a good do. A family get-together too, their eldest boy home for The Games, grown-up now, independent, with steady work not too far south. Always a close family, a tight crew, their lives lashed together, part of the same mesh. And after The Games, the ceilidh. The Games weren't the same without the ceilidh after. Everybody spruced up, the men smelling of pine, the women sweet as clover, half bottles in hip pockets, a flame in every heart as the fiddlers tuned up, the grime and grind of work washed away as the dancers took their partners. The hours just birled away.

Of course some always drew the short straw. Folk had to

get home somehow and what did you do if there were no buses, trains or taxis? Not his own boy driving but a friend from school who'd sensibly stuck to orange squash and stewed tea. It could have been drink, drink took so many on the roads and off them. It could have been drink but it was a stag, hot on the heels of a hind, leaping blindly into the road, smashing into the windscreen. Four boys dead, the stag too, just before dawn on the coast road south.

– The wife won't stop crying. Folk from the church keep coming to the house and saying: God loves us, our boy is alive in our hearts... but when you're dead, you're dead, Blondie. And that's it... D'you mind me talking to you? The lads there, they don't hear me any more.

She looks out of the window. In the rain-washed evening light, the shingle glitters. Along the curve of the bay, draped between street lights, multi-coloured bunting flaps softly. People are out walking, locals in pastel jerkins, visitors in slime-coloured Barbours. She can see her car, parked near the war memorial. A stone soldier, gun in hand, searches the bay for enemies. An irreverent gull perches on his head. Beyond the purled, treacherous road, the setting sun has gilded the peaks of Assynt; Ben Glas, Canisp, Cul Mor, Stac Pollaidh, Suilven. Could there be anything more like heaven on earth than the light on those ancient, unique peaks? It's said that God was practising when he threw those lumps of rock at the land, one by one, like a novice potter chucking clay at a spinning wheel, hoping to hit centre. One-off mountains, mountains to fall down and worship, not for their perfection but for their endurance, mountains to love because they are there, have been and will be long before and long after everything imaginable...

But a mountain does not speak the same language, sky can't feel joy, hope, sorrow. Does sorrow only reveal itself through the eyes? What of the hands, which have held the loved, lost one, why do the hands not weep?

Andy's fingers are laced together like a cradle, or a net in which he has landed too heavy a catch.

Gynae

THE FACE WAS too big, as if the head had been rolled flat. Blurred; the eyes and mouth just dark smudges. And too close, almost touching her own. All she could see. Her hands went out to push the face away but as she reached out it backed off, ballooning up into the darkness.

– Just checking.

Night staff. In dark blue. The ones in white took temperatures, blood pressures, urine samples and sat on your bed with a clipboard and a list of questions. The ones in yellow brought clean sheets and tea, if you didn't have NIL BY MOUTH above your bed. Pale green for the theatre crew, plus masks and non-slip clogs. One of them held your hand, the others horsed around, while they knocked you out. They did their business while you were off in limbo land. The jolly butchers. What did the bluecoats do?

– All right?

There was a smell – not a bad smell – familiar, but she couldn't put a name to it. A free-floating memory. No connection, no link to a particular person, place, time. She rubbed her cheek against the pillow, trying to identify the smell. The night nurse must have taken her movement to be a nod because she moved off, a smile spreading like a stain across the lower part of her face. The soles of her shoes made a sucking noise as they detached themselves from the lino.

Calamine? Calendula? Something medicinal but gentle, a balm, not at all like the harsh hospital smells. Camphor, camomile, she had the feeling it was something beginning with Ca. Ca Ca Ca Ca... If she could name the smell, she'd be nearer to pinning it down but she went blank after camomile and that wasn't it. Whatever it was, it was comforting and she was in need of comfort. She wasn't all right but neither was anybody else in the ward and she wouldn't be as bad as some. The nurse was out of earshot. She'd have to raise her voice to be heard, which was bound to disturb other patients.

Was there a bell to press? On the wall behind her bed were a couple of unmarked buttons but nobody'd told her what they were for. After they'd taken her particulars – and asked her for the n'th time if she was sure she wanted to go ahead with it – they'd just left her there to wait for her turn to be wheeled along to theatre. Her mouth opened and made the shape of *nurse* but not even a whisper came out. Across the aisle, a woman howled. It was the bleak, naked cry of someone trapped in a bad dream.

She'd been sleeping, dreaming maybe, she couldn't remember, but it had been deep and soothing, the kind of sleep people talked about in books but didn't, in her experience, happen so often. A total escape from awareness. she owed it to the little sturdy nurse – bobbed hair, specs, the trace of an Irish accent – and her needle. She remembered the chill of meths on her skin, the steel point pushed firmly into her backside, a brief swelling as the morphine sank in, the seductive rush of numbing warmth.

How long had she slept? How many hours had passed? That

was what mattered, passing the hours, days, God help them weeks, staring at the telly or the ceiling, using up the time in baths, meals, medication, sleep. In Gynae people didn't talk much and didn't ask what you were in for. Too touchy an area: terminations and blocked tubes, women getting rid of babies, women desperate to conceive. If they could have done a swap...

Her back-to-front gown felt damp. She slid her hand over the sheet. Damp also. Maybe just sweat. Maybe that was all it was but she'd have to look, to check because the nurse hadn't. The light switch was in an awkward place, high on the wall behind the bed. She had to turn over onto her side and hoist herself up, supported by an arm which felt as if the bones had dissolved, as if it hadn't been used for a very long time. The stitches tugged as she lunged for the light. God Almighty. Worse than before. A flood.

She sat up in bed, holding the sodden red sheet away from her matching gown, staring at the strange brightness of the blood. How could it be her own, all that from a small incision at the navel? She looked like one of the battle victims she'd seen on the lunchtime news, when there was no lunch because they hadn't done her yet, hadn't opened her up. To get away from the tormenting smell of food which wafted into the ward from the corridor, she'd moved through to the patients' sitting room. Nothing like NIL BY MOUTH above your bed to whet the appetite.

An auxiliary had been dusting the seats.

– Glad I don't work *there,* she'd said, as footage from yet another war-torn city was blasted across the screen.

Bombs and bloody corpses. Hospitals bursting at the seams.

– What a world, eh? The things people do to each other. Never watch the news. Gets me down, so it does *Hello!* magazine, that's my cup of tea. Everybody's happy, that's what I like to see. Gives you a wee lift. Want a loan of this week's issue?

She'd said no to *Hello!*

Like a moth, the night nurse fluttered towards the light and drew the curtains round her bed. More red. Red and pink stripes to stare at while the nurse went off without a word, to find something or someone. At the far end of the ward a cistern hissed. Did she need to pee? The last time they'd made her use a commode. The swaying curtains were making her nauseous.

She shouldn't still be here, wouldn't have been if things had gone to plan. She'd told the nurse, the sturdy one with the needle, she'd told her she had to get home, the kids would be upset, she'd promised them a bedtime story. And anyway she couldn't waste any more time on all this, she'd have to be back on her feet the next day, or the day after at the outside, have to be fit for work. If she took the injection she couldn't go home…

– One thing at a time, Christine, said the nurse, the only one out of everybody she'd seen who called her by her first name. It had seemed more caring somehow and she had been in a state, the pain severe, and the morphine had taken it away, taken everything away for a while. Even now she still felt detached from her body, distant, except for the wound. All she felt in touch with was the wound, invisible under a sodden dressing, only the incision at the navel linked her with her body.

A low rumble of trolley wheels. The curtains parting like the Red Sea. Another face. Yellow coat. Armful of starched linen.

– What a state you're in, said the auxiliary, sighing at the sight of it, her, and she felt embarrassed by the mess, the trouble, about having to sit on a chair while a stranger changed her bed, covered the sodden dressing with a fresh lint pad – We'll leave that to the doctor – and dressed her in a clean gown. Like a baby, a bloody baby. She'd gone though a load of linen, made extra work for everybody.

Something had been taken away. That had been the point of the hospital visit, to take something, no, the possibility of something away from the invisible regions of her body. That had been done. She had been done. Doctored. She'd volunteered.

The decision had been made under no pressure from anyone and it had seemed like a good idea, a practical one at any rate, one which would simplify the future, make it manageable. But something else had been taken away.

A white-coated nurse breezed through the curtains followed by a young male doctor, in theatre green. He held out his hand to her but before she realised that she was meant to shake it, the hand was retracted. She could feel a wild giggle bubbling up from the pit of her stomach, trying to free itself, to erupt into the sleeping ward. She mustn't laugh. It would hurt to laugh and anyway, it wasn't funny, there was nothing at all to laugh at.

But God, he was so young to be left in charge. Just a boy, white-faced under the light, unruly red curls falling into his eyes. Not exactly Doctor Kildare. As a kid she'd watched the debonair Chamberlain on telly and – along with thousands or maybe millions of other female viewers – fantasised about being laid up with some critical (but not disfiguring) injury and coaxed back to health by a concerned and attentive Kildare.

But nobody in their right mind would want to meet a man they fancied under these conditions. A woman, even a very young woman, would have been better. A woman would have made more sense. Why were there so many men in Gynae? How could a man decide what best to do with bits he didn't have? And what in God's name attracted them to specialise in that department? Were they all perverts or what?

The smell was still there. Maybe it was in the linen. Knowing what it was wasn't going to help any but it was something to think about, something else. Maybe it was in the air. The flowers? Plenty flowers about the place, though none at her own bedside. She'd had no visitors. No need, she'd be in and out the same day, that was the plan. But the plan had fallen through and when they decided – the smarmy young surgeon who cracked jokes about bimbos and bikini lines and the nice nurse with the needle – when they decided to keep her in overnight, she'd wished to God that one of those fit people who filled up the ward after the evening meal with chat and chocolates, was there to visit *her*. But no flowers. Elsewhere she liked them; in the wild, in a garden, a vase on the kitchen table. But not in hospital. There was something stiff and lifeless about the florists' sprays, the functional bunches of cheery daisies, tight, fleshy rosebuds and papery carnations. Carnations. Could it be the carnations?

She felt stupid being wheeled through the ward flat on her back, tried to sit up, was gently but firmly restrained by the nurse, put in her place, in the hands of two tired-looking kids...

Notices in the corridor: NO SMOKING. GIVE UP SMOKING. PATIENTS' CHARTER. What did that say? She'd read it through that morning as she waited to be admitted, waited to hand over her body... courteous... prompt... ensure. What was it that they would ensure? What was it that she had a right to expect?

The overhead light in the theatre was weak and ineffectual, sick-looking. Gone the bright daytime buzz of the operating-room, gone the loud, hairy porter who showed off his tattoos, leered at the *ladies* and jollied them along to the chopping block. At night the room was grey and dreary and deserted.

She was rolled off the trolley onto the table, a surprisingly narrow metal and rubber affair, and left on her own again. It was the way of it. Entrances and exits. And then the voices off – whispers, laughter, the well world going on as usual on the other side of the curtain. Had they gone for a tea break?

She could do with a drink. Nothing all day. NIL BY MOUTH. A drink would make her feel better. And a bite to eat. Bread and water would do fine. If she could get hold of the one who'd changed her bed... Why hadn't she thought to ask at the time? She was the one to ask. Tea was one of her duties. No point in asking the wrong person, the doctor, say. Doctors didn't deal with tea.

There was something worrying about the way the two of them were passing instruments back and forward. And all that rattling and clinking. It seemed… experimental, like kids making up a game, a kind of medical Mad Hatter's Tea party. The nurse couldn't find the scissors. The doctor was holding a length of catgut which looked like a guitar string. He was squinting at the stuff with the curiosity people show for something they've never seen before. She felt horribly alert. She'd seen more than enough and they hadn't even started yet. If they'd just give her a general like the first time, instead of a local, all she'd know would be a fizzing tingle in the veins, then blackout.

But it was the nurse who blacked out, just after the doctor peeled off the dressing. He held it out to the nurse for her to dispose of but she shook her head. Her eyelids flickered rapidly. Her face turned the colour of the walls. She stepped clear of the operating table and flopped on to the floor. The doctor gawped at the body on the floor and the body on the table, stupefied by panic. The desire to run away was written all over him, yet he did nothing except stare at his hands as if he were counting them and wondering: Why so few?

Beneath her dressing the blood had pooled thick and dark and in an alarming quantity. As the doctor dithered between cleaning up the patient and resuscitating the nurse, she lay on the table and looked up at the ceiling. Again a giggle – or was it a scream – bubbled up from her guts.

– Can I do anything to help? she said. Help was undoubtedly needed and at that moment she was the only person available.

This is Tomorrow

THOUGH SHE LAY with one pillow under and one pillow over her head, she could not block out the nasal warble of the DJ to which Frankie, who lived on the floor above, was crossing imaginary lochs on his rowing machine, his trim moustache glistening with sweat. She glanced at the luminous digits of the clock which stood on the bedside table, ticking its own small contribution to the pre-dawn chorus. It was six a.m., as she knew it would be.

It was too much, being woken again on top of the baby roaring for feeds all through the night. She pressed the top pillow hard against her ear and pulled down the blanket but now that she had been woken there was little chance of getting back to sleep again, little chance of being able to muffle the rousing words of the DJ and the brash music he fed to his early-morning listeners. To the mother, this assault on the ears was worse than any alarm clock. It didn't simply shock her awake then leave her to gather her senses but insisted, like a stubborn child, until she felt her body stiffen with a hopeless and distressing rage.

Rage was an emotion she has not really known in herself until she became a mother. Coolness had been her characteristic response. Temperature control. Emotions on hold. But nowadays rage took to bubbling out of her like a hot thick soup, spurting its burning broth and scalding at random.

She wriggled on to her back, taking care not to disturb the baby who lay like a starfish between her and her husband, snoring softly, hogging the best part of the bed. The mother huddled on the edge. It was still dark outside when the upstairs radio was turned off. By this time she had heard – between exhortations to leap out of bed and jog round the nearest available open space – that roadworks on the M1 were causing lengthy tailbacks, that a leading brand of breakfast cereal had been taken off the market due to the discovery of carcinogenic additives, that bags under the eyes could be reduced by wiggling the nose, that commuter stress could be alleviated by early baroque flute music, that the number of hedgehogs killed on the motorways was at an all-time high, that an artificial Christmas tree was more environmentally sound than a real one. And a dozen golden oldies, songs which had been hits when she was an idle teenager: *Wild Thing, Dedicated Follower of Fashion, Lazy Sunday:*

> *got no time to worry*
> *close my eyes and drift away*
> *close my eyes and drift away*
> *close my eyes...*

Seven a.m. Still an hour in which to catch some more sleep, an hour before the morning routine need be set in motion. If she could lose consciousness quickly she might feel rested by eight. But if it took too long the cat-nap would only make her feel worse when she did have to get up, so was it worth trying? She closed her eyes and began to breathe slowly, deeply, the way she had been taught at the ante-natal refresher classes, amidst a roomful of women propped up on cushions, rehearsing for pain. But this only emphasised the tight knots of tension which snagged across her back from her neck to the base of her spine. She shifted, shifted again, rotated her shoulders, made her mouth hang open to prevent her teeth grinding together. She tried to make her mind go blank, empty.

That was what the mother was seeking, an emptiness, a void into which nothing would flow, fill up and demand attention. A clean dry basin with no dirty dishes in sight. But it wasn't easy to empty the mind. Not easy at all. The more she tried to clear it the more cluttered it became, each thought jostling for attention, the essential and the junk, the things she must remember and those she'd be better to forget.

Just as she began to sense her aches and pains retreating, the tensions loosening off, the mind sifting its jumble, she heard the familiar sound of her three-year-old racing down the hall, pushing open the creaking bedroom door and skidding to a halt at the bedside. And then the high, clear voice:

– I want breakfast. Is this a nursery day? Is the baby in your bed *again*?

– Shush. Shush.

– I'm hungry. Is it morning time? Is this a nursery day? Mummy? Mummy!

– Shhhh. You'll wake the baby.

– Is this a nursery day, Mummy? Is this tomorrow?

– No, it's today. The day you're on is always today.

And then she remembered what day it was, leaned over to switch off the alarm before it began to bleep – it would wake the baby but not her husband – and with more enthusiasm than usual, dragged herself out of bed.

Her eyes were still half-closed as she stepped into the shower. Today she must fight her craving for sleep. Today was a day to be alert, to savour each moment. She had things to do other than washing, cleaning, shopping, cooking, feeding, clearing up. She had people to see. A life of her own for a day and a night.

– Corn Flakes, Weetabix or Honey Smacks? the mother asked as her daughter trotted behind her into the kitchen.

– I want porridge.

– Please.

– Porridge *please*.

– I don't think there is any.

– Yes there is. It's in the cupboard.

– I don't think so.

– Yes it is. So there! I want porridge I want PORRIDGE!

It was going to be porridge or a tantrum and porridge took less time so she put on a pan of milk to heat and began clearing away the clutter from the night before. As the milk frothed over the lip of the pan, she could hear the baby begin to cry, its whimpers building up to a full-throttled scream. She lifted the milk pan off the heat, stirred in the oats, turned down the gas, filled a beaker of juice for her daughter and gave her a book to look at while the porridge cooked, while she got the baby up and washed and dried its hot pink bottom, changed the nappy and dressed her in fresh clothes, threw the nightsuit into the laundry basket, slid the jiggling body into the highchair, while she filled a kettle and switched it on, found the baby's plate and beaker, cut a slice of bread for herself and put it under the grill to toast. She dropped a dollop of porridge in the Peter Rabbit bowl, added milk, sugar, spoon, set it down in front of her daughter who screwed up her face and began to whine:

– But I wanted to put in the sugar BY MYSELF!

– Next time, okay? Tomorrow.

– But this is tomorrow. THIS IS TOMORROW!

– This is *today*. How many times have I told you, the day you're on is always today.

– It is not! Don't you dare say that! said the child.

The bottom lip was pushed out and a couple of large tears pooled in the corners of her angry eyes. The baby laughed and banged the table with a chubby fist.

– It's not funny, said her big sister.

– She's just trying to cheer you up, said the mother.

– She is not! But anyway anyway anyway, how can I cheer up when I've just been upset?

As the baby girned in response to her sister's sudden gush of tears, the toast began to smoke under the grill but the mother turned it over anyway, poured boiling water into the baby's mush and – to avoid lumps and choking fits – stirred as patiently as she could. She fetched a couple of rattles from the toybox and put them in front of the wee one to keep her occupied while the food cooled. She made coffee, took the toast out from under the grill, spread it with butter and bit off a large chunk. Her daughter was dragging her spoon through the porridge, turning what had been a fairly appetising plateful into a lumpy, sloshing mess. She had not yet begun to eat. The baby was hitting itself in the face with a rattle. The mush was still too hot for the baby so the mother finished her toast, gulped down a mouthful of coffee, walked briskly through to the bedroom and shook gently, the exposed shoulder of her husband. She shook the shoulder again, firmly. She spoke his name gently. She spoke his name firmly. She announced the time then went back to the kitchen.

Five minutes later, after managing to aim a few mouthfuls of food into the baby's roaming mouth, she returned to the bedroom and went through the shaking-waking process again. This time she was shrill. Her husband's eyes and mouth opened suddenly, as if she had dunted his skull with a mallet. His body jerked into a sitting position, then slumped back against the pillow.

– What day is it?

– My day, said the mother. My day away.

– Right, said the husband. Right. He shook himself and rolled out of bed.

Back in the kitchen the mother said:

– You haven't touched your porridge.

– My spoon has, said her daughter. You've got a dress on.

– Eat up now.

– You've got a dress on. Why have you got a dress on?

– Yes I've got a dress on.

– Are you going to a party? Can I come too? Can I wear my party dress and my tights with the Silver Minnie Mouses on the legs?

– It's nursery today. I'm not going to a party. I'm going to a conference. Cold porridge tastes horrible, you know.

– You know, this porridge tastes horrible and it's not even cold. HA HA HA HA. What's a confrence?

– Eat up now.

– What's a conference?

– A kind of meeting. Lots of people meet and talk. I have to stand up and talk. About children. You don't want me to tell them that my little girl doesn't eat her porridge?

Slowly her daughter raised a loaded spoon to her mouth and turned suspicious eyes on her mother.

– Are the people strangers?

– Most of them will be.

– I'm not allowed to talk to strangers. Why are you going to talk to strangers?

– I'll tell you tomorrow, said the mother.

– But this is tomorrow! You said last night you were going away tomorrow!

In spite of a last-minute panic search for her purse – her daughter had hidden it inside one of the baby's socks – in spite of having flown into a rage, threatening to take off her dress, her make-up, to throw her conference notes in the bin and the uneaten porridge at the wall, with apologies and goodbye kisses and an additional load of guilt, the mother finally gets out of the house.

The train is delayed and by the time she arrives in the city it is rush hour. The portion of her day set aside for a light meal and rest before the evening event has been lost through the hold-up. The streets are dark and crowded with nudging irritable queues of people, all trying to get home before those ahead of them. She is hungry. The small cafés have closed and there is no time for a sit-down meal so she buys a sandwich from a takeaway, cheese and ham – a striped slab of orange, pink and white and tasting of soap – and gulps it down on the way to her hotel.

The room which has been booked for her is quiet, spacious and plush; a huge bed, carpeting into which her toes disappear, chintz curtains. She has a view of the river where brightly lit ferries paddle through dark, gleaming water. The room is also very warm. The mother phones the organisers to let them know that she has finally arrived. When she has unpacked her bag, she takes off her clothes and sprawls on the bed. This is just where she wants to be, on a bed in a quiet room, with the river rolling by outside the window.

Alone. Not that it wouldn't have been good to be with Jack, her husband, the kids' father, dad. They spent so little time together, just the two of them. But it is perfect without him. At that moment he would be bathing the children, bent over the tub, shirt sleeves rolled up, steam crinkling his hair. The kids would be pink and glowing, the older one washing her doll's hair, the baby splashing and squealing with delight. Bathtime was an oasis between teatime squabbles and bedtime tears.

The mother has only a few spare minutes before she must get ready to go out and she is just beginning to enjoy being where she is. She rotates the dimmer switch until the room is lit only by a faint orange glow from the river lights. She looks up at the dark ceiling and begins to drift into an expanding, enveloping emptiness. The street noise fades into a gently, rhythmical clatter. The radiators hum. She stretches out a hand, disconnects the phone for a few minutes of certain peace. Her eyes close.

She wakes from a vivid seam of dreams and feels refreshed. It is dark outside but she can hear birds. She checks her watch. She reconnects the phone and calls the service desk.

– That's correct, madam.

– Are you sure?

– Quite sure, madam. 6.15 a.m.

– You mean it's morning?

– Friday morning, madam. Breakfast begins at seven.

She goes to the window and drags the curtain open. Across the river, against the skyline, is the unmistakable pink smear of dawn. She has slept right through the evening, the night, the whole bloody conference, right through her first opportunity to escape the laundry, the vacuum cleaner, the lifting and laying, the first chance to break through the walls of domesticity which thicken as they stand, the first occasion to take part in something bigger than the house, to invade her mind with something other than the next meal, the next stack of dirty dishes, how to negotiate a buggy and a ratty preschooler across cracked pavements to the grocer's, the fruit shop, post office, bank, newsagent, how to juggle the chores of the day to fit in with the variable but despotic routines of baby. She has missed the first opportunity to be a person in her own right, to have some kind of independent presence, to be more than just a buggy-pushing, bag-laden donkey.

Even if the conference had been a washout, how the hell does she explain coming all the way here – at the committee's expense – only to fall asleep? Even if presenting her paper had been a disaster, at least she'd have done it, done something, something else, even if the party after had amounted to nothing more than chatting with other parents about the kids they'd left at home. Though even at the other end of the country, she hasn't really left her own kids behind. They're still around, dawdling invisibly at her heels.

The phone rings.

– Mummy? Hello Mummy. I'm having my breakfast. Daddy

made me my breakfast. Have you had your breakfast? Were the people at the confrence strangers? Did you talk to strangers? Daddy took me to the swingpark and I spoke to a kid I didn't know. Are kids strangers?

– I'll explain later, okay? I have to speak to Dad.

– No Mummy, explain now. Are you coming home soon, Mummy? Is this tomorrow?

– This is *today*. I'm coming home *today*.

– But you said you were coming home tomorrow!

The mother draws in and holds her breath, counting, clenching her fists, holding back her disappointment, gripping the phone, not speaking until she has dragged her voice down from its inner scream, not speaking until slowly, softly, with deliberation, with a raging love she says:

– It's OK. I'll be home soon. This is tomorrow.

A Little Bit of Trust

IT WAS ALMOST dark. The heat had gone out of the day and Malek had sold no carpets. He pushed his hands deep into the pockets of his Italian coat, savouring its warmth, its style. Maybe he'd have to sell it. His fingers rubbed against the flaccid, greasy banknotes. Twenty dirham. Enough for something to eat but not enough for wine and wine was what he wanted, needed. Tourists were thin on the ground now and the few backpackers who drifted round town day after day were a waste of time, spinning out their cash and days like threads, eating bad food which made them sick, so they could hang out in the sun a bit longer.

Malek had sold no carpets though he'd been pacing the alley since early morning. Now it was almost dark and there was nothing to be done but wait and see if tomorrow brought in a busload of Germans. The way things were, the bad situation getting worse from one newsflash to another, the world rushing towards war, it was not at all likely that tomorrow would bring anything better than today.

Maybe he'd visit his mother after he closed up. She'd feed

him. He'd get an earful of her worries about his bad ways but he'd still have money in his pocket. Yesterday Yousseff had sold a carpet, everybody knew it. It had taken him two hours, several pots of tea and a mountain of patience but he'd done it, he'd got rid of a carpet. Maybe Yousseff could spare enough to make up the difference on a bottle.

Jane had been wandering the town for hours, trying to acquaint herself with the medina, to fix in her mind the maze of twisting alleys within the walls of the old town. In spite of assuming an air of determined confidence (as recommended in her guide book), in spite of having done this kind of thing before – in places where more overt hostility had greeted her, where the stares had been more accusing than curious, the swearing more vehement, the spitting more accurate, where worse horrors had swarmed in the shadows – still the place evaded her.

Every alley seemed the same, crammed with people and produce, the air heavy with smells – spice, petrol, perfume, drains, everywhere the jangle of horns, bells, cart-wheels, and radios blasting out a jarring mix of eastern and western music. So many people extended a hand – a beseeching, scabrous hand or firm insistent trader's hand – everyone saw her coming, her skin pale as a mushroom, her hair an ashy blonde. She stood out from these people like an aberration.

Turning a corner and finding herself out of the medina at last, back on the main street not far from her hotel, looking up and seeing the clocktower black and solid against the last dregs of sunlight, Jane's eyes began to water. Perhaps it was the dust. There was a great deal of dust, of course, dry red dust, like the paprika and harissa which the spice merchants piled into fiery pyramids, the sky was thick with dust, the light a colloidal orange as the sun dropped behind the ramparts.

Jane's eyes hurt. They were tight, stinging around the rims, contracting in on themselves, shrinking into pinpoints. For several nights she had barely slept. She had gone beyond normal weariness into a fatigue which brought with it a surreal super-awareness, an ultra-sensitivity. Everything ached and clenched, from her bones to her guts to the pores of her skin. Her teeth ground together as she held a tense pained smile. In addition to fatigue an indefinable sadness.

The muezzin's sunset call from the clocktower reminded Malek that drinking was bad for body and soul but Allah says everyone is free and drink he would if he got the chance. Others did. Tourists came to town, ate in restaurants every night and drank in the waterfront bars until they couldn't walk and had a taxi take them a hundred metres to their hotel. Tourists could do what they wanted, no problem. All they had to do was pay; tourists in their designer clothes, haggling over the price of a carpet, happy only when they came away with a bargain, settling only for the cheapest price, never believing that when the vendor got down to his last price he sold for no profit, only for ready cash – because you can't eat carpets – tourists hiding their money as they counted it, as if the very walls of the medina were out to cheat them, tourists excited and happy, making a transaction, rolling up a carpet, imagining going home to their cold grey country with the bright, beautiful thing, spreading it on the floor, pointing out aspects of the handiwork, urging friends to feel the quality. Later they would walk all over it in their dirty outdoor shoes until it was dull and threadbare, by which time they'd be thinking about another holiday in the sun, about living it up in a place where for them everything was cheap, dirt cheap, thinking about buying another carpet. Tourists – he wanted to piss on them all.

She had come for a rest and here she was, walking down the street with tears springing from her eyes, keeping on walking because if she stopped she would crack, right there in the middle of the street. And if she cracked, would she mend? She put on her sunglasses. Here women hid their entire bodies beneath wraps and veils: all she could hide was her eyes. But it was too dark for sunglasses. She could barely see. She was bumping into people. The tears were already trickling below the black plastic frames and spreading over her cheeks so she removed the sunglasses, wiped her eyes and – seeing a pretty courtyard draped with carpets – left the main street again.

He was just about to lift the carpets off the wall and take them inside for the night when the woman came by. It was her jacket he noticed first, a loose, shimmery black thing which picked up the reflections from the coloured lights in the rubber tree. New to town, he could tell. She walked slowly, only the blue eyes raced, scanning walls and shop windows. Nervous, he could tell. Clutching her purse so hard her knuckles shone through her white skin. She held herself straight, stiff, but when she turned to watch as he unhooked a handsome silk kilim, her jacket rippled, softening the angles of her body. Not French. Not German.

– Hello! How are you? Welcome!

She looked at him, straight at him.

– I like your jacket, he said and – knowing the answer – added, Did you buy it here, in Morocco?

Of course she shook her head and at that moment he should have asked her into the shop, offered tea, pulled out the carpets but she was already past the door, he had been too slow, too taken up with admiring her jacket, wondering what it cost, too busy looking at her eyes, mouth, breasts, legs, and trying to think of something else to say in English. But his English was not so good, he was out of practice, so when he finally called:

– Come please. Only for look, no for buy – it was too late.

The moment to embark on a sale had passed, the moment when their eyes had met. Now her back was to him, her long shimmering back, and she had to look over her shoulder to reply:

– Another time perhaps. I need to eat.

That was when he should have let her go and find the ugly overpriced hole she'd circled in her guide book but no, he'd taken hold of her arm – and she had put up only a little resistance – and guided her to Restaurant Yasmine.

– A clean place, no expensive, very near.

– Your brother's place, is it? she said, but not nastily, not like a smart-ass tourist, not that hard, knowing tone he had endured day after day before all this talk of war killed off business. He denied any connection to the patron of Yasmine though, of course, Amal would slip him a couple of coins for bringing in a customer. With weary amusement she let him settle her at a table, summon the waiter, shake her hand as if being led around was all a harmless little game, no big rip-off.

– Bon appetit, he said, and went back to close up the shop.

She had gone past hunger. Eating was an effort. Her hand shook as she lifted forkfuls of spicy stew to her mouth. Though the restaurant was deserted, though there was no one to notice her except the waiter, she felt too visible, too conscious of every movement, as if she had lost the habit of eating. Food fell off her fork, stringy bits of meat and vegetables lodged between her teeth, her cutlery rattled against the hot clay bowl.

The commotion outside was a convenient distraction from the gravy-spattered tablecloth and the embossed wallpaper. A procession of some sort, announced by drums and demented pipes, passed the open door of the restaurant. From her seat she could see a long table being carried through the narrow alley, a table set with cloth, candlesticks, flowers and utensils, held aloft, rocking by on the swell of the crowd, a table and then a calf, skittering behind.

The wedding feast, on spindly legs, pissed with abandon as it was nudged towards its own slaughter. Malek hammered home the lock on the shop door. When he recognised the wedding party he spat loudly into the dust. The husband, an English with wispy hair and a belly like a woman with child, a forty-year-old English marrying a local girl, a virgin of sixteen years. He'd come here for that, lived half his life doing whatever with women and now he wanted to buy himself a child bride – and of course these poor people had given him their daughter – he wanted feasting and dancing, the *mariage typique*, the big ritual, he wanted his guests waiting outside the door so he could go to them with his bride's bikini briefs and say: See? I have made a woman from this girl. See, the blood of my wife.

Jane put the change from the large bill into her wallet, left the restaurant and walked straight into the path of the man from the carpet shop. He was walking between a young man and woman. Their arms were linked. They were laughing. When he saw her he broke away from his friends.

– Did you enjoy your meal? You want to drink something?
– Where?
– Where you like.

He felt for the money in his pocket. A crisp fifty – thanks to his good luck of running into Yousseff and Fatima – and twenty of his own.

Without thinking she had responded, without making any decisions Jane had begun to walk in step with Malek. His friends had gone.

– Not far, she said. I don't want to go far.
– Of course. You want to be near your hotel. I know this. No problem.

When the first bottle was empty he wanted to order another but she said:

– I'm tired. I should go now. Back to my hotel.
– Stay longer, please, just a little longer, he said, reaching for her hand, which she withdrew. Please, he said, I like you, you understand? We drink one more bottle then I take you to

your hotel, no problem. Please, he said, and when he spoke he seemed so sad, so hurt by her refusal, as if all he wanted was a little bit of trust, a little more time together, nothing else, no sex adventures, he knew her situation, knew she was not free, she had made her situation clear before they reached the bar. And it was better sitting here, drinking wine and looking out at the sea, better than huddling under too few blankets in the gloomy hotel room with its maroon curtains and dirty yellow walls.

– Please, because for me... you know what is *coup de foudre?*

She didn't. And she had left her dictionary in her hotel room. And his explanations involving a flash in the sky did not clarify anything. But when the waiter appeared with another bottle she remained seated and let her glass be refilled. When the wine ran low, so did his English and her French. Arabic had always been out of the question. She took to looking out at the boats in the harbour, he to watching her. He could tell that in her mind she was far away from this place, this man she didn't know, in her mind she was on another shore, in another bar, with another man, her husband, an English, maybe like the one in town who'd be at that moment dancing with his Moroccan bride, preparing to penetrate her body and no questions asked. The family and the nation had given their permission, opened their arms and said: Come in. Welcome. Take what we offer. You can pay the price. It is a good price, special price for special person. Nothing to you.

She was looking out to sea and he was looking at her elegant jacket and the fat purse at her fingertips. How much did she have in there? And at home? A car, a video, hot water day and night, a wardrobe full of good clothes? The Italian coat was all he had and maybe he'd have to sell it. And what would she take home? What would she take from his country? It was always take with tourists. Souvenirs, photos, memories.

A carpet would look good in her house. Maybe she had a big house, maybe she'd take home two, three, four carpets, maybe he could really make a sale. If everything was nice for her tonight, maybe tomorrow she'd come to the shop, he'd serve her with tea and they'd make some good business, enough to keep him going for many weeks. But she hadn't said anything about buying a carpet. In fact, she'd said many times already that she had not come here to buy, that she did not want to buy, she hated bargaining, it was not her way. She was clear about that, about her way, definite, as if at other times – when she was not so tired and so far from home – her life was a neat and intricate pattern, one she had chosen from a whole range, the way she might choose a carpet.

– Your jacket is like the sea in moonlight, he said, touching her sleeve, but his pretty phrase didn't bring her eyes back to his and now that the wine had been drunk and paid for – he had offered to contribute Yousseff's fifty but she refused it – now he should take her to her hotel.

The night air bites as they walk across the uneven cobbles of the harbour. Her jacket is thin. She is cold. Though she protests, he takes off his coat and drapes it over her shoulders. The waves smash against the sea-wall. The boats creak and scrape together. Away from the bar the harbour is badly lit. No one is about.

– Come and hear the sea, he says, as they veer away from the exit towards the far side of the harbour.

– I can hear it, she says, and stops, but he is pressing her to go further, to give him just a little bit of trust, and just as she is thinking that it would be good to feel the spray on her face, that had she been in her own country she would have gone – accompanied or alone – past the dark huddle of boats to the sea-wall, just as she is beginning to feel sick of her own fear and suspicion – she has been saying No, No thank you, another time perhaps, since she arrived – just as all this denial is getting to her, he grips her arms.

– Come please. You come now, please, he is saying but the tone has changed, the *please* is no longer a polite request, he is pressing her towards the dark and she knows she has already taken a step too far, such a short step and yet everything has changed... but how can she push him away now, she who'd sat all night asking questions about the crafts, the spices, the economy, the lives of girls and women, the *mariage typique*, the war, and he had told her everything he knew. It had not been easy for him to say so much in English and she had wanted details, wanted to take from him so many details, he had given and she had taken and now... he lets go of her.

Moving away to the sound of his urine hissing over the cobbles, walking fast, she puts a distance between them. When she reaches the exit to the harbour, she begins to run across the lorry park. She remembers that she is still wearing his coat, she throws it off her shoulders, the ground is muddy, her shoes become caked in mud, the mud slows her down, her feet drag but she doesn't stop, with each step she is nearer her hotel. He picks up the coat. He continues to follow her but is too far behind to catch up, close enough only to wave his muddy coat in the air, to wave his coat like a flag and roar his contempt at her shimmering back.

Barely an Incident

SHE RAN INTO the station just in time to see the tail-lights of her train being sucked away into the dark throat of the tunnel. Above the shuttle platform, blue banners swayed in its wake like drunks. More time to be put to no good use. It had been one of those days already, without missing the bloody train. The evening meeting had dragged itself to a close with nothing resolved, except where and when the next meeting would take place. It was part of the job, showing her face, putting in hours in the windowless meeting-room, as one after another suggestion was passed around like an unwanted parcel. If we get A from B and C comes up with D, if E is prepared to give F to G, and so on through the directory of funding bodies to be begged, flattered or bullied into parting with a chunk of the tightly clutched and hopelessly insufficient budget. The notepad with damn all on it but doodles and queries. Nothing but coffee and cigarettes since noon. She was a wide-awake zombie again.

The station was deserted and freezing, as only a station could be, icy draughts snaking in from all corners. Snow had fallen earlier, turning to sleet and finally rain. Wet dripped through holes in the roof, where neurotic city birds were twittering away, duped by round-the-clock lighting into believing it was day and time to sing. The lino-tiled concourse was slittered with coffee, beer and slush. In the far corner, a hunched woman was pushing a brush, eyeing the floor with contempt, as if there were no point in doing what would just have to be done all over again.

The station was bleak at the best of times and if you couldn't face the bar and its odour of weary, anonymous transience, there was nowhere to sit, except the dank Superloos or the slippery metal seating rings, stuck out on the concourse like high-tech doughnuts. Whoever designed those seats must have been convinced that the last thing a traveller wants is to be friendly. Folk fanned away from each other, like spokes on a wheel, points on a compass. A deliberate effort was required to catch your neighbour's eye.

Her hands were a blotchy tartan and burned. She couldn't feel her feet. Trails of melting sleet squirmed through her hair and dripped down the back of her neck. Time to kill but she wasn't going to pace to and fro like that commuting musician – there was always one around – clutching an instrument case to the chest like a mummified lover. Nor was she going to peer at the small print on the posters advertising weekend breaks in Paris or Amsterdam. She'd seen them all before and anyway, they'd only make her restless or miserable or both. That was the trouble with stations – there was always a more tempting destination than your own.

It was too cold, exposed and lonely out on the doughnut seats so she stood in the entrance to the burger bar, where an overhead heater puffed out stingy clouds of warmth. She should eat, but one look at the blown-up photos of buns oozing melted cheese and sweaty beef and she was digging in her pockets for cigarettes. The news-stand, coffee bar and fruit barrow were closed and barred for the night. If you really needed to spend money, you could still get passport photos from the curtained booth, business cards from the autoprinter, donate to city hospitals by dropping money into a Howitzer shell or 'Test Your Emotional Temperature' on The Passion Chart, if you were prepared to squeeze a couple of phallic handlebars. Nothing else to do but look at the clock, the Arrivals and Departures board– on which nothing was imminent – and the people.

Apart from a bag lady who was curled round one of the ring seats like a seal, asleep – or trying to be – the only people using the seats were a young couple: Japanese perhaps, or Malaysian, she couldn't tell, couldn't really see them clearly because three lads, lager cans in hand, had rocked to a halt in front of them, stamping their boots and splashing filth from the floor at the small, compact couple and their tidy bundle of belongings.

– Sorry pal, one of them said. Ah mean ah'm really fucking sorry but.

He squinted at his can – it had a pin-up on the back – took a swig, tipped it so the dregs dribbled onto the girl's shoes, staggered back a couple of steps, steadied himself briefly, then reeled in the direction of the taxi rank. The other two were still standing over the seated couple. One of them bent down so his eyes were on a level with the boy, and inches away from his face.

– Heh heh – WHO FLUNG DUNG?

There was a flurry of movement on the seats, a flash of white shirt as the boy twisted to get a better grip of his girlfriend, jerking her towards him. His eyes batted from side to side as if they were on elastic.

– Ah said, WHO FLUNG DUNG?

– Don't know, said the boy. Sorry. Don't know.

His panicky vowels rolled around the empty station like skittles.

– That's a good one, eh Barry? Bastard doesnae know.

– Does he no?

– No. Nothing like ignorance, eh?

– Put him right, man. Put him in the picture.

– Nah. Wouldnae waste ma breath.

The girl began to cry, quietly. She had taken her glasses off and was plugging up the tears with her fingertips but the shiny drops kept oozing through, breaking up and trailing down her cheeks. The boy circled her with his arms, putting his body in front of hers, as if by enveloping her he could mend the damage, make the tears stop. He was talking non-stop into her chest, rocking the girl against him.

– Ah'm starvin, man, so ah am.

– Fancy a chinky, eh? Deid cat chop suey. Hey – WHO FLUNG DUNG!

The automatic doors wheezed open and shut the three of them out, leaving behind the sour echo of their laughter. And just as they left, in walked a couple of the boys in blue. It was farcical – the timing was spot-on – but not funny. They were doing the rounds, a gangly one and an older, stockier one, strolling, chatting amiably. They were not looking around much, just glancing here and there, as if they didn't want to notice anything they might have to deal with, as if they were actually trying not to pay attention.

Should she report the incident, get the bastards booked? Names, addresses, questions, notes in the wee black book. It was provocation, no doubt about it. But it could have been worse, what might have happened could have been so much worse. No blood, wounds, no visible damage, nothing you could put a finger on, barely an incident and yet anger welled up in her – anger and hatred. She wanted revenge, reprisals, wanted them dragged back and paraded through the square, chained at the neck, their tongues cut out and all the other atrocities race had committed on race. But mostly she wanted the girl to stop crying.

It was terrible, seeing the boy trying so hard to comfort the girl and getting nowhere, the pair of them a contorted huddle of distress, shipwrecked on the concourse. The boys in blue ignored them. The gangly one jerked a thumb at the bag lady humping about under her coat. The stocky one checked his watch and shrugged. They'd shift her later.

She was standing right where they had stood, in a puddle of spilt lager.

– Excuse me...

– ...

– Excuse me, but were those people bothering you?

– Don't know, don't know!

The boy sprang up from his seat, fist raised, eyes flashing. She jumped back, expecting a blow, but the boy checked himself in mid-swing. The girl stared, open-mouthed and impassive. Up close she could see how young they were. Pimply kids in thin clothes. First loves maybe. Wanting to draw a curtain on the world. But the world wouldn't be shut out, go away or mind its own business.

– Those people...

She pointed in the direction of the automatic doors. She hadn't even thought of what to say, just walked right up, intruded, forced herself on them.

– They're just drunk. Don't pay any attention. Please.

But that wasn't it. That wasn't what she'd meant to say at all, and she could hear the plaintive whine in her voice. The boy lowered his arm slowly, sat down and resumed his grip on the girl. She fiddled with her glasses, clicking the legs against the frames, lifting them to her eyes then changing her mind and slamming them into her lap. What's it to you, her eyes demanded, what's it to you?

– You are very kind thank you for your trouble.

The boy's words rattled out, a memorised response, polite standby for any occasion.

– It's no trouble, she said, To me. It's you who had the trouble. Sorry, she said. I'm really sorry.

There was nothing more to say and she was getting uncomfortable and embarrassed by the whole thing. There was no sign of her train yet, so she walked back to her spot outside the burger bar. She was tired, of people, herself, of hatred and stupidity, wasted time and missed connections, the weight of work in her bag, tired of being out.

Maybe the girl had been upset about something else, maybe they hadn't even understood the insult, maybe the two of them had been fighting, or somebody they knew was sick, or recently deceased. Maybe she'd failed an exam – they looked more like students than tourists – or lost her job, or even just been to see a film with a sad ending. What did she know? The girl could have been crying about all kinds of things.

As she hurried across the concourse towards the train pulling up on platform six, she glanced back. The girl was still crying. Her blundering spiel had done nothing to help. Maybe even made things worse. After all, when did anybody ever thank you for poking your nose in, interfering. And what she'd said – *those people* – what did she really know about them? And *just drunk*. Just? What kind of excuse was that? Sorry, I don't know, don't remember, am not in control of what I'm doing because I've had too much to drink – the national excuse for everything from bad-mouthing to murder. And she had gone along with it, just like everybody else.

Friendly Voices

I HAVE BEEN here too long. The city has shrunk to a village. Incestuous is a word bandied about the place by the stretching web of people I know. Not that I have a wide circle of friends – I have never been especially liberal with my affections and intimacy is something for which I have always had a certain reserve. Incestuous is not an exact description but close enough. Unwholesome enough. I and those like me are not people who wish to be associated with the dirty underside of life, the margins of existence, the underdog, subculture. We talk about it, of course, we are all too aware of our tenuous position and ambiguous relationship and sympathise with those who, through no fault of their own, have found themselves on the fraying edge of our society.

It's the dug. Feart for it. Doesnae say, like but Raj knows well enough. Raj can smell the fear on her. Dirty big bastard that he is, makes straight for the crotch, pokes his wet nose into her baggy jeans. Ah let him sniff about a bit until she starts to get panicky, then ah call him aff and slap his arse so the both of them know who's boss around here. But ah'm an animal lover, a big softy where Raj is concerned. Love me, love ma dug.

We talk about it, about them but keep our distance. We have created areas of safety for ourselves or at least put in speak-entry systems and requested unlisted telephone numbers. We take certain routes through the city, avoid others. We know well enough what those other routes are like. We've seen them all before; in our student days when everything was briefly, falsely equal and later, as young professionals, early in our careers when we preached and practised and hands-on approach. Grass roots. We got down to grass roots. Not that grass was a particularly common feature of the landscape.

Once Raj has settled at ma feet, the doctor crosses her legs and clutches the top knee. Funny, never seen the wummin in a skirt. Probably a policy no tae send them up here showing a leg, in case us lot, us *animals* get funny. Funny peculiar but. No supposed tae come up here on her ain, anyway, supposed tae have a mate wi her, for protection like. Ah tellt her she should get a dug of her ain. Hours a fun and guaranteed tae keep trouble at bay. Unless trouble's got its ain dug.

There's no need to be reminded. It doesn't do any good to be reminded of things we can't change. We're not heartless but practical, having learned from experience that we can only function efficiently by maintaining a certain distance. We have our own problems – who doesn't – but we are, at heart, solvers, not sinkers.

When she comes in, she gies out this big sigh, like she's been holdin her breath all the way up in the lift. Probably has because the lift stinks. No all the time, no every single day. You might be lucky and catch it just after it's been washed, in which case you just about choke on the disinfectant. Me, ah'm used tae it.

Doesnae mean ah like it, but some things you just put up wi.

Anyway, after Raj has had his wee thrill, ah let her settle intae the comfy chair and look around. She checks tae see how ah'm keepin the place, see if she can find clues as tae how the medication's workin afore she starts asking questions. No daft this one, knows fine I'm a bloody liar, knows I'll say the first thing that comes intae ma heid tae confuse her. Tries tae get an idea of her ain, tae read between the fuckin lies ah spin her.

Shouldnae come up here by hersel. Tryin tae make oot she's brave n'that, but she's crappin it all the same. She's all edgy, hinging aff the chair, eyes poppin oot, kinda glaikit like, crossin the legs one way an the other. Her jeans rub thegither at the crotch and the denim makes a kinda scrapin sound. She gies a wee kid-on cough and pretends to be dead interested in ma latest picture a Christ on the Cross. Crucified in a field full a sheep. Quite pleased wi that one when ah done it but now ah'm nae sure. Ah've got hunners a crucifixions anyway. She looks at my picture and ah look at her crotch. The dug has left a damp patch on her jeans.

We've looked over the edge, know what lies there. We keep ourselves under control, in check, watch out for the signs, of losing the place, letting things slip. We know what to look out for. We're trained to spot the signs, like the weatherman is trained to read the clouds. It's what we do; spot the signs, make a forecast, though we like to think that the meanings are not fixed, that there are options involved, possibilities.

No ma type at all, very plain. Nae make-up, jewellery – bet she's got plenty jewellery but leaves it at hame in case somebody gies her a doin – cropped hair, wee tits – ah mean, no a lot goin for her, tae ma mind. Money but, she'll have plenty a that, plenty dosh for putting herself out for the likes a me. Nice car. Nifty wee two-seater. Seen it last time she came. Frae the windae. Pale blue convertible. Can just picture her on a sunny day – the sleeveless top on, something loose and cool, the open-toed sandals – pullin doon the hood and belting oot tae Loch Lomond. Bet she's a fast driver. Bet she gets a buzz frae rammin the accelerator intae the flair. Wouldnae mind a whirl in her motor masel. All ah ever get's the fuckin ambulance or, for a treat, the paddy wagon. Ah'm no complainin but. Never say no tae a wee bit drama.

Of course everything's relative. One only has to pick up the paper to be reminded just how much worse is daily life elsewhere: the Brazilian goldmine, say, where there is more malaria than gold; the bloody streets of Jerusalem or Johannesburg; the duplicitous back alleys of Bangkok or Rio; the hungry pavements of Bombay, New York, London. There are no goldmines on our doorstep, or war zones, no tin and board barrios, food queues. Yet.

She gets the chat going so she can start tae suss oot the state a the hoose. Sometimes ah clean up for her comin, sometimes ah dinny. Depends. The place is a pure tip the day. Even if ah'm feeling no bad ah sometimes let the mess lie anyway, just tae see how she takes it. Like tae keep her on her toes. Dinnae want tae make her job too easy for her. Thinks she can tell the state a ma heid frae whether ah've washed the dishes or no. And the chat's aye geared tae pick up clues. Thinks she can earn her dosh by droppin in for tea and chitchat. Tries tae guess how ah'm daein frae what videos ah've watched, what magazines ah've read. Ah like it when she gets on tae that. Get a chance tae use ma imagination. Make up some brilliant titles, all horror and porn. Like tae get a wee blush goin on her, see that pulse start up at her throat. It's no a lot a response but she's no meant tae respond at all. It's her job tae stay neutral.

She's no bad, but. Means well. Heart in the right place and all that guff. Wants tae help. Ah mean, she could've gone for one a they plum jobs in the private sector, analysin the rich and famous in some plush place down south. The nurse who comes tae gie me my drugs, ma monthly jab, he tellt me she's top-notch, expert in her field. Could've been rakin it in, sinkin the excess intae a second hame, somewhere aff the beaten track, far way frae the hurly-burly a Harley Street, or wherever they doctors hing aboot these days. But no, she's chosen tae make her livin frae the likes a me.

We complain, particularly about the larger issues, particularly on behalf of others. We are outraged about what is happening in the world, indeed the state of the globe is one of the most popular subjects of conversation amongst people like us. We lie awake at night and worry about the depletion of the ozone layer, preservatives in food, the destruction of the rain forest, the incidence of cancer near nuclear sites and the latest epidemics, about religious fundamentalism, neo-fascism, wars, riots, strikes, demonstrations, disasters natural and man-made – hurricanes, droughts and floods, about aphids, wild dogs and mad cows.

But we get up in the morning, the sun is shining, a scent of blossom is in the air, the grass is fresh and green beneath the litter and dog shit we are growing accustomed to in municipal parks. Under a clear sky joggers, dog-walkers, cyclists, down-and-outs, students and parents with young children take the air together, at their own speeds. There are cycle lanes, walking lanes and jogging tracks. A bird sings. Blossom drifts in pink clouds above our heads. A man on a tractor cuts the grass and cleans up yesterday's mess. Another day passes without event, without people like us overstepping the boundary between the solvers and the sinkers. We have accumulated the life skills required to keep our individual globes turning fairly smoothly. We stay clear of the edge but don't allow ourselves to forget what lies beyond it. We care. People like us care.

She's near drunk all her tea by the time she gets on tae the voices. Just about time for her tae get going when she brings them up. Have they been friendly? she says. Eh? Your voices, she says. Aw aye. Have they been friendly? Aye, ah says, nae bother. Ah'm gonnae tell her about the state a ma heid when the singin starts up. My ears go that plugged up way like when you've got headphones on and the singin loups roon ma heid. It's that kinda auld folky stuff, nae many words you can make oot, just a miserable kinda moany sound but sorty nice wi it, soothin like. The doctor's askin me somethin. Ah cannae hear what she's sayin, ah just know it's a question cos she's got her heid cocked tae the side, like a budgie. Raj is sitting at ma feet, looking up at me wi big sad eyes, daft dug that he is. Sometimes ah think he hears ma voices tae.

My office is bright, sunny. The walls are painted a pale, buttery yellow. On the wall facing the door is a small watercolour of a decorative plate and some pearly mussel shells. Behind my desk, above a shelf where I keep a constantly updated selection of leaflets (and my shade-loving ferns) is a calm abstract painting: Contemplation 4. There were three other remarkably similar paintings in the small gallery where I bought it. Any of them would have done just as well. Buying paintings is not a particular interest of mine. But I like those I have and they brighten up the office, give my patients (clients) something to look at while they try to untangle their troubles, sort them into words, order the chaos of their minds into sensible phrases. People don't like to look you in the eye when they tell you their troubles.

It's no ma kind a singin but ah'm sitting here, hearin it, nae movin a muscle, an ahv'e got this amazin glow all over, ah'm feelin pure brilliant. Ah cannae explain it, ah've just got this kinda swellin in my chest, like my lungs is blowin up wi pure clean air, not the usual muck we suck in up this way. It's a gloomy auld tune, right enough, but it cheers me up no end. Here's this doctor, this consultant, sittin in ma chair, in ma hoose, which may be a tip the day but isnae always. Next time she comes ah'm gonnae show her. Straighten it up, clean. Aye well, sometimes it doesnae seem worth the bother just for me and the dug.

Just like me she is, this doctor, on her tod. Naebody tae cuddle in the night. Least ah've got the dug. What's she got? What does she snuggle up tae on a cauld night? A hot-water bottle, a teddy bear, a sex-toy? Nae sae young neither tae be alane. Better get the skates on if she wants tae tie the knot. But then maybe she's one a they solitary types by choice, Christ. Or queer, aye that's a possibility. No what ah'd call a man's wummin.

Considering the design of the surgery, I'm fortunate to have a window. I've lined the sill with plants, the hardier varieties, those which require the minimum of attention. When I'm there, I play music, Baroque mostly, at low volume. I read somewhere about experiments on house plants to see how they responded to different kinds of music. Rock music made plants wilt whereas Baroque made them flourish and wrap themselves lovingly around the source of the music. I try to give people the same opportunity to flourish. I listen, offer tea, an old but comfortable armchair, now and then a sympathetic nod. Mostly I listen until my client had told me the first version. It's usually a slow, tiresome process, for both of us. I ask a few more questions and the client redrafts the problem. I try to give people an opportunity to flourish but don't claim a high level of success. The nature of the task being what it is and nothing being absolute, even an accurate assessment is rarely possible. My plants do better, when I'm around to tend them, though I'm rarely in the office these days. In the catchment area served by our practice, those who need me most rarely come looking.

It's that singin. Ah just get this overpowerin... ah just get this feelin that she could really dae wi a big hug. Ah get tae ma feet, cross the room and lift her aff her chair. Ah'm staunin there, huggin her, fair away wi masel till ah see the look in her eyes and Jesus fuckin Christ it's pure terror, the wummin's scared rigid, like a big cauld stane in ma hauns afore ah let go a her. And then the singin stops. Just like that. Like a tape being switched aff. Nae mair glow. That fuckin singin.

Doesnae say anythin about it, no a fuckin word. Just picks up her briefcase, tells me tae mind and be in for the nurse themorra, and goes. Raj chucks hissel at the door then slinks aff tae the kitchen. Needin fed but he'll havetae wait. Ah'm in nae mood for the fuckin dog. Ah hear her panicky wee steps as she hurries along tae the lift. She'll no notice the stink on the way doon, she'll be that happy just tae get the fuck oot a here.

There she goes, marchin aff tae her motor, aff tae her next patient. Maybe she'll need a wee pit-stop somewhere, tae pull hersel thegither, get hersel nice and neutral again. When she's through wi us lot, put in her time, done her bit, she's gonnae nip back tae the surgery, tae her cheery wee office, take oot ma file and bang in a new prescription. She's gonnae up the dosage, up it enough tae take away ma voices allthegither, blot them oot, kill them aff. Didnae mean her any harm for fuck's sake, Christ ah was tryin tae be nice but she'll no see it that way, will she? She'll see it as a fuckin problem, and up the dosage. Tae bring me back tae ma senses, back tae The Real World. Tae this. Themorra. Jab day themorra. Ah get the feelin my voices arenae gonnae be fuckin friendly the night.

Repeat Please

SHE RINGS THE doorbell. She speaks through the entryphone. It is noon. She is always on time, sometimes a little bit early. She says *Hello it's Jane. Teacher.* Teacher Jane thinks I do not remember her voice from one week to the next. I press the button and the downstairs door opens for her. I wait for her to knock on my door.

When Teacher Jane knocks on my door I open it. This is the arrangement. She comes once a week to teach me English words. She says *Hello how are you.* She smiles a big smile. She wants that I say *I am very well thank you.* I say only *Come* and she follows me inside.

I am not so very well thank you. I am cold. Since I have been here, since I came down the steps of the plane at London three years ago I feel as if the sun has not touched me. It rained the day I arrived, not the rain we have at home, not the big bright drops which crash down and vanish. Here the rain wraps itself around you like a wet sari.

Ali met me at the airport. He was holding an umbrella and a

raincoat. He gave me the coat. He told me I would need a coat. He took my suitcase and began walking. I followed him. We travelled by bus, by train. We walked up a windy street and stopped at the downstairs door. He showed me my name next to his on the entryphone. We walked up the stairs. He took me inside. The flat was empty. He told me this would be home. It is not home. It is only a house.

When Teacher Jane comes I am tired. Since Izmir was born I do not sleep. I try to sleep but the baby wakes me, or my dreams do.

I am walking, feeling the hot earth under my feet. I am walking to the river, the wide slow yellow river. Beside me is my sister. She has her small pitcher on her head. A plane crosses the sky and we look up. It is not one of the great white birds which bring wives to husbands across the world. It is small and black, buzzing. My sister does not know the difference. She waves at it and runs down the bank into the water.

When Jane rings my doorbell I do not want to answer it. I do not want this to be my door. I cannot step outside into the yard and throw rice to the chickens. I cannot pick fruit from the tree. Teacher Jane says *Hello how are you.* I say only *Come* because that is all that is necessary. Jane is not doctor. She is teacher of words only. She cannot make baby eat, cannot mend my dreams. Cannot find Ali a better job. He goes out in the morning, early. He comes home in the middle of the night. I get up, prepare some food. He eats, he tells me how many curries were sold at the restaurant. He smokes some cigarettes and goes to sleep. Ali goes to sleep and I lie beside him, waiting for the baby to wake up.

We wade until we are waist deep. We begin to wash, my sister splashing and ducking her head underwater. On the far bank the ferry is loading up with passengers, the local ferry which has standing room only, in one straight line. I count seven women, one little old man.

On the far bank it is peaceful. There is a temple, a small tea plantation and a forest of tall trees. My grandfather told us that these trees came all the way from Scotland. He would go to the forest often, to walk, he'd say, but with only one leg he did not walk so much. Mostly he would sleep in the shade of the Scottish trees.

Teacher Jane sits on the bed and opens her bag. She takes out a notebook and a pencil. This is the lesson beginning. She empties the contents of her bag onto the floor, piece by piece. She stops at each item and says its name. She says this name two or three times then I must *Repeat Please*. When Jane's bag is empty – and my room is once more untidy again – she asks me the names again and I remember one or two. *Paper, pencil, book* – always Jane has books and newspapers and magazines. I think in her house she must have only books and magazines because each time she brings different ones. In my house there is only the newspaper. Ali reads it. I use it to wrap up the vegetable peelings.

After I have said *paper, pencil, book, diary, hairbrush, cigarettes, matches, keyring,* we do her shopping. She holds up a carrot. *Carrot,* she says. She lays it beside the hairbrush and points to the hairbrush. *Carrot?* she says. She wants me to say, *No, it's not a carrot, it's a hairbrush.* I say only, *No.* This is not important to me. The baby is important, and Ali. I have no room in my heart for carrots and hairbrushes. I will not make this house into a home because I know the English word for a vegetable I do not very much like.

Ali says I must learn to speak English so that he can go on longer trips to his brother's house in Leeds. There is not enough room for all of us to visit. Anyway, Ali is going on business. I do not know what business. Ali says I do not need to know. We do not agree about this and I worry in case he is maybe doing something dangerous. But money must be sent to our home town somehow and in the restaurant he earns so little.

Baby wakes up. *Baby crying*, says Jane. I too say *Baby crying* and Jane says, *Good.* But now she must sit, not teaching while I feed Izmir. I do not have enough milk. I am a poor cow. When Izmir has emptied each breast he cries for more. I get the tinned milk. They gave it to me at the clinic. I show it to Jane. *OK?* I say. *Sorry,* says Jane. I point to the writing. I want her to read the instructions on the tin. I want her to teach me the right mixture but she doesn't understand. Why does she teach me the words for carrots and hairbrushes and not *Help me please?* All Jane does is stare at Izmir's tiny crumpled face and be afraid. Afraid that just by looking she will make the crying worse. Afraid that if she held him in her arms he would break.

The ferry is standing at the platform. And then the sudden disturbance at the bank, the ferryman running into the forest, the boat sliding away from the bank without its oars, the boat rocking, the monkeys screeching as the black plane returns, low this time, roaring, trailing a filthy ribbon of smoke. And then the rattle of gunfire and the ferry passengers tossed like logs into the water. The river is streaked with red. This is my sleeping dream. It will not go away. It is the past and the past will not go away. My grandfather was dead by the time he was brought ashore, the river mud streaming over his body.

My waking dream is of the future. It also will not go away. Ali tells me I live too much in my imagination and that I will be happier here, will feel safer here once I have learned more about this country, once I learn the language. He says I must put everything from home behind me. He says I must spend more time outside, looking around me, and not so much time inside myself. He says when Izmir is older, he can play in front of the house. There is a small concrete yard. I have planted some flowers out there, by the wall, but I do not sit in the yard and

Izmir will not play there when he is older. I will not let him. My waking dream will not let me leave him there. In my mind I see a car stopping, a grey car with dark windows. Two men get out. I cannot tell what they look like, only that they are dressed in suits and wear dark glasses. Everything happens in a flash.

When I tell Ali my dream, he asks me if they are Asian men or white men. I do not know but I know there is a reason and it is Izmir they want, not the fair-haired child next door. There is no accident. They pull Izmir off his toy train, bundle him into the car and drive off. Ali says these things happen here only on the television.

The lesson begins again when Izmir has cried himself to sleep. Jane fetches the clock from the window ledge and point to the time. *Half-past twelve*, she says. She makes the hands move round the clock and tells me the time. *One o'clock. What time is it?* and I must *Repeat please*. At one o'clock Jane will pack up her bag and go away. I want her to go because I am tired yet I do not like to be alone, in this house which is not a home.

Jane sees me yawning before she has finished with the time, so she puts back the clock. She smiles and says *Sleepy?* and I say *Sleepy*, then *Tea?* and she says *Thank you very much*. We go into the kitchen, leaving Izmir asleep in his pram. There is now a table and two chairs. While we are drinking our tea I hear a small noise at the door. *Postman?* says Jane. *Postman*, I say. *Letters*, says Jane. I will fetch the letters when Jane goes away.

Jane wants to show me something special. She has a magazine with a shiny cover. She turns the pages. There are pictures of watches and cars and men in English suits and girls in shorts dresses. Also of perfume bottles and underwear and big country houses. Also of soldiers and operations and mountains. She stops at a photograph of a mountain covered with trees. These are the Scottish trees my grandfather was so fond of. I have been living in this country for three years now.

I have not seen any of these trees, except in December when little ones are taken indoors and dressed up.

Look, says Jane. She turns the page and points. It is my own village, my own river. There is no ferryboat at the landing. There are no people laying out laundry on the bank or washing in the river but I know they are all there somewhere, out of sight, watching the pictures being taken, standing maybe right behind the photographer, telling him what to put in his picture. Did my sister too run over and watch or was she still too frightened of that spot?

Your home, says Jane. She is very happy to be showing me the river, but I cannot see that peaceful empty river. The noise is in my ears, the buzzing and the roaring, the rattles and the screams. The smell of burning fills my nostrils. I close my eyes to block out the bloody picture I see taking shape over the peaceful one and I am thinking yes, Ali is right: I live too much in my imagination, and then Jane is jumping up from the table and shaking my arm and shouting *Look! Look!* and I see smoke creeping round the door and I know that the smell of burning is not a phantom from the past but is the present, is here, now, in my house. Jane stands back as I run for Izmir.

The hall is black with smoke. At the door is a burning ball of rags. The carpet and the wallpaper have caught fire and I know now that it was not the postman who came today. I am filling up buckets of water at the sink and Jane is throwing the water at the fire in between shouting through the open window, *Fire! Fire!* and *Help! Help!* and I am repeating again and again everything she says as loudly and clearly as I can.

Human Interest

THE NOON SUN shoots through the window of the Queen's Hotel Bar and a thin rod of hot light bores into the dark mahogany table. Before Julie is able to set down her shopping bag – between the empty beer glasses and full, filthy ashtrays – Sam Cox has his broad, stubby hands in it and is pulling out a wad of chapatis, a pineapple, two tiny cooked chickens, a tub of buffalo curd.

– Hasn't she done well! says Alphonse.

He curls his arms round Julie's waist and eases her on to his knee where, after leaning forward to smack Sam Cox's hand away from the supplies, she settles briefly.

– Good on you, kid, says Findlay Sneddon. I'd say a wee toast is in order, eh Alfie? One for the road?

Alphonse raises his eyes to the ceiling, points at the bar clock. Joan fires a column of cigarette smoke across the table.

– What *did* you do to lay your hands on chicken? Or are we not allowed to ask? says Joan.

Julie giggles, springs to her feet, picks up the picnic and leads the way out of the bar...

The sky is a vast, white glare. A map is spread across the dashboard of the jeep. With one hand Julie holds down the flapping sheet. With the index finger of the other, she follows the twists and bends of a road, the only road, going north. Alphonse drives. His shirt sleeves are rolled up to the elbows, his dark glasses spattered with the corpses of small insects. In the back, Findlay Sneddon sleeps off his lunchtime beer. Joan and Sam Cox smoke and pass a water bottle between them.

Apart from the occasional rickety buffalo cart or sleek dark limousine, the road is empty. Due to recent events, normal travel on this road has been severely curtailed. Only those with urgent need to reach family or friends cram into the sagging, bulging buses, resign themselves to being driven at full throttle, to duck and pray at the sight of any approaching vehicle, to be hurled round blind bends, a sheer drop on one side of the road, the threat of ambush on the other.

This is stark, open country, contrasting sharply with the sun-drenched beaches and lush tropical vegetation of the south, which formerly lured tourists from colder climes. Tourism, in fact, had only recently increased to the point where it account for 40% (check) of the gross national product (is tourism a product? subst. income?) The rhododendrons and Scotch pines – planted by homesick Brits (in the early days of the Raj?) – are thinning out, the sugar pink and duck-egg blue ranch-style bungalows giving way to flimsy shacks huddled along the roadside. There is little sign of life from the sad little thatched hovels. It is as if the invisible occupants are holding their breath...

Joan taps the back of the driver's seat with her pen.

– Alphonse, sweetie, How about stopping for a quick look? Stretch our legs. Piccy or two. Calm before the storm and all that.

– Or the aftermath, says Alphonse.

Findlay Sneddon opens his eyes as the jeep skids to a halt.

– Background, says Alphonse. Want some?

– Thanks, says Sneddon. But no thanks. A bite to eat wouldn't go wrong.

– That lot's got to last until tomorrow at least, says Julie.

– Besides, says Joan, Today's the lady's birthday and who wants to eat crusts and chicken bones for their birthday tea?

Julie springs down from the jeep, smoothes out the creases in her shorts, fondles the focus ring of her camera. Good legs, Sneddon observes. Neat little arse too. If somebody else hadn't got in there first. Young and new and oh-so-keen, just about wetting herself every time she catches a whiff of copy. Unlike some. As the others scout around, he extracts a chapati from the packet, tears off a piece, inserts it in his mouth and chews, with contempt.

Crouched down, going in for close-ups, knees parted, smooth honey-gold thighs against rough dry dirt and criss-crossed cane wall, a bowl of chillies left to dry in the sun, as fierce a shade of red as her lipstick. A satisfying composition of colour and texture. A fetching little scene. Fuckable, thinks Sneddon, definitely fuckable. But then he always finds himself thinking about sex en route to an assignment.

The shacks appear to be deserted. Doors swing open at a touch. The dark interiors give out a rancid odour. At the entrance to one lies the infested carcass of a dog. Julie clicks away at bits and pieces until Alphonse, resting a hand on her shoulder, advises her to go easy on the still-life compositions. There's a chance of a big story up ahead, a big, fast story where every split second might offer up a new angle and the last thing she'd want is to be taking time out to reload. Action is what they're here for. It's what they live on, how they eat.

The sun is merciless. The paddies and plantation are behind us. There is neither a scrap of shade nor a breath of wind.

Ahead the vista is dry rolling scrub, cracked earth and bleached outcrops of rock, like some elemental graveyard. and indeed, in the endless desert, nothing seems to be alive except us and we're not in the best of shape. Throats parched, nostrils clogged with dust, heads throbbing from the pulsating glare, clothes crushed and sweat-sodden, exposed areas of skin sticking to hot upholstery, bellies rumbling. We fantasise about food and the supplies in the back – procured with considerable difficulty by our enterprising photographer – present an almost unbearable temptation. On my left, the truculent Scotsman constantly mops his face with a hanky. On my right, my old buddy from Boston hogs the water bottle. In the front, the photographer and the driver are too listless to pursue their ongoing romance...

– You can't say that, Joan.

    – Hmmmm?

    – That last bit. About our lovebirds.

    – My readers will eat it up. It's what they want. Human interest. A bit of life ongoing. In the midst of crisis, what is more uplifting that a budding romance?

    – Even you must be able to see that it's out of context.

    – Listen, Sam-Sam, too many hard facts and my readers turn over to Food, Fashion and Fiction. Still, out of respect for your unwavering sense of propriety, I'll give it a query.

The sun is going down and the sky takes on the quality of a sluggish, churning liquid, as the dust does its hazy aerial dance. Visibility is poor. Without switching on the headlights, Alphonse continues in low gear along the deeply furrowed dirt track. He stops the jeep behind a mound of rubbish and switches off the engine.

    – Charming spot for a pit stop, says Sneddon.

    – This is it, you cretin. Our destination.

    A short distance away is the village; no more than a dozen

shacks, clasped in a bracelet of tiny fields.

– Helluva quiet, says Sam Cox.

– Looks like it's all over, says Sneddon. He leans forward and prods Julie between the shoulders. In which case, dearie, I'd suggest you get a big swig of the local gutrot down you before you leap in with your glass eye.

– I've seen dead bodies before, says Julie, adjusting her lens to the fading light.

– Yes, dear, says Joan. But there are dead bodies and dead bodies.

– Aye, says Sneddon. Whole ones and ones with bits missing. Broken jigsaws of bodies. Bits you couldn't put a name to.

– Cut it out, mate, says Alphonse.

– Only telling the truth, pal.

– Try putting it in print. Try that for a fucking change.

– Boys, boys, says Joan. No fighting, please.

The light has almost drained from the sky when the reporters reach the edge of the village. Apart from a thin bleating – of a child or animal it's not certain – and the rasping crackle of their own footsteps, there is barely a sound.

– Evacuation? says Sam Cox in an undertone.

Joan indicates a thin coil of smoke.

– Another bloody red herring, I'd say, says Sneddon. Might as well get it over with and get down to the food, eh? I could eat an elephant.

No one answers the lumbering man in khaki fatigues whose pen swings on a chain from his thick, red neck. There's a general feeling of indecision. No one suggests splitting up. If there had been something happening, if there had been noise, action – they'd expected troops, stone-throwing kids, mothers with babes in arms running down the street – they'd have been up and away on their own, propelled by adrenalin, fear and the promise of money. But there are no streets here, only narrow tracks between black, empty fields. It is too quiet.

At the flickering heart of the village burns a small fire, the only apparent source of light or heat. Around it, the villagers are gathered, sitting or lying on the ground. Here and there a limp figure is briefly lit up by the flames it stretches towards, before becoming once more absorbed into the still, silent congregation. There is a hazy, unreal quality to the scene; the twitching flames, the smoky air, the hush. What the reporters are witnessing is not another eruption of the trouble which has been flaring up elsewhere, not the terror of night raids, but the life of an entire community reduced to terminal torpor. Slow motion is what has happened to this isolated village on the dry plains.

Above the fire hangs a cooking pot filled with boiling, stinking roots. Those who have the strength to crawl, scratch at the hard ground in search of insects. There is nothing else. The village has run out of food. The crops were torched by soldiers or rebels, no one seemed certain. They came at night, lit up the sky with fire and left. In the morning the fields were black as night. Bloodshed has passed by, but not the protracted agony of starvation.

Several miles from the village Alphonse pulls the jeep off the road. Findlay Sneddon unpacks the food from Julie's bag and begins to pass it around. Joan takes a small candle from her purse, pushes it into the centre of a chapati, flicks a flame to the wick, holds up the token cake:

Happy Birthday to you
squashed tomatoes and stew
bread and butter in the gutter
Happy Birthday to you

Julie snuffs out the candle with her fingers, pushes away the food held out to her, bites her lip until she tastes blood.

– If I eat anything I'll throw up.

– I wouldn't count on it, says Sneddon. He bites into a chicken leg. Your guts might be more pragmatic than your conscience.

– Fuck you! Julie's voice is thin, brittle as glass. Fuck the lot of you. Knew fine what they wanted. Staring you in the face. Doesn't need translation. Same in any language...

– A dreadful business, says Joan.

– The eyes, flies gorging on babies' eyes, heads drooping like dried-up pods. You sit here stuffing chicken into your faces while back there they're filling their mouths with mud. Are you going to put that in your columns. Are you going to tell your readers that?

– We really couldn't help, says Alphonse. Sometimes you just can't. Not directly.

– Might have made matters worse, says Sneddon. Got them killing each other over a few chapatis. Or us. Think about it.

– Did nobody ever teach you, says Alphonse, Not to speak with your mouth full?

Sam Cox looks into the darkness. Something out there is moving. Lean, dark bodies circle the jeep, picking up their scent, the smell of food.

War Dolls

OSWALDO IS LATE. Maybe he forget how quick the jungle grow; it creep up while the back is turn, the eyes is close. Me, I no sleep good. Some nights, no sleep at all. Always is possible Angél show up but Angél is *nada*. Is no from fear I lie in the dark and listen to bugs and dogs, the scrip-scrip of geckos, the soldiers' boots. People say I have no fear.

Angél no agree but Angél no here. Angél have other things to do than wait in this boxroom above the *zapatería*, breathing in the stink of leather and burnt rubber, crazy from the smell and all day the tap tap of the hammer. Angél, he away, always away. He make plans, I know he make plans for a better life but me, I sit on my ass, wait for Oswaldo and wonder why he no come.

Long time ago, when we was kids, was the other way round; Oswaldo staying, me going, me coming back with apologies or gifts or nothing but a kick in the pants. One day you go, amigo, but we, we still here, with the soldiers' guns ready for us, the soldiers' hungry eyes following our girls.

My people wait too long. The map of their waiting is drawn

deep into the skin; faces like dry riverbeds, eyes without interest or hope. In the plaza everywhere you can see the same look in the eyes. You people, I think you find it... convenient. The sun throw light on white shirts, black hats and slow, sick eyes – dramatic, no? And of course the military, the military is another take.

Is impossible to describe to you this pain of waiting. You see poverty, disease, death – of course, is all here, looking back at you. Accusing. And you, with the expensive camera, are you thinking about the soundtrack? Are you trying to decide which tune from your collection of world music is best with this *foto* tragedy – some mountain flutes, some *canciónes de los poetas revueltas*, or maybe better, as contrast, some drunk and crazy mariachi... Or maybe no music, maybe you let the moving pictures speak for theyself?

I have my own ideas. I too plan to make a film about this situation. You see, I know you will take these little bits of me talking – and maybe Oswaldo, maybe even Angél if you lucky – and twist them into a story but your story, amigo, is only a scratching in the dust. A puff of wind, the whisper of trouble some other place and it will blow away.

You want Oswaldo to take you to Angél. You want me to help you do this. People say our leader is *recluso*. Also that he has beautiful girlfriends and many important international contacts. They say he like late-night parties but also early mornings in meditation and the study of philosophy. Believe what you like. Maybe all true. But no important. Our leader is *nada*. I only half year in school but I see and I think, fuck. My people still waiting; on every street in every town. Look outside – I am fortunate to have a window – so many poor people, like me and Oswaldo, be born, grow up and die on the street, in public.

You want Angél be star of your movie, me I want Oswaldo. That boy; I want make film of he, in the mask and balaclava, eyes straight to camera, voice fuzzy because of the mask, a toy

MI6 in his hands. No joke, amigo. Is never enough real guns for everybody but can do much with wood and shoe polish. Is no too much problem for Oswaldo. Oswaldo a smart bastard. Me too, eh? Well, me and Oswaldo, we still alive.

Emilia is also in this town now, but alive? *No sé*. Maybe you go find her in the plaza, look, and decide for youself. When Oswaldo and me was kids, if we no get money from gringos, Emilia, she kick us out the bus station like dogs. Then Emilia have good job, sitting behind window of ticket booth, taking money and giving tickets. Then Emilia young and pretty. She have eyes for Angél and Angél, he make promise he no can keep. America. *Téjas*. The same promise everybody make, same made-up story, same lie, amigo. But people believe what they want and now Emilia she all day in the plaza with the other mothers, sewing, sewing, sewing; no eyes for nothing but pesos and war dolls, pesos and war dolls.

How to find Emilia? No so easy, maybe. So many like she, head turn from the sun, back bent, busy making doll smaller than a match, hands quick as fish but the eyes; look in the eyes. I tell you for nothing, Emilia no so old as she look, no the wise *vieja* you people like put in *documental*. Maybe to you she look like she already live a long and interesting life but Emilia only thirty-five years. And now Angél no have eyes for she, Emilia's life is *nada*. Remember, amigo, if you find she, remember when you pick up a little stick soldier, say the price too high and put it down.

Eh, even the air is slow and heavy from waiting for change. You see the way the dust hang over the square like sorrow and the leaves on the trees droop like dead men's fingers? The soldiers is bored, bad-tempered. This week they shoot many many dogs and Emilia, she fear for her daughter. Never I like this town. Too high up, too many churches. You visit the churches already; you see all the gold inside? Eh, make me crazy. And too quiet. When I was kid I come here one time, to steal for Angél.

Now I wait for Oswaldo. Maybe wait all night and Oswaldo no show. You know, amigo, I think Oswaldo not too far away. But even if he come tonight, maybe he no speak, to me, to you, to nobody. Maybe nothing to say. Wait and hope is all. Soon is darkness. If you want sleep in hotel bed, go now. For soldiers, curfew is time for badness. Soldiers too is poor kids; killing work put food in the belly and boots on the feet.

In my head I see Oswaldo's death many times; so many ways to die. And if Oswaldo no come back, I alone. Si, I have the compadres, I live for they but sometimes I feel too much alone, too far away; the compadres is not enough. This boy. I no sleep because when I close the eyes, I see Oswaldo die, and me, I see me filming the death of this brave and foolish boy. I see my people waiting so long only newsreel left; the dead total flash on screen, mothers scream for bleeding *niños*. But no sound; only voiceover story. No real screaming on the news. And me, I see me fall down dead in the dust, still holding a camera, still making movie. Or the only one alive, only one still walking, walking across the plaza; the ground red, shadows crawling over the dead as *los cóndores* come down from the sky in a slow black spiral and I no can stop looking, I keep filming, because no one else is left to see. Eh, but this happen when you wait too long, you imagine the worst things.

All day I have this pain like a toothache, like my mouth is shoe-leather and somebody hammering nails in. Maybe it's just the stink of *huaraches* or the heavy air, maybe no more than that. But we have always been close, Oswaldo and me, and sometimes we know things about each other without speaking. Is not so crazy, amigo, to feel pain when someone you love is hurting.

Eh, this talking is thirsty business. No water; Coca and Fanta only. Warm fizzy shit. It blow up the belly and rot the teeth but what else to wash dust from the mouth? Beer, tequila? Sometimes I want drink, drink until the walls spin and sleep come quick as a kiss but for me, no drink, drugs. And no women. People say Angél come a long way but really he is like always, he push people around. One time Oswaldo and me, we steal and sell the skin for Angél. Now, for Angél and the people, maybe we die.

To die no problem. I tell you already, people say I have no fear. Maybe is true. Only, the movie. I no make my movie. Eh, you talking to one dumb *chico*, no? One more loco think he can change this world when he heading *rápido* for the next. In the next world, no Coca and no Angél. Or else I also quit that place. But you no interest, eh, no interest in Oswaldo, Emilia, me. We nothing special, eh, nothing special. Is Angél you want on film; mystery man.

Is smart to take it easy, amigo. All this up and down to the window like you waiting on a girl. Rest the feet; maybe you need the feet *rápido*. Sit. Drink a fucking Fanta. Count geckos on the wall. You no like the smell from downstair? You want your hotel room? If no go now, you miss dinner – Emilia's daughter carrying big tourist plate of meat, beans, rice. You see this girl already, eh, the beautiful Angelina? Touch her, amigo, I feed your balls to the dogs.

So; you and me till dawn? You, me and five hundred pairs of *huaraches*. I think it will be a long night. In the night, time grow like the jungle. In this town, even before the soldiers, is quiet here, so quiet, any sound at all can stop the breath, if you have fear. And you, I can see you have plenty fear, amigo. Not in the eyes – you know to make the eyes steady – but on the mouth I see a little twitch. Fear make you hold on to life.

Me, maybe I no want hold on. Is cold, eh? Feel the walls. Is like inside a cave, wet and cold. This place, eh, this town above the clouds. I come here first when I eleven years. The bus it drive right through the clouds and keep going. I think maybe we drive to heaven. Funny, eh, amigo? Then, I no want go to heaven, only *Téjas*. This gringo in the bus station, she say maybe Téjas, maybe. She like me. I hope and hope. I smile. *Nada*.

Only this place. maybe, if she had take me to Téjas, I be president of USA by now, or big movie maker, driving three days non-stop in my Cherokee Trailblazer back to my home – only here is no my home and no my people, no really – I have only Oswaldo.

You hear boys whisper Téjas, Mister, Téjas, in your ear, you still hear them? How you shake off the smiling boys who drift around the bars like smoke? And your *documental*, how it help they? No your problem, eh? Your problem is how many days, how many dollars. You buy your *información*, your story, get out. Because if you wait, fear grow inside, creeping and choking. Is when you begin to feel naked, when the breath burn cold in the throat and you dream of home, your girl. Is when you go to the bar for American beer, American whiskey and wonder if our girls is worth the risk... Eh, amigo, you have standards, I know. But standards like road signs, they change with the road. On a big highway the signs are bright, see easy. On a little road some signs is eat up by jungle, fade from sun. The path Oswaldo must take have no sign.

How to pass the hours? Maybe you tell me about your life, home, your girl. You have a girl, yes? Tell me about your girl. No problem, amigo, is just for me something to put in the head, a picture to put in the head. And why not a picture of your girl? Tell me, is she blonde, blue-eyed? I like to think of this girl. What she do when she happy to see you? I been here a long time, a man must do something to pass the time. I tell you already, no women for me. Is better I am alone but desire no rest, amigo, desire has no walls, checkpoints, is free to go where it want, to climb into Angelina's bed and breathe in the smell of her warm, oiled hair, eh, the beautiful Angelina.

So, when you no make *documental*, you do home movies? You shoot your girl being sexy? She like do dirty things for camera? No? She no like, or you no like say? What girl like a man who chase other people's pain? You know they say a man alone is *poco loco*, and a *loco* with a gun... my gun is no toy, amigo. Is better to keep happy a man with a gun, no? Show me your camera. Let me hold it in my hands, amigo, look through the lens... Good quality, very good. *Muchos dólares* for this camera, no? More than a gun. More than two, three guns, maybe. Be careful where you go. Somebody maybe try to steal it from you. Very good. I can see all the way to the plaza. But tell me about your girl. You think about she when you lie in your hotel bed? If no go now, amigo, no bed for you tonight, only little broke chair. Unless you want lie with me?

When Angél come here – only one time – he no like. Too small, smelly, too dusty. He cough, cough. Is the land here – dry, dry. In America, good land, plenty land, fields so big you no see the end. Angél always he think big. But here is small people, small farms, fields like bed sheets spread out to dry. Angél have big ideas but me, sometimes now I think pesos in the hand is better than bodies in the street. But if Oswaldo take off his mask, put down his toy gun, will gringos buy Emilia's dolls? If no war, what will Emilia sell?

Before the fighting, the women make trouble dolls, tiny tiny, for help *niños* sleep. Little bit magic, eh? You tell trouble to doll, the doll take away. But now, too many troubles, maybe only guns and *documentales* can fix things. Listen; it begin already. You no hear nothing? Your ears is block? You no hear the dog cry and the clock-clock, like chopping wood... eh, but is no dog, is girl; the soldiers take a girl. *Madre de Dios.* Better she die now, before they put her in truck. You ever see a cat catch mouse? It catch, it let go, catch again, throw in the air before it bite off the head. Even after the mouse no can crawl, no can squeak, the cat play. The girl is mouse for the soldiers. To know and do nothing is terrible, terrible. If I no wait for Oswaldo, my only friend, I say fuck Angél's orders, fuck the big plans.

You hear now eh, you hear now? I think is big mistake for you to stay here, tonight. This no safe house. Me, I stay and cry for this girl and hope Angél have good plans. You, I think you must go now. But the camera is problem. Soldiers, they no like *documentales*. They see camera after curfew, maybe you roadkill. Must be very careful, very quick. Maybe hotel door already close, *no sé,* but listen, I make deal. You give me camera, I give you gun. My gun is no toy, amigo. Also plenty ammo, see? Is time to leave your story, eh? So give, take, go.

Swan Lake

I HAVE A memory from a long time ago but so clear, every little detail. France in springtime, early spring when the world was just coming to after the winter. There were violets everywhere pushing through the dewy grass, their petals uncurling shyly, opening up little by little. A grey, still morning, birds everywhere; on the ground and the water, in the trees and the sky. I've never seen so many birds; finches and woodpeckers and doves and many I didn't know. The trees were completely still, the new catkins drooping like little monkey tails and fat, green-tipped buds thrusting and glistening stickily and making me think of sex, that luxury denied to many of us itinerants. The domiciled world finds it objectionable enough to see us eating, drinking and sleeping on the streets but sex – the homeless fornicating in public? I don't think so.

An old steam engine stood on a narrow track – TACOT DES LACS – as advertised on a rusty sign which might have dated from the nineteenth century, idling there until Easter when day trippers from Paris would come and pay to be chugged round the water.

So early in the morning, the mist still drifting over the water like breath. Away from the road and its disappointments, there was no one around. One lake led on to another, each glimmering its own grey tones, drawing me away from my destination, away from the chance of a lift, though after walking all night a lift had begun to seem like a very remote possibility. The long silky fingers of the lakes beckoned and it was easy to imagine a sprite in the mist, luring tired, hungry people deeper and deeper into the forest until they were lost. But that's not the way it was; that was tiredness playing tricks on me. I found out later that the path formed a long loop round the lakes which eventually led back to the same spot.

It was not because I was drunk that I had that idea. I don't drink. Many of us do but not me. I don't swear either, unless I am very angry, and then only under my breath; I never ever shout. For some people shouting is a liberating thing, a way of getting things out, spring-cleaning their heads and starting afresh but for me, the sound of shouting... no, I don't like the sound of shouting.

There was no human noise at all except the crunch of my own feet on the path, my own stomach growling for food, my own breathing heavy and hard as if my chest were full of lead. I found an empty cartridge on the path, a little steel-grey plastic rocket, and picked it up, I don't know why, maybe just for something to hold. The woods turned out to be a game reserve. It happens everywhere; you see somewhere which from the distance looks free and welcoming but when you get closer there's barbed wire or an electric fence or a wall with broken glass along the top. And signs, of course. RÉSERVE DE CHASSE in this case. With a gun or a fishing rod – and a permit, mind – there would be plenty food to be had. But I had stopped thinking about food; the thought of eating a bird or a fish was not in my mind at all. I was too caught up with watching the swans. There were other birds on the lake too, little black moorhens puttering about, geese and ducks all making ripples on the calm water but it was the swans I remember most vividly, gliding across the water so poised, clean and white, swivelling their dangerously beautiful heads.

Some were feeding too, backsides exposed to the sky, fluttering like flowers. And being spring the mating season was on the go. On the trees the ladybirds were stotting about, stuck together, bum to bum. Odd to just continue going about your travels while having sex, but maybe they're a tribe of itinerants and if they stop too long, some other kind of insect will want to know why.

The swans; they seemed to be moving at random, ripples fanning out behind them. One of the males had begun to pursue a female, casually at first but determinedly skimming along behind her. It's easy to see why dancers try to imitate swans, all that stylish swishing. But isn't it always the males who do the showing off, fluffing themselves up, coiling their necks back and tucking their heads into the feathers? More like fan dancers than ballerinas, really. It was a subtle, casual pursuit, the male showing off, the female paddling on apparently unconcerned but keeping her distance all the same. And then the male rising out of the water, huge and heavy and slow, wings creaking, neck straight as an oar, flying barely a hand's breadth above the water, the female continuing, playing hard to get.

It's the swans I remember most, and the shy violets, and another all too familiar sign: STATIONNEMENT INTERDIT AU NOMADES. Sounds less harsh in French but the message is the same in any language: keep on walking, mate, don't stop here, take your carcass someplace else. I can't remember how I got to where I was going or even why I was in France in the first place. There must have been a reason but... when you move around so much the road becomes not so much a route from one place to another as a place in itself and moving along it is just part of survival, like breathing. One thread of tarmac leads to another, they are all part of the same loop. The places on the way only matter to those who live in them or come to visit and compare their lives to others in the domiciled world. It was the same that day, nothing has changed other than the place, the time and my method...

Then it was water but the thought of fouling up the lake, of distressing the birds put me off. As well as the violets I remember another plant which, unless my nose was deceiving me, smelled a bit like piss. Anyway, it reminded me of a good few stairways and closemouths; the perfume of the streets...

Here, the city streets are stuffed to the gills with visitors and the police have been doing their annual clean-up so the tourists' views aren't ruined by too many of us lying around, living our distasteful, disturbing lives in public. One year somebody made a show about us, put some of our more colourful characters on the stage. It was very popular and even won a prize. People laughed and cried and clapped like hell at the end. A full house every night, television interviews, photographers and a good tap for some. It's one thing for tourists to pay money to see us on the stage, another to trip over us on the street.

RÉSERVE DE CHASSE. Hunters don't mess about. They see something moving and contrive to stop it moving. Maybe that's what gave me the idea but it didn't fucking work and I'm angry which is why I'm swearing, angry for failing yet again.

It's so clear. I keep thinking there must be something else about it which is important. Just the flat grey water, the swans, the violets. I had stopped at the woods to get away from the road where nobody'd picked me up all night. Not the first time that had happened; walking at night was something I knew pretty damn well. On quiet roads it wasn't too bad; just the headlights to contend with, the weather and the lack of decent footwear. The usual. Where I was coming from or going to who knows, it was quite likely that I was just keeping on the move because it's safer not to stop anywhere too long. I can't think why I was in France. I don't know anyone in France. It was probably just something about the place, the way one memory leads to another like the lakes, on and on and then, without warning, you find you're back at the beginning again, neither lost nor found.

The swans: they mate for life. But how do they choose their partners; by the way breast feathers fold into each other like heavenly pillows, the quality of their dry rattling calls, or the sight of another's backside waving in the air, an unearthly feather flower? And once they've chosen a mate, are they happy? Is spending your life gliding across the lake more bearable when you've a partner to share the moving around with?

Not France, or Germany. Spain, of course it was Spain. Was her name really Violetta, or is that just me making things up again? Violetta and the cheese – a wedge of pale, moon-coloured cheese, creamy like her arms, Violetta talking to me and never for a moment looking away, making me listen to words I couldn't understand, holding me with her eyes. Violetta, the cold winter sun on her hands as she sliced the cheese.

Spain, down on the south coast somewhere. Africa across the water. I didn't go to Africa. You can't walk to Africa. I did ask. I did go down to the docks and see if there was anything doing on the boats but there were plenty other needy people who could understand orders and curses, so fair's fair, nothing doing.

Sitting on the sea wall, the breeze ruffling her hair. I asked her where I could buy some food. She took one long steady look at me, cut off a slice of her cheese and handed it over, talking talking talking, God knows what she was saying, I just stood there chewing and nodding and wanting to squeeze my thanks into her... but instead, when I'd finished eating, I shook her hand, turned away and in on myself once more.

Maybe her name wasn't Violetta and the connection with the lakes is something else altogether. Violets. African violets. Oh yes. African violets. All wrapped up nicely in shiny cellophane, a little card with a picture of the flowers I'd bought, a printed LOVE FROM... and my name crushed alongside in my best seven-year-old handwriting.. Thanks son, she said, but violets are useless, too fragile for this climate. Just keel over and die if you turn your back on them for a moment.

Warm, too warm in here. I'm used to the cold more than heat. But the bed is good; a little pillow with a disposable paper cover, a clean crisp sheet and a rubber mat underneath for any mess. I've made plenty mess already. The lovely Indian woman with a long plait, gold rimmed glasses and shy violet lips like those little flowers in France, has gone to get help. To have a woman like that touching me, to have any woman touching me now... God, I must smell a bit too.

It was the lakes and the swans, the thought of someone shooting a swan. I don't know, I just thought that a crossbow would at least do the job properly, and maybe also that there was some point to it, some significance – the hunter and the hunted in one – I don't know. The bow was too heavy, I was weak, my hands shook like a drunk's...

My mother thought the violets were too fragile to survive the harsh, inhospitable climate so she didn't want them, didn't want to be bothered with a plant which hadn't the will to live, she'd had enough of things keeling over. Maybe if she'd just tried to like my present a little it would have opened its heart-shaped petals and stood up straight and brave.

And me, even if I was too shy and too quiet, curling into myself, turning my head away and stopping up my ears... it was not my mother, I kept telling myself, it wasn't her, it was just a noise which would pass over like a plane and everything would be all right again. But soon the plane didn't pass over, it began crashing around inside the house, the room, my own head, crashing and exploding. One day somebody from the social came and dug me out of the wreckage.

The lovely Indian woman has returned, with help. She tells me I look like a saint in a painting she saw in Florence, from the Renaissance. The arrowhead burns my chest, my blood blooms on the white sheet... Did I see a wounded swan crawling to its nest, wings torn and bloody? Did I hear a shot? No help for the bird, no knives or needles... nothing for the pain. I'm so lucky.

She is above me, looking down, her eyes deep and dark behind her glasses. She is holding my wrist and telling me to count backwards from a hundred. Her hand is small and warm like a little bird. She is smiling and looking at her watch.

Africa is across the water. Grey shawls of mist wrapped around the thin limbs of the trees. The flowers too fragile, not worth the bother. Violetta cutting cheese on her open palm. The cheese smooth against my dry, swollen tongue...

I turn away and into myself, and my own white-hot ecstasy...

A Living Legend

LISTEN, IT MUST be almost a full house; can you hear the deep rumble, the unspoken communion of strangers, of people who've paid good money and come out on a bitter stormy night to hear *A Living Legend*? This is how Clem bills Belle on the posters. What he called her when she locked him out of the dressing-room tonight was not so grand. Belle yelled back something even worse through the closed door. I laughed – quietly – and swept up the remains of the broken glass before she could do herself, or me, any damage.

Belle doesn't like my trilling, nervous laughs. Nor Clem's chewed, sour snorts. The only sounds which please her are the whoops of a full house. Don't you think it's odd, really, when Belle is in the business of tears? I have never been able to understand how it can be good to feel bad but that's what her audience pays for, every time. When Belle sings cheerful songs people shift in their seats and clear their throats. It's sadness which makes hundreds – of course it used to be thousands – hold their breath as one, the sadness of this difficult, contrary old woman who can barely remember her own words and may have trouble staying on her feet.

Belle's sadness is not a stage act, turned on to please the crowd, no, it is real and has been so right from the beginning, sadness she couldn't disguise even if she wanted to. In every photo, every film clip, even when her mouth is stretched into a wide glittering smile, her eyes shine with tears. And anger, too. Belle's sadness and her anger know no limits. They have accompanied her around the world, her invisible baggage, her demons, the blue moods and the black.

It took the entire journey here for Clem to persuade her not to cancel; Belle yelling, Clem slapping the steering wheel, the van roaring up the motorway at I don't know what speed. I prayed for deliverance and looked out of the window at ribbed brown fields and fat factory chimneys, at more fields, bridges and a long steel-grey curl of coastline. These dogfights must be endured, they are part of the job, but to be trapped in a van smelling of cigarettes and too many years on the road, hearing Belle and Clem pound each other with words blunt and heavy as bricks – it makes me shrink inside. Though I believe that everything is ordained, it is not good to be enclosed in a speeding capsule of rage.

In a way it is a good thing to see a piano on stage. Belle can lean against it for a song or two. Otherwise, by about halfway through the set, she might begin to totter a little. The audience might not notice but Clem, later, will curse her every unrehearsed step and fluffed songline. He will scold her like the unloved child she has always felt herself to be. She will purse her lips, scowl and possibly break something else. Clem says he would prefer an impersonator to the real Belle. An impersonator, Clem says, could do a better job of being Belle than Belle can now make of herself.

The bad thing about a piano being available is that Belle still has the unfortunate desire to play. I can see it in her eyes when she goes on stage, that invisible thread, pulling. Belle loves the piano better than any of the men who have passed through her life and are now no more than half-forgotten lyrics. The piano has been her solace, her confidante; the white in Paris, black lacquer in Tokyo, the walnut in Rome. But now, in her hour of need, the piano, too, betrays her. I expect you are wondering why I use such a gloomy word as betrayal. An old-fashioned word, and an old-fashioned idea. But Belle also talks about betrayal; by lovers and managers and recording companies. When she is allowed to. She is under contract not to speak about any of these things in public but, as you might expect, Belle has little respect for contracts. Contracts have cheated her too many times, kept her in her cage of pain. But she has lived like this so long, captivity is what she knows and, like a bird hurling itself against the bars, Belle bruises herself more than anybody else.

Tonight's venue is a church, at least it used to be a church; now it's a concert hall. It's fresh and bright, not at all the kind of place to which Belle has become accustomed. Most of the audience sit in hard, high-backed pews. The rest – who paid more for their tickets – cluster round candle-lit tables in front of the stage. Drinks can be brought through from the bar so people can pretend that they're in a nightclub even though the ceiling is arched like a gothic heaven and smoking is forbidden. A proper nightclub would have been more appropriate. I don't like the sham of the place though the dressingrooms are clean, chilly but clean. Belle likes the venue, the churchy feel. Uplifting, she says, and the acoustics are good. Maybe, but the PA system's so fuzzy that the acoustics hardly matter. And the band – I am not musical but even I know when a rhythm guitarist can't keep time.

Belle should not be blamed for the band. Clem hired the musicians and Clem cares more about cost than quality. He must have scraped the scrapings for this lot. Clem says Belle is lucky to get any kind of band at all with her reputation. I don't deny that she can be difficult. I know as well as anyone just how difficult she can be. But we were not put on this earth perfect, our purpose is to grow towards perfection, however long it may take. Belle believes this too and knows it may take more time than she has left to reach a state of grace.

I do not talk to Belle of faith. It is she who talks of such things. The further she strays, the more she talks about needing to get back to the fold. It is never too late, I tell her, but Belle is scared of her sins, scared to look them in the eye, to name them. It breaks my heart every time I see her turn to the mirror, stare into her own sad black eyes, clip on big, shiny earrings, slick her mouth with lipstick then unlock the box where she keeps her needles and powders, the only comfort Clem has ever provided. It breaks my heart because, for Belle, happiness is no more than relief from pain.

The house lights are down and from the stage, Belle is looking out on a swaying sea of flames. Maybe the candles will help her forget Clem's threat that this may be the last night of the last ever tour, that if she screws up one more time, or blabs about business, she'll never see the inside of another dressing-room, never mind step onto a stage. Clem has said this before, countless times, but this time I think he means it. Clem has plans for the future which don't include Belle. Lately he has been doing a lot of talking on the phone; he is hunting down a new name, a new girl to groom for fame, a new voice to pour its heart out for a miserly percentage. If the deal goes through, Clem will have no more need for Belle.

Earlier tonight I had to stand in for her because she wouldn't do a lighting test. Clem had been rude to her and, of course, she was rude back. Belle has never been a good friend to herself, which is why I stay by her side, even when she hates the sight of me and curses me for shadowing her like the devil's own disciple. I know why Belle hits out at me; this, I understand. Other things are beyond me, but it is not for me to question what I don't understand. I do what must be done and so I walked around the stage, stopping where I was told, watching as a cool, serene space put on its red dress and pretended to become a nightclub.

Belle is wearing indigo. It's a soothing colour, indigo, deep and dark as the night sky but Clem doesn't like it, says it's too heavy, too ethnic; he wants her to shimmer in champagne silk and oyster satin, wants to put the Living Legend on stage, not the crazy old woman in an African wrap, with sharks' teeth round her neck and demons in her head. But Belle will not be told what to do or what to say; she has always been a woman with a will of her own. And a mouth as big as the Mississippi, says Belle. Which is true, and why Clem sits in the wings, head back, eyes closed, still as a dead man, listening hard, missing nothing.

Belle has been warned often enough that some things are okay to say out loud, others she must try to keep to herself. If she wants to talk politics, the history of oppression, black pride, the blues, she can go right ahead. She can talk about race and colour, poverty and inequality, conspiracy and murder. She can talk about Brother Malcolm's vision blurred and soiled by treachery. When she talks about Brother Malcolm, her eyes always search the darkness for me. It was he who brought us together all those years ago, who gave us each other. She can talk about her own attempts to embrace the Nation of Islam, and her failure to find redemption in faith.

Belle is free to talk about anything but business. She can complain all she wants about the injustices of the world as long as she doesn't mention the injustices of her own life. Clem will not tolerate this. He will hold it against her; on this he will not be crossed. As he sees it, Belle belongs to him because nobody else wants the trouble of trailing a has-been round provincial venues. Clem no longer cares for Belle and she has never cared for herself. All I can do is tend her wounds; I cannot cure the disease.

Tonight, the crowd is on her side, easy and kind, cheering

wildly at every opportunity, hanging on every word, thrilled to be in her presence, no matter that the musical arrangements are harsh and ragged, that Belle's voice lost its wings long ago, its dip and soar, its ability to hover on a high note long enough to reduce a house to tears. This is a crowd which is trying hard to believe in the beauty behind a cracked voice and a band which sounds like the garbage being taken out, a crowd which strains to hear traces of Belle at her best and makes allowances for everything. These people want to cherish this shoddy performance, to take home personal memories of their idol, to talk years from now about the night they saw, in person, *A Living Legend*.

If only Belle could lose her need to gaze into darkness and flames; if she could take pleasure in other things, daylight, for example, birdsong, spots of sun marking out her kitchen floor. It is not my place to suggest this. It is only my place to be by her side when she needs me and absent when she needs to be alone, to stand in the wings while applause and the storm compete in rattling the roof of this deconsecrated place. Belle takes another bow and another. When the storm overwhelms the applause, she steps down from the stage, takes the glass of rye from me and the cigarette I have already lit for her. I offer her my arm. Wearily, we pick our way through darkness towards the glowing buzzer on the dressing-room door. Nearly there, I say, nearly there.

Glancing

RAIN GLANCES OFF shiny pavings at a crazy angle, wind slashes her face, her city clothes useless against the unrestrained elements of this wild, exposed island; she should turn back, make a dash for the green door with its B&B sign swaying above it, take the steep narrow stairs two at a time to her tasteful verging on twee accommodation, strip off the wet clothes, snuggle up and listen to the racket the rain makes on the roof and the sea makes on the window, try and get used to it so it doesn't keep her awake like it did the night before. But she's been in the room enough, too much, and the solitude hasn't been soothing, in spite of cute little abstract collages, perky pot plants, an efficient heater, a sea view.

The people she's come to meet haven't arrived yet and the place is so dreary it would be funny, had there been anybody to share the joke with. Six lone lads hunch on bar stools and mutter curses. At home, it's the kind of place she'd walk into and out of again and feel relieved to be standing in the rain. But she's here to meet people more prone to the animated huddle than the lonely line – and who should arrive shortly – so she buys a drink and takes it to the table facing a dormant jukebox. Even silent, the jukebox is better than nothing; modern, hundreds of songs to flip through, the casing dayglo pink and yellow; as out of place here as happiness. A deserted pool table fills the back room. Above it, a lamp with a fringed shade casts a thin smoky beam across the baize.

She didn't think to bring anything to read so reads the bar, which has been hammered together from fish crates: ABERDEEN, WICK, THURSO, 2 doz COD, 2 doz WHITING. Reading the bar involves craning her head sideways and attracts attention. One of the boys at the bar glances round, his head swivelling slowly from the neck. Surreptitious. Reptilian. She concentrates on not meeting his eyes. To do this without obviously looking away, and maybe setting up some unspoken game of chase, she stares at the gap between him and his neighbour. Her purse is heavy with coins, the jukebox enticing. She leaves her seat, feeds in a handful of change and begins to read the song titles, taking her time, reading slowly, re-reading, becoming deliberately engrossed in the business of choosing, flicking the card index forward and back again, making a pastime of indecision.

She must have pressed the wrong buttons. The jukebox plays nothing she chose, though the selection it thumps out could have been worse and the element of surprise is a distraction. The volume alone improved the place, for her if not for the others. It's good to be filling the dull air with the illusion of somewhere else.

She doesn't blame the locals for being gloomy. The day has gone from sodden grey to bruised blue. Who'd fancy the prospect of darkness for months on end? In a place like this, an island off the scrag end of the country, weather matters, makes a difference. There's a lot of it about, and when the sky's bright enough to see anything at all, you can see the weather coming. Rain clouds wheel, snow flurries shear over the hills, greybacks wail across this exposed, battered island and there's nothing to be done but stick it out.

Her drink's nearly done. She's going off the prospect of meeting people. Friends of friends. Theatre people on tour. She could go now, skip out and miss them. She's come all the way here for peace and quiet, after all. Many do, in summer, and clutter up the narrow streets. Off season, she's one of a handful of visitors. The tourist shops are deserted or closed. What she'd wanted. But peace and quiet haven't been having the desired effect, the jukebox is still playing and she hasn't had her money's worth yet.

The lad with the lank, sandy fringe is getting bold, letting his eyes linger, willing her to look at him, to adjust the angles of her eyes just a fraction, and meet his. Eye contact, coinciding lines of vision, that's the game, but she's not playing. After two more random selections and several failed attempts to catch her eye, he cracks down his glass, scowls in her direction and lurches out into the rain. Behind him the door bangs, predictably.

Another lad strolls over to the jukebox. Smallish, dark tidy hair, white shirt, denims. The disc drops, clicks into place, makes a couple of scratchy revolutions. A piano mourns, brushes drag over a drum, lead in to Joe Cocker's melancholy squeal.

– I like this one, he says.

He shifts his hips to a couple of bars then turns to face her. A pinkish baby face, squint smile, bright eyes. Clean-cut. Fresh-faced.

She likes the song too. Didn't choose it. *Night Calls*. A song for the lonely, the heartbroken, and she isn't that.

– Come and play pool, he says. It'll cheer you up.

She makes excuses to stay put – doesn't need cheered up, wants to listen to the music, can't play pool – but he's persistent and points out, in a light, easy way that she can do what she's doing, feel what she's feeling and still knock some balls across the table.

He chalks cues. Big smile.

– So what's your name, then?

– Joanne.

– And where're ye frae, Joanne?

– Edinburgh.

– Edinburgh, eh? Ah've a half-brother doon there. Muirhoose. And whit're ye daein here?

– Getting away from Edinburgh.

He draws in his breath, lines up his cue, fires at the racked balls, sends them rocketing across the table.

– And what're ye daein in the pub? Ah'm nosy by the way.

– Having a drink and playing pool.

Big smile again. Shirt sleeves pushed up to the elbow.

– Aye, ah ken. But aboot here lassies dinna come intae pubs on their ain.

– I'm meeting people.

– Local folk?

– City people. In a show at the town hall.

– Ach weel.

He's got an appealing, wee-boy cheekiness about him, and dimples.

She hasn't played pool for years but begins to enjoy the geometry of it, the way you could see one action causing another, the contrast between a direct hit and the knock-on effect of a duff shot. If you could lay your life on a table, work out the angles of contact, predict the knock-on effects… And circling the table fills time better than staring at the jukebox or the fish-crate bar.

– Ah'm a butcher, he says. Wis on the fishin but oot a work mair than in it. It's a job. Jimmy's in Muirhoose, like ah said. Except he's no there that much ah dinna think. No that ah ken how he comes and goes. No seen him in five year. In the forces, like, been all over the place. Belfast, Falklands. The Gulf. In the paras now. A hero, he is. Medals and everything. Shot! Tch, and you said you couldna play!

– Cracked up one time. Lost the place, like. Hit the deck every time a bloody car backfired – thought it was gunshot, ken. And a pure mental temper he had, ragin. Put a boy in hospital and himself in the cells. Better noo, ken. Been asked to join the flying squad, sas, like.

He goes for hard shots, spinning out the game.

– If he goes for it, if he signs up, they give him this contract which says – ah'm no supposed tae ken this, top secret like – but if somethin happens to him, if he gets done in, all his faimily – mither, faither, wife, bairns – they'll all be taken care of. A pension, ken. And protection. No that he's got wife or bairns yet.

She's taking her time too, eyeing up possible angles. The dreary little back room is warmed by the boy's island voice, easy smile, his ready confidences.

– No me, like. Half-bloods dinna coont. Last time ah saw him, ah was in the shop – new tae the trade then but an auld hand noo – ah was standin at the coonter'n this big laddie – a full six inches taller than me – is standin on the ither side, sayin: Get a fuckin move on there, Alex – that's ma name by the way – and ah'm thinkin, How does this laddie ken ma name? So ah says to him, Do ah ken you? and he says, You fuckin should, ya cunt, ah'm yir fuckin brother.

– Excuse the language but you shoulda seen me. Stopped in ma tracks, rigid, ken. The cleaver above ma heid and ma mooth wide open, like ah'd seen a bloody ghost. If there hadna been the pork chops and the big high coonter atween us ah'd have thrown ma airms roon him right there and then. When ah got aff ma shift, we cam doon here, drank pints and pints, then staggered up the brae, huggin each other and greetin like bairns. Hadna seen each other since primary school, like.

He misses a shot. Still grinning, he points the tip of his cue at an easy ball.

– There you are. Ah'm givin you a chance... Jimmy hung aboot awhile, hiked over every incha the toon in his DMs – it was pissing rain the whole time he was here, like tonight. Liked the place, so he did; slagged it off, ken, but jokin like. He was a laugh. Ah miss him. Dinna really ken him, but ah miss him.

A lucky shot wins her the game. The remaining balls are returned to their pockets. Without their rolling geometry, the click of contact, the room resumes its usual dreariness.

– Are ye for another lager? he says, but she's ready to go, to get out...

– Ach, weel. At least ye're smilin noo. When ye cam in, ken, ye had a face like thunder.

The room is warm. She wraps a towel round her wet hair, pushes her toes into thick, dry socks, cups her hands around a mug of steaming tea. She'd missed the theatre people, after all, missed them on purpose. As she turned back along the street, she'd heard them straggling down the brae, their sharp city voices cutting through the island storm. Lowering her head into the rain, she kept on walking.

It is a good room. She was lucky to find such a good room. More home comforts than home, in some ways. Simple. A clean, calm room in the midst of a storm. She wipes the condensation off the window, looks past crooked chimney stacks and sagging walls, looks through shifting masses of darkness towards the rain-streaked lighthouse beam way out in the bay.

Red Tides

THIS DAY THERE's no swimming because of the red tides. At the town end, First Beach is covered with noxious algae the colours of rust and blood. A thick band of the stuff clings to the high-tide line like a scarf or a bandage. A big stretch of sand is messed up by clots and spatters. Sumbums have moved further along, making our patch less private than usual.

But it's a good day for the beach: hot, with a fresh breeze blowing off the water. Lois, Carla and I are face down, flat out on our towels. We're lying in a row, like a tanning chart – Before, During and After. I'm white and pink in bits, Lois is light honey, Carla olivey bronze. We could soak up the sun all summer and our skin tones still wouldn't even up. We're different, that's all. Around us is the usual litter of clothes, tanning oil, snacks, cold drinks, cigarettes, books. We've been coming here between shifts since the good weather began. We've got our beach needs sorted out.

Carla and I do other things together when Jimmy's out of town. Lois stays home and waxes her furniture or her legs. Or dates Andrew who's definitely a hot number. The girl wriggles when she says his name, stretching the A around her mouth like gum. His name comes up a lot. Doesn't matter what we're gabbing about, Andrew has seen it, done it, or got an opinion on it. You can see the frisson rip through the girl every time she stretches that A. No problem in that, I mean, everybody likes a little jolt. But when you're between men the eternal mention of somebody else's really gets to grate and right now that's my story.

There's a piano player in one of the wharfside cafes who's kinda cute – plays moody Van Morrison numbers and smiles to himself while he's tickling the ivories. Sometimes I drag Carla down there after the beer bars but I know she hates it. The décor's repro deco, straight lines everywhere, nothing fancier than the odd triangle, and that goes for the clientele as well. Basically Dorothy's is full of jerks, but because it's pricey it's never so bombed you can't get a seat, and at the end of a shift that's something. I guess I'd have settled for the crush at the beer bars if it hadn't been for that little blond guy with the nimble fingers. Looks good in his tux. So who doesn't, Carla says. And you've only seen him late-night. This is true and I've been fooled before by candlelight, dimmer switches and booze.

The reason Carla and I don't go places with Lois – apart from the beach – is basically Andrew. She keeps the guy out of sight but can't shut up about him. We know his height: six/two; hair colour – chestnut (not just brown for God's sake, chestnut); eye colour – hazel – Andrew the nut, as Carla says. We know what kind of car he drives, what he likes to eat: littlenecks and bloody beef; how many times he brushes his teeth, what he likes about Lois – her body, hair, clothes, apartment, personality, in more or less that order. Lois tells all. Can't help herself. Andrew is way up on her priorities. Otherwise, she keeps her business under wraps. Like what she did before she moved to the coast. One time Carla asked her straight out. Lois closed her eyes, turned her neat nose to the side, blew a slim line of smoke through neat, glossy lips and said, Streetwalker – dead serious – Fall River.

We got the message. Sure there are places to be a streetwalker but Fall River is not one of them. Stinks of sulphur from the mills when they're open and hard times when they're shut down. This girl wouldn't drive through the streets of that town, never mind walk them. Her favourite slogan is a store sign outside a dry cleaners: GRIME DOESN'T PAY. And does she believe it. Her apartment has surfaces which glow like the heavenly bodies are supposed to and her soft furnishings have a nurtured look, like pets.

Lois has manicured blonde hair which turns into her neck in a single wave and looks metallic in the sun. She's pretty in a regular front-of-house way – even-featured, nothing lop-sided, nothing too big or too small, medium height, leggy, looks good in clingy T-shirts, skimpy sun-dresses and the high-cut frosted bikini she's wearing. She's undone the back strap and halter neck so she won't have any paler strips of skin around her tits. In case Andrew doesn't like it.

There are things we don't know about the girl. We do know she's recently divorced. Alan (another A name), the husband she ran after for years, ran off with a girl the spit of Lois but younger and with money. Lois threw all the frozen dinners she had prepared – a month's supply of planned, balanced meals – into the waste disposal and moved to the coast for fun, sun and fucking. What she got was Andrew.

After our shift at Neptune's Carla and I sometimes go drink beer, listen to the band, bitch about this and that – the slow eaters, cheap tippers, the pains and the real assholes. Maybe we'll let some guys buy us a beer. But Carla won't fool around. It's not safe and she knows it, she's no fool. Jimmy drinks Old Bushmills and sings slushy Irish songs with some touring band, Retro – or Repro – something they call themselves and it's what they are, old-style fake. Jimmy's never been within a thousand miles of the Emerald Isle but turns on a brogue at the merest sniff of whiskey. And gets punch drunk and jealous in a big way. Carla's a whole lot better than he deserves.

Our place in the sun is at the end of the comfort zone. Further along the coast it's too rocky for stretching out. There's a big cruising scene down by the changing huts but where we are, next to the big rock and high, scratchy dunes nobody can just stroll by and parade their tan and muscle tone. They have to say something and better have some good lines. Carla gets off on crucifying cruisers. She's right, sure. But sometimes when it's hot like this and there's nothing to do and the sand chafes the bikini line and grinds its way under the swimsuit legbands, mixing with slicks of tanning oil, sweat and other body fluids, I'm personally not in such a hurry to chase away an okay guy.

But here we three are on our own little tail of beach and who's there in the distance but Monsignor Zyw. The black skirts of his coat wing out as he picks his way over the wounded-looking beach. The Monsignor is a regular at Neptune's and everybody's favourite customer. What a treat he is, a real sweetie. And so easy – orders the same meal every time.

– The scrod, bless your heart.

Scrod – no such thing. It's a made-up name for baby cod, a restaurant fiction. But this little guy with his tinkly voice – who gets the giggles halfway through his second Martini – makes us all try to be a bit nicer than we really are. Even Gus: his usual cynicism crumples like a dishrag at the sight of old Zyw perched tidily at his table for one, hands clasped round each other, bird eyes sparkling.

– And how are you tonight, Father? says Gus, dipping his voice to the carpet and tipping a two-fingered salute at the worry waves rolling across his forehead.

– Wonderful, my son, Zyw answers every time, Bless your heart.

While Monsignor Zyw chews at his scrod and the Ballams pick at their lemon-dressed salad and probe sensitive areas of their marriage, blind Bill likes to give us girls a hard time. We forget to turn our heads when we speak to him. Thinks we don't bother. Look at me, Goddammit, he says. You think, what's he getting at? He can't see. But Bill can say exactly where your voice hits the wall. Tunes pianos. Looks like Roy Orbison.

– Take a look at who's cruising, says Carla to Lois. Doesn't it kill ya?

Lois takes forever to see the vertical, buttoned-up Monsignor among the horizontal bodies. When she does, instead of going coy and cutesy – like she does when she waits on him – her face goes kinda cloudy. I mean, I'm looking up thinking the weather's about to break but no, the sky is pure blue – then she's twisting about on her towel, hooking up the backstrap and halter, squeezing into a tight T-shirt – Lois doesn't own any baggy ones – then she's stashing the book she's been reading in her bag.

– Must be raunchy stuff, says Carla. Lend it to me when I'm feeling deprived.

– I could use it right now, I say.

Lois ignores us. She lies down on her back. A frothy red scarf lifts and ripples and veils her face.

We always bring books and read for a bit before we get too hot and sticky, before the print starts to jump in the sunlight and it becomes too much effort to turn a page. Carla picks racy new fiction and crime stories set in exotic locations. Lois goes in for sex disguised as romance and romance disguised as sex. Me, I never know what I'm looking for and never seem to find it. I get through a load of books. Don't read them. Start plenty but mostly give up quick. Short attention span. Or something.

– So what's the story? says Carla. Picking up tips on new ways to fuck, or what?

– I wish you wouldn't call it that, says Lois, who's no stranger to the word – It sounds so ugly.

– You want it to sound like eating ice cream?

– I gotta go.

– No you don't.

– Ice cream sounds good. Black walnut with blueberry ripple.

– Butterscotch fudge.

– Who's going to stand in line?

– Think you could give up sex if you had a constant supply of ice cream?

– Think you could give up ice cream if you had a constant supply of sex?

– Really girls, I gotta go.

– Things to do.

– People to see.

– Anyone in particular?

– No prizes for guessing.

– Please, says Lois, will you please knock it off?

Some nights just don't work out, however you look at it. It's like there's something in the air, some kind of virus which hits out at everybody. A hot day, a hotter sweaty night, the cooks stripped to the waist, Gus running out of ice and running off at the mouth at blind Bill's sister. Somebody screwed up on the reservations. It happens. So what's the big deal? Everybody gets their Goddamn dinner sooner or later but regulars don't like it, regulars get ratty real quick about folks from out of town taking their tables. The Ballams get stuck by the kitchen and Jeez do they bitch and bicker and hassle us girls, sticking a fork in the air every time we go by. Monsignor Zyw gets wedged between the crab tank and the air-conditioner and the kitchen runs our of scrod just before his order goes in. The night is lousy all round. By the time we get our aprons off we're ready to kill or sink some drinks and think about it. I'm speaking for me and Carla. Lois has other plans.

This town is too small. I mean first we meet the Monsignor on the beach – he finally gets through all those bodies to us, raises his hat, bows and walks around the rock, to peace and quiet and an empty stretch of shingle. Carla and I wave, Lois crosses herself. Chrissakes, we should have known something was up with the girl. I mean, it's just not something you do when you're wearing a bathing suit.

After the dinner shift our feet are burning up, so I persuade Carla to start out at Dorothy's instead of ending up there and who do we meet but blind Bill. He's sitting right by the piano, alone at the best table, on the prawn-pink sofa. He picks up on our voices and calls us over. Bill order highballs for us without asking, pats the sofa on either side of him in invitation. Carla stays on her feet. I sit. The guy doesn't bother me. He's got some good stories about old jazzers he's tuned pianos for in New York City, I like his line about seeing with his ears, he doesn't say stupid things about what you're wearing or how you've fixed your hair – well, he wouldn't but still. And I get to see the piano player.

Carla sucks down her drink.

– I'm out of here, she says.

Jimmy's doing a spot at O'Malley's. I've heard Jimmy's band enough to know I can miss it. And O'Malley's has the worst seating in town – high-backed pews some nut saved from a burning chapel and stuck in the bar when old-style was new. After tonight's shift, I'm happy to stick with the sofa.

Maybe Lois tried calling the bars, she knows where we go. Maybe she tried a couple and gave up. It's always the same, isn't it, I mean, where's anybody when you need them? More likely she couldn't get near a phone. On the beach, at work, she said nothing and Lois never liked to be asked. She'd tell you a thing in her own time, if at all. We should have known. But say she'd come looking for us, what would she have found? Jimmy going loco with a broken bottle, carving up Carla's ex for buying her a beer. Me out of it on the beach with Bill and the piano player – Lyall – all three of us blind drunk, stumbling, lurching, swaying into another kind of crazinesss. Carla at the hospital, me on the beach, Lois out of her mind in her glossy apartment. Some night. Must have been a full moon or something, but I wasn't paying much attention at the time.

The sea is warmer than earlier in the summer, the beach clean and swimming good. These days, mostly, I'm alone, though once in a long while Carla joins me. Carla doesn't get out much and when she does, all she wants to do is sit in the dingiest corner of some tired, empty bar and worry about Jimmy. Something's got to give. Her ex now has a ragged scar across his neck and he's been spreading the word that Jimmy better quit town, which of course he won't do while he can still camp out at Carla's place, eating her food, drinking her booze etc. I reckon she'll go south at the end of the season, if she's still got it in her to make the break.

The red tides haven't been back and neither has Lois. She quit Neptune's and got herself some kind of day job. Andrew doesn't like her working nights and what Andrew doesn't like, goes. Her name comes up from time to time. Gus says she's giving out to half the cops in town. Andrew's father is chief of police. Andrew admires and fears his father. Andrew has a Dobermann, a shotgun and a taste for pain games. That day on the beach, the girl was reading de Sade. Nobody could say she wasn't prepared, but still. Lois. I reckon she's gone over the limit.

I miss the company down here, by the black rock. Just me and the gulls is getting kinda dull. I've given up books. Too much trouble. I eat, sleep and cool off in the water. The gulls clean up my crumbs before the breeze got a chance to blow them away. We had some good times, the three of us, and when times were bad we kept each other from going under. Laying around, flaked out in the sun, it seemed like no matter what was happening in anybody's life – if we could just laze around and talk it through, or just talk, about anything, it didn't matter, almost any kinda mess could be straightened out. At the end of an afternoon, we'd take home our trash, our oily, gritty towels, our hot tight skins. Also some kinda plan for the future: no big deal – some way to get by for a night, a week, month, season. A season at the outside.

I miss the girls. Don't miss blind Bill or the piano player much. Don't remember much. There's a blank where there should be a weekend. Bill's eating someplace else these days and I steer clear of Dorothy's. Not much to miss, I reckon, either of them. Nothing I couldn't find elsewhere. But I don't know for sure and right now I've nobody to talk it over with. Maybe I should move further along the beach, meet some new people. Or on. Maybe move on.

Landa Opportunity

NO KIDDIN, PSYCHOLOGY major? My kid brother's a shrink.
Up in Boston. Me, I'm more the philosopher – self-taught –
freelance observer of my fellow man, woman, kid, dog – always
on the look-out for life's basic ingredients. Which is why my
brother's filthy rich and I'm clean broke. But me, I got
imagination, whereas my brother, he don't even know how to
dream without all kindsa deep meaning messin up the action.
Dreams, he tells his patients – at around ten bucks a word –
are where it's at. But mostly, I reckon, my brother dreams about
bucks, big bucks, thousand dollar bills swirling about on the
sidewalk like food wrappers, drifting into the trash-can which
– pity it only happens in dreams – turns into the night-deposit
chute at the bank. That's where my brother goes nights – the
Goddamn bank – once his patients have dumped their dreams
into his dictaphone.

Wanna try one of my meatballs? I need a second opinion.
So I guess you'll quit waitressing at the enda the summer? Back
ta school in the fall? College must be a lotta fun. I never did
bother with it myself – my kid brother's fees ate up our parents'

savings – but I'll bet all that studying pays off. That's one thing you can still say for this country, you can go places with an education. Doesn't matter who you are or where you're comin from – the highway to the top is straight ahead. Yep, one thing's for sure, this is still the landa opportunity, and don't let anyone tell you different.

Landa opportunity. Landa power. That's my kid brother's trip, power. He gets off on playing God to psychs. Who wouldn't, if you reckon up the leisure time. Short days in the consulting suite and long weekends on the sailboat with his shrink wife. That's the only catch, the wife. That dame's close to the brink herself. Crazy shrink bitch. Excuse me, but really she's the kind who'd throw herself overboard if ya looked at her the wrong way. Like you tell her you dig her outfit, she gets mad at you. Shit, I mean, what kinda reaction is that? I mean, why wear a dress that looks like cling-wrap if you don't wanna be noticed?

But I tell ya, I'm not so crazy about my brother's lifestyle. Nor his wifestyle. No friggin way do I covet my brother's wifestyle. Don't get me wrong, I don't say every dame in the brain business is looped out. You sure don't look like you fit that bill.

So whatd'ya reckon? Does my sauce need a drop more love and affection? Or maybe a dasha the spice a life? My taste buds are dead. I can always tell a Saturday. By Happy Hour I can't taste a friggin thing but garlic. I ask myself, why bother with hors-d'oeuvres? The jerks we get in here for Happy Hour just suck them up three at a time and don't give a shit what they're eatin so long as they don't haveta pay. Not one a these guys knows howta savour a thing. It gets to me, this place. You take a buncha trouble ta get the flavour spot on. It figures you'd appreciate some kinda acknowledgement for improvin on potato chips, right? But all that crummy bunch out there see is somethin to soak up their beer between lunch and dinner. A little appreciation is all I need.

My kid brother doesn't need appreciation. If his clients don't dig his analysis, they sue, so if they leave his office without a scene, he's happy. Goes home to his deep, big buck dreams. Shit, I gotta get outta here. A guy's gotta have a whole buncha imagination to stick around in this clapboard acropolis. It's OK for a young person like you, I guess, and anyway you've got school ta get back to, but for a guy like me, it's really the pits. I mean, they hire me ta cook Greek and then what? They ration the friggin olive oil. I gotta substitute corn oil and low-grade corn oil at that. Olive oil, corn oil, Jeez, it's like givin a guy water and askin him ta turn it inta wine. Lemme tell ya, I'm an inventive guy but some things ya just can't fake. Jeez, they hire me ta bring up this joint from the third-rate liquor hole it's turned into since Benny hit the rye and Stavros got dropped from the Fall River Flyers. I tell ya, I perform miracles in this Goddamn kitchen.

I gotta give ya a piece a advice, babe. Watch out for Stavros. He's one horny motherfucker when he's lit, which is most nights around the time you girls knock off, know what I mean? Benny, now Benny's a different ball game. He won't try nothing like that but he can be real mean. I mean really. Last waitress he hired quit on her first night. She screwed up on a couple orders and Benny wouldn't lay off bustin her ass about it. So look out for yourself, babe. And watch out for the brothers Constantinos.

So what makes a good-lookin lady like you go in for pokin inta folks' brains? Typa women in the psych world – I gotta be frank about this, I mean they're so friggin extreme. Ya got frigids, ya got nymphos and not a whole lot in between. And eating disorders – stuffin and starvin. That kinda thing sure is no recipe for a good time. I mean, I'm the kinda guy who likes to cook dinner for a date, give her a tasta my style. But with a woman like that, what happens? Ya get the place all set for a neat little love feast – candles, flowers – me, I go for tiger orchids, they sure beat roses for sexiness. Ya sit the lady down to an aperitif – I have the best recipe for screwdrivers you'll ever taste in your life. Ya bring on the food and the next thing ya know you're date's tellin ya she can't touch a forkful of any friggin dish you fixed. Or ya get the other type who homes in on her plate and eats until she has to excuse herself and go throw up in the washroom.

For me, a woman should be like a good steak, medium rare. No way do I go for overdone – steak or dames. Some sauce, maybe. I like a little sauce. Go easy on the mayo, will ya. That's tub's gotta last the night.

My brother, he always had a tough time with dames. One would check him out – he always had looks on his side – they'd date. She'd find out he was a shrink and the next thing ya know she's thinkin: I'm a real screwed-up person. Right now, I don't need romance. I don't need sex. Right now, what I need is analysis. Here's a guy who can supply it for free so I'm gonna go for it. So my brother gets himself all tied up in sortin out her head and misses out on any kinda fun. Me, I may be a little past my prime – know what they say – used to be a Greek god, now just a Goddamn Greek – but I've still got an appetite for a tasty lady.

No way would I trade places with my kid brother. Sure, I wouldn't say no to his padded cell. Ten rooms, five acres and half a lake. Way up in the mountains. Plus a condo in downtown Boston.

Hot plates! Use your napkin if you don't want blistered fingers. Now remember, it's Saturday night. You got no timeta hang about shootin the breeze. I need those orders in double quick. We're gonna be busy busy. Sure is a bad night to begin but make it through tonight and you'll make out OK in tips.

What's this you're givin me? Another order for steak? What's with these guys. They go eat Greek, then order a friggin steak. I got two trays of pastitio to shift tonight. You girls are gonna haveta push the pastitio, right?

Jeez, I been here way too long, working my butt off for

these cheapos. I gotta keep tellin myself, Nico, you're a smart guy, you can rise above this shit. Hang in there, make your stack then get the hell out. I'd get a better job in the city any Goddamn day. Been thinkin about movin up to Boston. I could hang out at my brother's place until I got set up. Except that crazy wife of his would drive me nuts. One thing's for sure, I won't be wastin my talents in this joint much longer. Right now, I'm gettin psyched for a shift and lemme tell ya, the next move I make's gonna be the big one.

The way I see life, it's having collateral that counts. You can grab a hold of collateral. My brother and his buddies, they got it wrong. All that psychobabble about attitude. Money in the bank is where it's at – and a warm woman on your arm.

Day off tomorrow. You too, right? Gonna fix me a late, late breakfast and just laze the day away. Maybe take a drive by the beach. Ya like the beach? Take it or leave it? But, hey, ya should get down there and tan up while the weather holds. Lemme tell ya, nothing lasts forever.

Say, ya know what? I just had a great idea. You're new in town, right? Don't know your way around? Why don'tcha let me show you the sights? I know this town like I know my apartment – too Goddamn well. My apartment's neat – and real cosy. Tiny, maybe, but it's got class. I don't deal with shoddy goods unless, like here, I got no option. But one place ya gotta see around here is Ocean Drive. Ten miles of pure money. Makes me green as hell but I love it all the same. When I'm real low I go take a drive out there and remind myself I'm in the landa opportunity. And a citizen of that land. Nobody can turn me out. Those mansions on Ocean Drive are wild. Like everyone's got their vision of what they'd build if they hit the big-time but these guys did it. Who knows, maybe a coupla them started out skewering souvlaki. All kindsa movies've been shot in the mansions.

We could drive around a while, take in a few aperitifs, then go back to my place for dinner. I got some tenderloin just beggin to be smothered in mushrooms à la Grèque. Whatd'ya say? Gonna give it a whirl.

Table Four ready to go. Gimme your answer later, okay?

I get the picture, sure. Ya gotta study. Even on vacation ya gotta study. Ya got such a tight schedule ya can't spare one Sunday, right? Sure, I believe you, but don'tcha reckon a break for a day might be fun? I mean, all work and no play... but I'm a philosophical guy, like I told ya... at least ya didn't say ya hadta wash your hair. I can handle a knockback. That's somethin a guy like me gets to be real good at, a guy like me who hasn't a lot going for himself in the first place. But all I'm saying is, it's too bad ya wanna pass up a good time.

Don't reckon ya'd miss much? Listen, babe, I got no shortage a lady friends. No way would ya be doing me any kinda favour by comin along for the ride. I gotta whole lista lady friends. Wanna see my address book?

My attitude? Whatd'ya mean attitude? I wasn't aimin at comin on heavy, I mean, I just had it in my mind – as you're new and all – to show ya some hospitality. Shit, you psychs are all the same, tyin your friggin brains in knots. I tell ya, babe, you're beginning ta sound like you really need a night out.

Hey! Get back here. Just where d'ya plan on headin with my souvlaki dinners lookin like that? Bring that order right back here, d'ya hear me? Garnish, babe, ya hearda garnish? Ever done this kinda work before? Too busy book readin for the real worlda work? Look – lettuce here, half tomato here, couple slices cuke on the side, chunka lemon sittin on the lettuce. Always lemon with souvlaki. Shit, the things folks don't know. Forget the lemon and you lose the friggin flavour. Besides, ya gotta pretty up the dish, see? Dress that naked meat. Ya do it for yourself, right? Try ta show yourself to advantage? When ya serve the food, my food, ya give it some presentation.

Psych women, shit. I clean forgot about depressives. How could I forget about depressives. Ya must be that type. I thought there was somethin weird about ya. Folks who go in for psych always got some kinda personal problems. Depressives are the worst. Hell to live with. I should know. My second wife was one. Pure neat hell. Was I relieved when she packed her bags. I mean, my first wife got crazy now and again, like if I quit my job or blew the rent at the bar. She'd break a few plates around the house but she was okay. I knew where I was with my first wife. Always knew she'd go look somewhere else for a meal ticket. Didn't take her long, I tell ya. And then my second wife comes along and things go from stormy to friggin hurricane weather. Shit, I'm the kinda guy who wants an easy life, no heavy-duty interaction.

OK, move it now, move it. Food's getting cold. Shift your ass out there. And try a friggin smile, babe. Nobody's gonna tip ya a red cent if ya don't quit scowling.

Maybe you should give my kid brother a call. See if he can help you out. In his professional capacity, I mean.

Limo

THE WHITE STRETCH limo is sinking into the mud. If Logan doesn't get some planks under the tyres, it'll sink so deep he'll need to hire a forklift to get it back on the road, the rutted track which even a jeep finds hard going. Blue leather seats, pale blue. Powder blue, Logan says, Popular in the Presley era. Before my time. If you tug a flap, the back seat pulls out into a king-size divan. Powder blue blinds slip out of the padded roof and clip onto little metal studs. Sometimes they slip off the studs and spring back up again and Logan curses, colourful full-bodied curses most folk haven't the energy for.

When Logan is really angry, his voice shuts down completely. Words snag and rasp in his throat, dry and scratchy and I listen to the dew drip from the rhododendrons which are rambling over the car, burying it in dark green dribbles.

My head is pressed against the cool blue blind. Logan is running his thumb down my back, pressing the vertebrae one by one, all the way down. His thumb circles the lowest bone and I wriggle and imagine a tail, a tail which could twitch and curl and slap his heavy hand away. I would like a tail, a real one. Not that horsehair thing Logan brought back from Soho. Not that – it's fake and stupid and I stuck it on my head like a wig instead of where he wanted me to put it.

If he really wants a pony, there are plenty in the stables. Pretty speckled ponies, shipped from Argentina or Arizona, I've forgotten but somewhere hot and dry. They trek around in mud here, most of the time, slogging up slippery tracks, their hooves rotting, while bulky beginners whip their haunches, kick their sides and yank on the reins. I never ride. Sometimes I go to the stables to smell the sweet piss-wet hay, to feel the ponies' steamy breath on my face, to look into their big troubled eyes. On cold days they cough and shiver under their blankets and I am sad for them.

There's rain, today – usually there's rain, which makes it green here, and beautiful – and Donny the piper is wheezing into action as dawn crawls over the hills. Not the piper's fault, morning, I know, he's only doing his job and if Milly could think of some better way to start her day, the students could get some peace in the mornings, not to mention those of us who also live here all year round without a suite of rooms in the west wing and an uninterrupted view of the islands. Logan says being woken by a piper is Milly's only extravagance. He says Milly hates the sound of the pipes so much that she gets out of bed to shut Donny up. People are strange.

Dawn, in the rain; the piper on the grass in full Highland dress underneath his dripping cagoule, playing another of his rousing laments. I wrap my blanket around my shoulders and sneak down the horse-track to the shore, leaving Logan to tidy up his limo. Sneak. Not my word for it but one overheard: *I saw her sneaking down the track this morning, Logan, at dawn, in a blanket, barefoot. What the hell was she up to, sneaking about the place?* Milly. He says she doesn't know about him and me but even if she did, she wouldn't care too much. Milly cares about paying the bills, Milly is too beat at night to want him near her, he says. She might even be glad, he says. I can't imagine Milly glad. Too much stone in her, too much endurance; no gladness left. Milly has no desire and, Logan says, no appetite for games.

Logan, I think, lives for games. Sometimes one of his games is such fun that I laugh too loud and he has to put his hands over my mouth. And then that becomes another game. There are good games and bad games and some very boring games as well. The limo is where we play them, me and Logan, the limo which can't go anywhere until Logan gets his road built. When he gets his road built, he wants to use the car as a swish taxi service for the students. He says I should learn to drive. Milly would buy me a tartan suit and a frilly blouse with pearl buttons and I could pick up the students from the railway station. I used to know how to drive but I've forgotten. And I don't want to meet anybody off the train.

You'll never know. You can see the contours of the islands; their fleshy curves, the soft pinks and greys, milky blues – the colour of a breast, an eyelid – the gradual slip from light to dark, you can see but you'll never know. You trek down with your sketchbooks, cameras, greedy eyes noting line, tone, the misty fingers of land. You search for the perfect angle, considering whether the gull which wheels between you and the view might be captured in a couple of swift, reckless brushstrokes or whether such a sudden, living movement might mar the composition. Your sturdy all-weather walking shoes crunch over the shingle, crushing lilac crabs and sea pinks underfoot. Piss off.

Some days here it's just never-ending grey. I like those days. Nobody comes clattering over my bit of beach when it's grey and damp. The seaweed smells good. The tide has washed the shore clean. I don't want any of your shitty litter on my beach, not a scrap, okay? Not a ring-pull, a fag end, nothing. Only the litter of history for me; bleached bone, smashed china, shattered glass, trundled by the tide into cool smooth jewels.

The students come and go. Just faces round the table, voices. A name or two makes itself known to me though I make no effort to know it. No need. All day working on the assignments they've been given and in the evening they can't wait to get at the food, at Milly's pretty dishes, Milly's own little works of art. I cart the veg from the kitchen to the dining room where Logan is carving the meat, smooth, thick slices of breast and leg, for those who eat it. Between us, we pile on the nosh and get back to the kitchen.

Milly sloshes pots in the sink. Logan hums tunelessly, scrapes plates and slams them down on the draining board. Milly has a way of scowling which makes you feel like her life is your fault. Mostly, she's cross at Logan but everybody else has to put up with her crappy moods too. Maybe, if Milly hadn't been so sour from the start, I'd never have seen inside Logan's powder blue limo. She never liked me. Maybe she knows Logan too well, knows the tracks his mind takes him down, dark thorny paths which all lead to the limo. His mind stays locked behind the blue blinds while he serves up Milly's food and listens to everybody rave about it. Milly is a very good cook. Tonight a woman clawed my arm with her blood-red nails to tell me how good Milly's cooking is. I hate that, a person taking hold of me like that. I don't know why.

Logan needs to fix up the dining room ceiling. The cornice and centre rose are hanging from threads of plaster, like garlands left over from a dance. They used to have dances here but now it's courses, courses, courses. A few more courses, all those feet dunting the floor – one day the rose will come crashing down on Milly's wonderful food. I never eat Milly's food. Usually I serve it and help with the dishes but Thursday is the Life Class and once the coffee's done I'm in the toilet, undressing for the benefit of this week's students.

Kyle, the course tutor, says he's asked Logan more than once to fix up a proper changing room. I believe him. I always believe Kyle. I don't know why really, maybe because he has no reason to lie to me, or because his voice is high and light, girlish almost, or because he reminds me of somebody. It doesn't matter. But so far, it's still the crappy kitchen toilet with the broken window and midges whirling in when I switch on the light.

The studio is filling up. Easels scrape across the floor. The heater hums. Already, there's a hot flush of anticipation as the students set up, jostling for a good view of the empty dais, its scatter of cushions. They've been reproducing sunsets and tree lines all week, mottled urns, pearly shells, sedge grass, dead crabs, bladderwrack, the roofless water-mill, half-buried still, the rusted catch of a redundant gate, a mossed panel of drystane dyke, all in painstaking detail, but tonight their subject is a living body, a nude: me.

Kyle has offered me one of the kimonos he uses for background colour to wear between the toilet and the studio, a black one with tangerines on it or a blue one with lime-green hummingbirds but I prefer my scabby old blanket. It smells of smoke and salt, of home.

When Logan found out that I lived in a cave, he offered me a caravan, like Kyle's, but nearer the big house. Milly didn't say anything except that I could use their facilities; a washing machine would clean my clothes better than the sea and surely a hot shower would be nice? Milly worries about the guests complaining about me and wrinkles her nose when I come into work, checking to see that I smell okay. She hates my clothes. Almost every week she reminds me that MacRae's do a cheap, smart line in polyester, machine-washable skirts. More than once she's offered to drive me to town – on payday – but I never go. I think about a trip in the jeep but Milly curses worse than Logan when she's behind the wheel and it's been so long now...

It's not the town I don't like, it's no worse than any other, no better either, except that it's by the sea and the ferries come and go from the mainland to the islands and the gulls make as much noise as the people; big fat, well-fed gulls which loop around the docks. But no city, town, village, no place big enough to have a name is for me. Not now.

But Milly's right about the shower. Sometimes when it's damp like this I feel so chilled, as if my body is packed in ice, like a killed fish, and I shudder and shake and can't hold the pose. Kyle is kind. He turns up the heater until the room is hot and the students start to sweat – well, they say it's the heat as they loosen collars, roll up sleeves and drag limp hankies across pink foreheads. But some sweat at the sight of a naked body – no, a *nude* body – stretched out on the couch. Kyle says there's a difference between nakedness and nudity. I don't think there is but he's the teacher and he pays for nudity. Logan must think there's a difference too because he doesn't pay for nakedness.

At the Life Class nobody talks. The room holds its breath; all its energy is concentrated in a dozen sharpened sticks. Sometimes I can tell by the sound of charcoal dragging across paper which part of me they're drawing; long flowing strokes for legs and arms, finicky flicks and dabs for head, hands and feet, an intense, concentrated rubbing and scratching for the crotch.

Kyle picks his way though the easels, stopping to comment on a line, an angle, a patch of shading. *Draw what you see*, he says, *not what you know*. He says this time and again in his kind, papery voice, without sounding bored of repeating himself. I'm standing, holding a broomstick above my head, left leg bent, right leg stretched back. *Liberation*, Kyle calls the pose – it hurts like hell. I count seconds and minutes and concentrate on keeping still. After a bit, Logan slips into the studio, pretending to hunt for stray coffee mugs left over from the afternoon's bowl and bottle exercise. It's his excuse to sneak a look at the sketches. Sometimes I think these crude likenesses of me whet his appetite more than the real thing.

Milly never ever comes into the studio but I can picture her scowling in the kitchen and can't help laughing. The broomstick wobbles. Chairs scrape, the students keek round their easels to stare at me laughing at nothing. I'm supposed to be looking up at the bloody broom I'm trying to hold steady, looking liberatedly upwards, but I hear them turn to each other and nod. Laughing out loud at nothing is what madwomen do and I must, after all, be mad.

Lives in a cave, you know, along the beach. No facilities whatsoever. A city kid, on the run. It's just not natural, is it? Somewhere warm you could almost imagine it for a while but here, for so long, in this sodden climate? Must be touched. Wanders around at night, too, half-dressed, bedraggled. I'd lock my door if I were you.

It's true, I don't sleep much at night. Other things to do, always other things to do. There must have been a time when I slept like other people, but I can't remember; it's gone, lost. Long after the students have gone off to their rooms and locked their doors in case the madwoman goes walkabout, I pose in the limo, for Logan. Unlike my liberated, nude poses for Kyle, the naked compositions which Logan suggests are modelled more on the style of Knave or Fiesta than Amateur Artist. Logan has no intention of trying to capture a likeness on paper and I don't have to hold his poses for nearly as long as some of Kyle's but… Logan has become so greedy for sensation.

She pokes a finger under a smooth stone, overturns it and crouches down until her face is inches from the damp dark sand. The shore life which she has disturbed moves haphazardly, confused by sudden exposure to light, air. Raking through the wetness, she picks up a crab the size of her fingernail, blows on it to dislodge some of the sand, pops it into her mouth, feels it scuttle frantically over her tongue, spits it out again and laughs into the still early morning air. Her voice slithers across the shingle. She follows her own laughter to the water's edge where the sea folds in like a cool smooth sheet. She stretches out on the shingle, face down. There is no one to witness her nakedness, her first light prostration. Barnacles graze her breasts, nick her ribs. At her navel, something slimy clings and oozes. Her pelvis is jammed against a sharp rock. Gripping two large boulders, she drags herself forward, feeling the tug and scrape along the skinny length of herself, until her face is at the tideline; stones, water, sky, a pall of midges. She opens her mouth wide as a cave and the grey sea floods in. She holds the sea in her mouth for as long as her lungs will permit.

Maya

SHE CAME ON at some nothing town where the bus stopped late in the evening, a dusty hot town where tired indifferent men sat and smoked bitter cigars, in the dull square, on cement benches, under a string of dim lamps, their feet dragging idly in the dark red earth, their faces in shadow. There was nothing to stop for there, except the use of an unlit stinking toilet in the roadside bar, or the purchase of a sticky tamale, a bottle of fizzy water. There was nothing of interest to the tourist. No ruins, no chapels, no ethnic markets. The scenery was flat scrub and there was nowhere much to stay.

But she had stopped there for an entire week.

– I like it here too much, she said, in her slow, difficult English. She sat down after removing an embroidered rucksack from her back. Her face was flushed. She was sweating. She adjusted a spotted headscarf over straggly girlish braids.

She was travelling alone and so were you. To the same destination – Palenque – where you had both planned, for your own reasons, to witness the spectacle of Maya remains, immerse yourselves in the vibrations of another nation's history.

What were your reasons? Can you remember now as you sit in your newly-decorated flat, sifting through handfuls of old photos, deciding which to keep, which to throw out, which most closely match the memories you have preserved, though these, like the photos, are faded, ragged at the edges. Of that time, that place, that person.

Else was German, from a small town in the north which was, she said, a winter city, beautiful only under snow.

– I like the sun too much, she said. Also the jungle. The Maya. Maybe together we go to the jungle, yes?

– Yes. Maybe. Sure.

Anything was possible on your meandering itinerary. As the bus careered round bends in the road it was better not to see, you sat back, bracing yourself for bumps. You smoked cigarettes, Else hummed and nibbled on raisins. You conversed. Two among thousands, backpacking the gringo trail, two single women going solo – you had notes to compare.

– It is good sometimes to talk, said Else. Better maybe than making love, yes?

Your own contribution to the conversation: a string of tales of en route suitors who had sought consolation in your northern features, the English language, an unprotesting body – on buses, trains, public benches, in stations, chapels, bars, museums, wherever tourists could be found, suitors whispering their loneliness into your ears, stroking you with their needy fingers, clinging to some morsel of romance before you dropped them off, one by one, at the first convenient junction.

Else listened a lot. Her concentration was visible. It was hard work for her being confined to English. You knew no German so she had no choice. As the bus pulled into the station she said:

– I think we are making a different journey.

– *Have made*, you corrected her. We *have made* a different journey.

– Ah, my English is too bad, ja?

At the *hospedaje* a double room was cheaper so you took it. The town was pretty. There were some sights worth seeing. You'd stay a few days before embarking on the last stretch to Palenque. For your pesos you got two beds, two rugs on the floor, one table, one sink, a plaster cast of the Virgin Mary above one bed, a crucifix above the other. Else chose the Virgin Mary. It was all the same to you. The room was cheap, adequate, clean.

Else closed the shutters on the cool morning sunlight and quietly arranged some of her belongings on the table: some books, an old teddy bear, an ugly little clay figurine, a bamboo flute. The things people travelled with. You travelled light. Everything was disposable. Else's books were not the kind to be traded for anything going in one's mother tongue. They were the solid, worthy variety. She held up one for your approval, an anthropological study of the Maya. This girl took her travelling seriously.

When you woke up, it was to the sound of Else vomiting into the sink. You rushed over with your towel and pressed it into her hands. This was the beginning of your responsibility; the offer of a towel, the only towel you possessed and now soiled with a stranger's vomit.

As soon as she recovered, Else flushed out the sink, rinsed the towel fastidiously, wringing it until her knuckles went white, twisting the cloth until it was straight and stiff as a rope. You hadn't noticed but this wasn't surprising, considering all the layers of loose clothing she wore. You looked more closely then as she patted her stomach and smiled dreamily, giving the impression of being inside a bubble, a mystical bubble of expectation. But that kind of thing was outside your experience and you had every intention of keeping it there. To you, all she had was an inconvenient swelling which made her wear her patched jeans open at the waist and caused her to throw up.

In spite of an aura of spiritual well-being, Else still looked exhausted, though she had only just woken from a sound sleep. A bad sign. Travel could take its toll at the best of times, especially travel on the cheap, when an overnight bus ride or a few hours' kip on a bench often took the place of a good night's sleep. What was she thinking of, going on a trip of this kind, in her condition? Shouldn't she be resting up, feathering her nest, knitting bootees and matinée jackets? Shouldn't she be staying within reach of an antenatal clinic, instead of tramping through Central America with a rucksack on her back and a baby in her belly?

Not that you knew the first thing about pregnancy, having pushed the idea far into the unimaginable future. People with babies – mostly – stayed at home and that wasn't for you. Not yet. People with babies dropped out of your life like unwanted baggage. You left them to get on with it. That was what whey wanted, wasn't it, to be left to roost under a cloud of talcum powder and nappies billowing in the wind like the sails of moored boats?

Not Else. She had taken the test, had her suspicions confirmed. She had given notice at the small knitwear factory where she worked, given notice at the house where she rented a small, cluttered room. She had withdrawn her savings of several years and packed her bag, filling up all the spare pockets with the decorative junk she couldn't bear to throw out. She carried her home on her back and – under her voluminous shirt – the biggest claim on her future.

– If I am well, baby is well, she would say, and you couldn't deny that she looked after herself. She possessed an extensive collection of vitamins, minerals, herbal infusions. She dosed herself with these each morning, after the sickness had subsided. And after the medicine, the exercises.

Rather than hanging around while she went through the procedure with the squatting, the stretching, the deep breathing, you began to go out on your own, dressing in slim-fitting jeans and a skimpy T-shirt – you didn't want anyone to imagine that *you* were pregnant – arranging to meet up later at a small cantina in the plaza.

It was an easy-going place which offered value for money and an open outlook. The waiters took their time and expected their customers to do likewise. Three days running he had been there at a neighbouring table, sipping coffee and observing the activity in the plaza. Three sightings and you felt you knew him. He was different from the others, wasn't he? You could tell right away that he lacked the restless, anxious gestures of so many on the road, those who at x were already on their way to y before heading for z, those who clung to a route as if it were a safety line.

He had seemed pleased to be just where he was, comfortable. He sprawled on his hard little café chair as if it were a deep, luxurious sofa. When he offered to buy you a second cup of coffee you didn't refuse. In a comfortable, containable way he turned you on, this man who became your lover by lunchtime.

When Else arrived Paul was sitting at your table. As she began to warm to her favourite theme, your eyes were on him. The jungle. The Maya. The gist of Else's conversation was: How does one reach this tribe who continue to live as they have always done, without the invention of the wheel, without Christianity, contraception? You chipped in now and again with cracks about machetes and banditos. You let Paul know that you didn't share Else's pioneering spirit, her passion for the primitive. You let him know that you had passions of your own and agreed to meet him later that day, when Else usually took an afternoon nap. You did not consult her. She did not complain.

Else's English was bad but her Spanish was non-existent, so when Paul bid his calm *hasta la vista*, you ordered breakfast, as you had ordered every meal so far. When you and Else had agreed to link up – only for as long as your routes coincided, without any commitment – it had been simply a practical arrangement, mutually suitable. You hadn't counted on becoming saddled with all these little responsibilities, like having to obtain not only your own requirements, but Else's as well. What had she done before she met you? How had she even obtained a meal, she who was so particular about anything she put in her stomach?

And she tired so easily. Your walks through the town were punctuated by her pauses. That day, the day you met Paul, she wanted to visit an obscure office where she thought she might pick up even more information on things Mayan. You would have suggested that she went alone but how would she have made herself understood?

The responsibility was beginning to chafe. You disliked the fuss, the effort involved in ordering complicated meals from simple kitchens and standing at the roadside while Else took deep breaths and clutched at her still insignificant bump, and using up a morning combing mucky back streets for an office that turned out to be shut.

Talking is better than making love, you had agreed. What did you talk about as you edged along the hot, narrow streets, avoiding skinny dogs and handing over the occasional coin to children pestering for pesos, pesos?

You talked about Else's future. She was vague. What would she do for a place to stay?

– Maybe I am living in the country. Maybe I find a little house, grow some chickens.

And the father?

– Maybe he make visit but I do not think. He likes too much the freedom. I understand.

Else understood everything. She would not stay with friends or family in case the baby might spoil anyone's sleep other than her own. And money?

– I am not needing too much money. I am baking the bread and growing the vegetable.

Vegetable was a word Else never could pronounce and it made you laugh, as did the way she unwittingly dismissed the future in every sentence. Yes, you had some good times together.

When you met Paul during siesta time, when the sunlight was cruel, he took you to a cool, dark café in a deserted plaza. You spent the rest of the day with him. And the evening. And the night. Creeping into his tiny room in case the señora caught you and turfed you into the street crying putana, putana at your back. Whispering, smothering your laughter in his lumpy pillow, throwing off all the blankets, lighting the mosquito coil and watching it glow in the dark as you passed the tequila bottle from your mouth to his.

The next morning you hurried back to Else, full of apologies. She had waited in, expecting you to return in the evening. But she understood. You spent the morning running little errands for her, being more responsible than necessary – expeditions to the post office, the market, the chemist. She had been more sick than usual that morning. And she had fainted.

– I go blackout, she told you, showing you the bruise where her head hit the sink.

And you thought that if you had been there it might not have happened. But you couldn't watch over her every minute of the day. She wouldn't have allowed it.

As you dotted in and out of the room, dropping off her supplies, you noticed that she was unusually subdued. She was someone who liked always to be engaged in some activity wherever she was: in the room she embroidered, she ate, she studied her picture book, blew on her bamboo flute. The flute playing got to you at times as she only knew a couple of tunes right through and played them over and over. But that day, remember? She wasn't busy with anything.

– What shall we do today? you asked, wanting to be obliging.

– Today, she replied, I am resting.

She lay down under a pensive Madonna and closed her eyes. You showered, changed your clothes, went out in time to catch Paul in his usual seat at the cantina.

On Paul's bed that afternoon, you ate tacos and listened to the thunder, the rain lashing the streets and whipping up rivers of mud. And behind the storm, Paul's even-toned voice telling you – as you talked of Else and her plans, Else and her baby, Else and her bamboo flute – that you had a choice and sooner or later you would have to come to a decision.

Paul... there he is, standing next to Else. He is holding her dripping rucksack above his head, pretending to be Hercules. Now that's a photo which doesn't correspond with the memory, such as there is. One for the bucket. You've even forgotten his second name. He lasted no longer than any of the others. What grand schemes were laid, yet by the end of the journey north, neither of you could wait to part company. With Else it was different.

You didn't know how to leave her there, at the station, in the rain, an hour before the train was due. Nowhere to shelter, nothing to say, no way of making amends. You were ditching her in favour of Paul and couldn't leave, not until Else insisted:
– Go now, please. It is better.

You scoop up the photos you've decided to keep, in the wooden cigar box, on the shelf alongside all the other decorative junk you can't seem to part with so easily nowadays. You are tired, nauseous. Inside you the baby twists and turns. It kicks. It flips about like a fish. You should put your feet up. Maybe take a look at that knitting pattern. At the clinic they told you to rest as much as possible.

That's the one you've been looking for... Else standing on the platform, twisting her braids, knotting them tightly around her head, ticket sticking out of a pocket, her huge anorak billowing in the wind.

Was the train on time? Did she find the Maya? And later, a house in the country where she could raise chickens and bake bread? Else... her hair plaited like a harvest loaf, arms folded across her belly, the darkness gathering around her, a squat figure on an empty wet platform.

You place the photo on the cluttered mantelpiece next to the keepsake she pressed into your hand as you left. You've never liked the crude little figure, its featureless face, stumpy limbs, broad belly, but you'd hang on to it a while longer. It is, after all, a doll. The baby might like it.

Little Black Lies

HE'S ON THE empty dance floor, alone with the spinning lights and the driving beat, doing what he does so well, making his body bend and sway to the rhythm of the song. The song's immaterial. He'll dance until he drops, dance until the beat stops pounding in his head, the beat of the drum, of the ocean waves on the shore, of his mother's spade hitting the hard ground, of his unbroken heart.

Sonny K. Lee was brought to this coastal New England town, a bright-eyed, black-skinned baby. His mother piled her five kids on to a Greyhound bus going north and stopped at Providence. As she had no money to travel further she hoped that, with a name like Providence, the Lord would provide.

After several months in a dirty city hostel, she and the children were allocated a house in Midtown, where she dug up the grass in the front yard and planted cabbage and potatoes. Midtown was not a town in itself but a cheap housing complex tagged on to the tail end of the handsome town of Freeport. The population of Midtown was mostly black; of Freeport itself, mostly white. Between welfare cheques, cleaning jobs in Freeport mansions, and later the eldest boy's wages from Specialty Pets, the family was fed, clothed, schooled and taken to church on Sundays.

The kids grew up and gradually left home. The eldest, Mikey, married a solid girl who cooked good cheap food, kept a clean house and had the faith. At the pet store Mikey was promoted from birds to reptiles and got a line going in crocodiles. As a youngster, Sonny would go along on Saturdays, flatten his nose against the glass and eye the weird birds and beasts with fear and wonder.

All the kids worked out, the way Sonny told it. Tillie was wed soon after Mikey. Babies came quickly. She got big and laughed like she was happy. Nina stayed skinny, single, busy, distributing religious pamphlets and organising outings for old folks. Will was going steady.

Sonny as a teenager, restless, sees a movie about a young black dancer, gets it into his head that the movie is speaking directly to him, flies the coop for New York.

He moves in with Charles, who keeps him in Levis and Cool cigarettes and lusts after his young black body. Perhaps there is more to it than that. Sonny believes so. Love is mentioned from time to time. Charles is thirty-five, white, a café-owner with friends in New York who do things in the arts.

Sonny is found a place in dance school, which keeps him off the streets during the day and in adorable shape for Charles, who likes to show him off at parties. Sonny in a white suit, high on champagne, flutters on Charles's arm, saying little, laughing a lot. Sonny, the well-behaved pet, plucks his master off the floor, takes him home when he's drunk too many cocktails.

His life with Charles didn't last. The older man tired of the social whirl – too many nights of idleness, too much wine – dried out in a detox ward, sold his café and opened a bookshop. Sonny had just found his wings, longed to flex them, to be out in the world. Charles's appreciation wasn't enough. The inevitable arguments ensued, Sony throwing his emotions around, Charles coolly backing off.

When Sonny's booking in the third-rate musical – which was all his dance training got him – packed up, and was followed by a year of no work at all and a trail of loveless one-night stands, he quit New York and returned to his home town.

His sisters swooped on him what questions. What you been up to? You got a honey down there? How come you so skinny? His mother eyed him reproachfully and forced him to eat a plate of hot chilli. The prodigal had returned. The word got round and the entire family, plus wives, husbands and even more kids, showed up first thing Sunday morning, dressed for church. The reunion was not a success. Sonny refused to attend the service.

When his mother came back from church, she told him calmly, that though it grieved her to say it, Sonny would have to find his own home. If he couldn't attend church, he must be some kind of sinner and she wouldn't have no sin in her house. He'd still be welcome for visits but had better not bring no wicked habits with him. Tillie and Nina tried to console him. Get yourself a girl, they said, and bring her home.

He got himself a job bartending at the Michelangelo, a gay place in town where they had disco music and dancing waiters. Sunday was the big day. While his mother was praying for his soul, Sonny stocked up the liquor shelves. What else could he do? Dancing, dressing up, drinks and men were what he knew. That had been his sentimental education. After Charles, though, there had been little sentiment involved. Was that what he came back for? Sentiment?

Though his mother didn't know the first thing about Sonny's life on the white side of town, his sisters kept tabs on him. Early on a Sunday morning, before Sonny had opened up, they'd slip into the bar to say Hi. Nina would bring her religious pamphlets and Tillie would bring hot doughnuts. Sonny made them coffee and made them laugh. They'd go away happy. They didn't ask too much about his life, just was he eating, was he having a good time, and where did he get those fine shoes?

Sonny was happy, happier than he'd been in New York, even with Charles. Here he wasn't just another poor boy, living on tips and invitations to dinner. He made his own living and his own friends. Sonny made friends without really trying. Having spent some years in the city and picked up some social skills, an extrovert style in clothes and a love of fun, he was in demand. He laughed loud and camped it up, sewed outfits to wear at work, rented a small apartment next door to the bar and often entertained after hours.

Although he was back more or less where he grew up, new doors were opened, old ones closed. In the black bars off West Broadway – the only black bars in town – folk like Sonny, whatever their colour, were not welcome. At first his life revolved around the Michelangelo. Men flocked to him, women too, even though for them there was never any question of a romantic or physical relationship.

As the years passed, Sonny gained a degree of acceptance in some of the town's fashionable restaurants where he entertained and overtipped. Also, largely due to Sonny's efforts, non-gays began to drop in to the Michelangelo. Some came only out of voyeuristic curiosity, some hoped for more, some simply came for the dancing.

It is a clear fall Sunday and the bar stays quiet until late afternoon, when the light begins to fade. Guy, Sonny's young man of recent months, plays pinball until the place fills up. Guy is twenty, restless. Sonny is thirty-five.

Robert and Donna are seated at the bar. They've been coming the last few Sundays and there's no mistaking why they're here. Robert leaves Donna seated at the bar for long spells while he cruises the dance floor. In idle moments, Sonny chats to the women. He doesn't like anyone to feel bad and she surely does, in spite of her smiles. The couple are British, over on vacation, planning to head out west to California. They're not married but had been considering it, before Robert began to take more interest in the Michelangelo than in Donna.

Late in the evening and the bar is still busy. Sonny's on the dance floor, taking a break from serving customers by entertaining them with an impromptu floor show. He spins the mirrored ball and leaps into the pool of coloured lights. Out of the corner of his eye he sees Guy necking with a blond boy, a boy his own age. It was bound to happen and now it has. And now things will change. Now Guy will find Sonny old, will no longer want him. History will repeat itself. Guy will find faults with Sonny, flaws. Love has not been mentioned between them for some time.

There's trouble at the bar. The English guy is slapping his girl about the head. She's yelling at him to lay off. Sonny leaves the dance floor and gently prises them apart. Robert is asked to leave. He attempts to drag Donna with him but Sonny prevents this happening. She'll see you when she's good and ready, he says. And not before. On his way out, Robert screams abuse at Sonny.

Sonny has just been to visit his mother. Her sight is failing. She's having trouble reading the hymn book. Them words keep dancing about and playing tricks on me, she says. I don't sing nothing I don't know by heart no more, lest I mess it up. Sonny is sympathetic. He has endless patience for the problems of others. For his own he has less time, less ability. Of his own he can tell his mother nothing. Guy has been messing him about lately, and there was the business with Donna.

She doesn't go with her English boyfriend to California. She turns up on Sonny's doorstep with a black eye and a visa about to expire. She wants to stay in town, get a job, but she's a foreigner and needs a permit. Sonny, without giving the matter much thought, offers to marry her. That way she would be a legal resident. There's no problem, he tells her. A marriage of convenience. People do it all the time. A wife on paper won't affect his life and apart from a blood test and some forms to be signed, there nothing to it. Donna without giving the matter much thought, gratefully accepts Sonny's offer.

Everyone in Sonny's wide circle of friends gets to know about the wedding. To some it's a great joke, to others a generous gesture. Guy is impressed by the outrageousness of it all, sees the occasion as a wonderful excuse for a party. Sonny's boss at the Michelangelo – where Sonny has worked for ten years – offers to pick up the tab for the party.

The day of the wedding is bright and clear. The maple in front of the Court House is golden. Sonny, Donna and their two witnesses – Guy and his sister – all dressed up and giggling wildly, enter the building. The registrar glances casually at the party and then looks again in disbelief. Sonny getting married!

Somehow Sonny hadn't expected a real ceremony, with real vows, and here he was, repeating them after the registrar with this girl he hardly knew. But when it came to saying the words Love, Honour, Cherish, he found he was saying them, not just as part of the arrangement they had agreed on. Saying the words, he was meaning them, feeling them. When asked to kiss the bride, he did so. He meant that too.

The party at the Michelangelo continued well into the night. When the guests had eventually gone home, Donna went to her bed and Sonny to his, with Guy.

As a result of the marriage several things happened. The first was that Sonny and his new wife began to be invited into homes where he had previously been unwelcome. It soon became obvious that his hosts believed that Sonny had gone straight for real. The second was that his sisters heard the news through a friend at the Court House and arrived the following Sunday. They ticked him off for not inviting them to the wedding then hugged him and asked a hundred questions about his wife. And Ma says hurry and bring her home, Nina added, before she and Tillie rushed off to church.

Why didn't Sonny set the record straight? Was it because he couldn't bear those doors to be shut again to him, door which had taken so long to open? Or was it his family? He hadn't intended them to find out about it but now they knew and were, in spite of not being invited to the wedding, in spite of the girl being white and a foreigner, delighted about it.

Donna, a little uncomfortably, went along with Sonny's story. She felt she owed him this much. Also, they were spending a good deal of time together with all those double invitations. Husband and wife were becoming close friends. Donna helped Sonny pick himself up when his affair with Guy ended, sat with him as he talked late into the night about wanting to settle with someone steady.

This wasn't the Sonny everyone knew and enjoyed. How much did he mean what he said, how much was a hopeless wish to please everyone, especially his mother? Her health was poor. She hadn't the strength to turn the soil in her yard but she kept on toiling in that patch the Lord – via welfare – had provided.

The time for coming clean about the whole affair passed, and, at Sonny's request, Donna agreed to meet his family. She even cooked dinner for them one evening at Sonny's apartment, giving his relations the impression that she lived there, reinforcing the unspoken lie. When they left, he turned to her. I want to make love to my wife, he said. Donna, thinking that her husband of convenience was taking the charade too far, lightly dismissed the request, said good night and went upstairs to her own apartment.

He's out on the empty dance floor, alone with the spinning lights and the driving beat, doing what he does so well, making his body bend and sway to the rhythm of the song. The song's immaterial. He'll dance until he drops, dance until the beat stops pounding in his head, the beat of the drum, of the ocean waves on the shore, of his mother's spade hitting the hard ground, of his unbroken heart.

The Four O'Clock Lady

ANITA DRAWS THE curtains, though there are only rooftops outside, pigeons and a couple of gargoyles. Frankie lets his head sink into the pillow and breathes in the smells of the room: lipstick, hot wax, nail polish, women. He tries not to look at the dreaded wall poster but, as always, he succumbs. It's like something from geography class at school, the earth sliced open like a layer cake, so that you could see how what goes on underneath the surface affects what happens on top. In this case it's a magnified cross-section of skin; pores like craters and thick, black hairs thrusting up from deep roots and covering the epidermal landscape with a horror forest of curving spikes.

Anita is her usual nice self, which is why Frankie always asks for her. It's bad enough coming week after week without having to suffer the blinking recoil of Karen, Pam, Angela. And Anita doesn't run late too often, which is another small relief. Waiting under the cruel lights of the salon foyer, which exaggerate every nick and bristle, is a humiliation he can do without. Waiting is hard enough without squirming on the dove-grey sofa under the disgusted scrutiny of the girls at the desk.

But the smaller salons were worse: poky, crummy little premises, where he had to hang about in full view of the street and worry about somebody he knew passing by and seeing him stuck there, waiting for a miracle. The treatments cost more in the department-store salon but the relative privacy was worth it. At least not just anybody might happen by and the clientele was mostly old dears who assumed, in an absent, self-absorbed way, that he was waiting for a girlfriend who was having her coiffure tidied up by Raphael or Rikki.

Frankie knows the names of most of the staff, at least those who stay and put up with the shitty pay and the snooty customers. Raphael's new and Rikki – who's been here for donkeys – is miffed that rather a lot of the ladies are asking for the new boy to tidy up their perms. Blue-black curls, chunky shoulders, a tan and a Venezuelan accent. And tight trousers, of course. Yes, Raphael is doing very nicely thank you with the ladies, cleaning up on tips and already picking up a few discreet requests for housecalls. Anita has told Frankie all about Raphael. Straight as a needle, unfortunately. It's only huffy, thinning on top Rikki who finds excuses to mince around the foyer, cologne floating in his wake like chiffon.

– Come as close as you can, says Anita.

The girls at the desk have a simple paging system: Pam, your three-thirty lady, Angela, your three-forty-five lady, and so on. The ladies whose appointments haven't yet been announced over the tannoy, politely ignore Frankie, as they do each other. Like him, they come alone. They gaze at anti-wrinkle creams and bust-firming gels, or else rake voraciously through fashion mags. What do they feel when they're confronted by all those perfect teenage girls pouting at them, girls without a wrinkle, an ounce of fat, or an unwanted hair in sight? Why do they peer so intently at images of beauty and glamour which, with all the money in the world, are beyond them? Are they just looking for reminders of their youth, or is there something more predatory behind old birds devouring those flawless teenage surfaces?

– Did your dentist friend give you something? says Anita.
– No.

Gold hoops their fingers, wrists, ears, throats; chains of the stuff but Frankie doesn't envy the ladies. Time, if not much else, is still on his side. Though by the end of the treatment, who knows? So slow, hair by hair, and how many will have to be burnt out at the root before he has any chance of becoming the divine creature he hopes will emerge from his superfluous forestation?

– That's a shame, says Anita.
– Mmmnnn, that little... arrangement fell through.

Such a slinky word, superfluous; it slides off the tongue like oil or honey. Realistically, it will probably take years to remove, patch by bristled patch. And the cost! If only Anita had something pretty on the wall, instead of that follicular nightmare.

– Oh dear, says Anita.

Anita doesn't wear jewellery. Just her white, short-sleeved overall, like a nurse's uniform. She even has an upside-down watch pinned to her breast pocket. Anita doesn't clink, like Karen or Pam or Angela, who flash cheap imitations of what their ladies wear against stringy old skin. Anita doesn't overdo the perfume or the make-up. The other girls wear foundation so thick you could scratch patterns on it, like tribal scars, so thick their faces have become as blank and rubbery as muggers' masks. But hairless. Utterly hairless. Anita herself has just the faintest shadow of a moustache on her upper lip.

– I'll have to turn up the voltage, says Anita.
– OK.

Anita adjusts the overhead lamp and picks up her needle. Frankie's eyes close as he feels the needle come in contact with the dimple immediately beneath his lower lip. He hears the click as Anita switches on the power, and braces himself, wincing as the charge burns out one single follicle. So many more to go. Tears ooze through his squeezed-shut eyelids. But pain, Frankie knows, is relative.

– Sorry, says Anita.

The shots of novocaine had certainly helped, numbing Frankie's face long enough to endure a double treatment session without so much as a twitch. It had been a good enough arrangement at first, calling into Mervyn's surgery an hour before his appointment with Anita. Merv, with the mouthwash blue eyes, antiseptic smile and surgical gloves, locking the door and cranking up the reclining chair so the two of them could exchange one good turn for another. But his dentist friend began stepping up his requests in a way which made thirty pain-filled minutes with Anita a safer option. Maybe in time he'd find another bent dentist for a trade-off but he's giving Merv the perv a wide berth. A chemist might be a better bet. One with a limited imagination.

Questions Frankie asks himself while Anita burns out hair follicles: *Why do you want to become a woman? Have you always wanted to become a woman? When did you first want to be a woman? Do you think your life will be better as a woman? Do you think a woman has a better life than a man? Do you realise that even with hormone injections, implants, surgery and years being Anita's four o'clock lady that you will still never be a real woman? Whose breasts will you have your implants modelled on, whose hips? Will the man of your dreams really want the manufactured woman-thing you'll become, or will you still, at the end of it all, be playing the same game without the equivalent bits?*

– Are you surviving? says Anita.
– Just about.

Anita will go on trying to help. That's her job. But she does more than her job. Anita, with her needle, in the tiny, curtained room high above the heart of the city, where every shelf is lined with creams promising epidermal miracles and the acned Anaglypta walls are blank apart from the awful poster. Anita provides a rest, a refuge.

– Those dizzies at the desk need specs. Four o'clock lady. I love it, really.

Once he's in Anita's warm, pink room, her little operating theatre, he's safe. Nothing she'll do, no matter how painful it might be at the time, will harm him. She knows and he knows that the treatment will take forever. She knows and he knows that, even with hormone treatment as well, the miracle might not happen. And even if it does, by the time it looks like taking, he might be past his sell-by date.

Anita is smiling and telling him about the suite she'd like; navy with orange pinstripes, from a place which specialises in Scandinavian design. She can't buy it yet, might never have enough spare cash, but it doesn't do any harm, she says, to keep a wee dream in your head. She knows and he knows that dreams are often better than the real thing.

– Sorry.

Anita says sorry a lot. Frankie knows that her sympathy is genuine. He knows, too, that it doesn't happen so often that you meet someone who means what they say. He knows about pretty promises, lovely lies he's wrapped around himself, nice nonsense said over showers, coffee, a line or two, get-up-and-go sounds, thanks yous and goodbyes, however they're phrased, the words like clothes are just a cover-up, but they get him up and out and home...

– Doing anything at the weekend? Anita asks.
– As much as possible.

Anita has a boyfriend. She is more or less living with him. They spend weekends in DIY shops, if you believe her. That is about as much as she'll say. Anita is really good at not talking about herself. And at not asking too many questions. Frankie imagines her on a Saturday night, out or more likely in with her nameless boyfriend – Frankie calls him Rock. A fire, a kitchen table, the flicker of the TV somewhere off to the side. A quiet, slightly boring Saturday night at home. She'll be in some kind of soft comfy jumper and Rock – he's probably called Colin or Sandy or Steve – will have his shirt open at the collar. They'll be sitting on the couch like an advert for cocoa, corny and cosy and just what Frankie would like for change; a cosy, ordinary, safe night.

– What about you?
– Oh, nothing much, probably, says Anita.

You have to talk, though there isn't much time for talking.

Only when Anita gives you a little break from the needle, which she always tries to do but her time is strictly limited. Anita's four-thirty lady has already been beamed across the tannoy, cutting in on a muted *Best of the Carpenters* cassette. Anita's next client is out in the foyer, early but nevertheless there, waiting on the sofa for her appointment, her miracle. The tannoy is an early warning that Frankie's time is almost up. Soon he'll be handing over his cash at the counter – including a generous tip for Anita – making his next appointment, nipping out the back door of the salon and down the stairs which lead directly to a side exit. In the early winter darkness, he'll slip, unnoticed, through the surf of shoppers and make his way, discreetly, to his next appointment.

Static

THERE'S SOMETHING I'D like to experience before I die. In some parts of the world, prairie, pampas, steppe, veldt – a wide open space where thunderclouds roll across the sky and dust balls roll across the ground – it happens. But maybe the place doesn't really matter, mabye it could happen anywhere and it would prove the thing scientifically, it would make sense of the invisible working of bodies and minds. At some time or other we've all felt the jolt and maybe we spend the rest of our lives trying to recapture that vital shock. You will know what I mean. We may have different ways of describing the sensation but both of us believe that it can be found, if the conditions are met.

One condition, an essential one, is not to try too hard, so I haven't gone to too much trouble, just a little trouble, in case you might think I hadn't made any effort at all. I'm wearing something nice but not too nice, not my favourite or my best clothes; that would be taking too much of a risk. Going through my wardrobe, I tried to imagine how you might react to the colour of a dress, the fabric of a skirt, the cut of a pair of jeans, discovering, in the process, that my wardrobe doesn't contain a great many articles of clothing that I actually like. Though I did buy for myself more or less everything I own, the choice, in the end, was limited.

I hope, too, that you'll wear something I like a little but not too much. I don't want to feel intimidated by your clothes. Or your appearance. Your appearance does matter – not so much what you've inherited but what you've done with yourself since. It's better you look quite nice but not perfect. Your voice, too, matters, your smell, the texture of your skin. Though I'm very far from perfect you might like some things about me. My teeth are reasonable and, as they are, I smile a lot, which makes me appear to be a cheerier person than I really am. I had my hair trimmed a couple of weeks ago so it's tidier than usual and I've found a rinse which replaces the grey with gold. Instead of dreary, wintry tones, I now have summery glints through my otherwise unexceptional brown hair. With the help of some inexpensive tubes of ammonia-free colour, I intend to go slowly blonde.

The flat – I've cleaned and tidied and spruced it up a bit but mostly because I prefer it that way; a clean house feels happier than a dirty one. I've watered the plants and sprayed their leaves so they glisten like freshly showered skin. Would you prefer my fleshy succulents or the feathery scented geraniums? Do you know that geraniums are named after crane bills? If so, do you find this fact as comical as I do? I considered buying flowers to put about the place but buying flowers for myself always feels dismal or extravagant and neither mood is appropriate. Of course I changed the sheets and aired the bedroom. No stale odours or memories cling to my dusted walls.

Of course you may not see my home. You may see nothing of my hand-sewn curtains my scrubbed skirting boards, my pressed linen and polished woodwork, or the tidy pile of ongoing projects which keep me busy and hopeful most of the time. You may not see any of it but if you do, I'd like it to be in reasonable order, I'd like my home to be wearing its welcoming, capable face.

If you are in my home you should be able to look around it and discover something – but not too much – of me. Rather a lot of me, possibly too much, has been put into paintwork and curtains and carefully considered linen but you have to put yourself somewhere, don't you? Some people leave themselves around all over the place but not me. I wonder whether you ever feel you have put too much of yourself into what could manage quite well without your efforts. Have you, too, come to the conclusion that all the bits and bobs around you might go on existing perfectly well without you taking any notice whatsoever? Do you, in greyer moods, feel this can also be true of people?

There is food, in case it's required, though sometimes food is just an added complication; accompanied consumption isn't always a plain, shared pleasure. Too much attention can be paid to the wrong details. Think, for example, about the crockery and ovenware, the clinking and pinging, the faffing around with ladles and padded, heat-resistant gloves. Putting a meal on the table involves contact with so many inert, cumbersome objects when they are not the point at all. And the eating itself, the chomping and chewing and swallowing, the forkfuls of food to be negotiated from plate to mouth; perhaps we should rule out eating. However, just in case food turns out to be an essential condition, I set the table, remembering to check the cutlery for streaks.

The food itself; if you didn't like my cooking, would it be something we could ignore or would it lessen the voltage ever so slightly? Would we find ourselves shifting in our seats and turning our eyes and thoughts to something other than each other? If there is food, perhaps it should have nothing whatsoever to do with me or you, food which has been purchased from a pretty boy or girl in a smart shop, though that too might be dampening, the lack of interest, effort. Even if the food is too wonderful and exotic for me to have attempted to make, offering you a precooked meal seems a bit like a trick, like cheating and cheating is not attractive unless it is clever and dramatic, the way it's portrayed in films and plays. In life it's small, mean and grubby.

The weather is good and it might be better to be outdoors although – as you'll have noticed – as soon as the sun shines, the world is crammed with courting couples and families milling around whatever green space they can find. All these other attached people might be a bit distracting, and the public setting might feel a bit obvious, contrived; strolling among so many composite blocks of humanity, maintaining a suitable, single distance... maybe not.

Thinking can get in the way, can't it, so once I've sorted out my thoughts enough but not too much, I'll slip you to the back of my mind, pop you into my mental glory-hole. If you could look inside, you'd see my most cherished moments all piled in together, squirrelled away, comforters to bring out on cold dark days when I can't see beyond my own blanket of boredom. Don't worry, I'm very greedy when it comes to cherished moments; I'll share them with nobody, not even you.

To think that such an amazing thing can happen in what can't by the sounds of it, be a very interesting place. Prairie, pampas, steppe, veldt. A whole lot of nothing much. A landscape of absence. But maybe absence meets the conditions, maybe a certain level of lack is required.

Friends, some of whom are familiar with the not-so-cherished moments of my life, have not been informed. (You, I promise, won't hear about those mostly minor calamities; there will be no sob stories, no confessions, above all not even the slightest hint of desperation because that would set up a different kind of circuit; one of sympathy, need.) I have managed to avoid any mention of you. Friends, I know too well, would gulp down all the details that I was willing to provide – as if they were olives, peanuts, popcorn – concerning your looks, personality, politics, bank balance and, of course, marital status. Married or divorced are now the most likely options. And then there would be the inevitable if tacit speculation on other intimate details. Friends would shuffle the facts and build up their own fancy-enhanced images of you, which I'm sure would be nothing at all like mine. They'd pass judgement. I don't mean to be hard on my friends – I love them dearly most of the time – but I've learned from past mistakes that it's not always beneficial to listen to advice. I can go into a day feeling briefly, recklessly engaged in it, until some good advice is poured in my ear and blights my little bud of hope.

So I have been keeping you a secret. There have been times when I've been tempted to slip a *By the way* into the many and interminable conversations about other people's husbands, wives, lovers, children, into which I find myself dragged like a recalcitrant mule. There have been times when I've had the desire to mention ever so casually that, even in the emotional desert – which, it's assumed, my industrious, single life has been for a little too long – between you and me, if the conditions are met, a literal, visible charge just might – as can happen in other, similarly monotonous landscapes – crackle and leap across the void.

The Worst of It

HE NAMED HIS son Freedom because that was what he wanted for him. The boy would wake when he was good and ready, wash, eat and sleep according to nobody's schedule but his own, roam wherever his childish fancy took him. He would have the horizon at his fingertips. And like his father, he'd go barefoot whenever possible. Folks might not like it, those who reckoned that what was needed in raising a boy was rules and training.

– Ain't no dog, Larry Myrtle would say, picking a strand of tobacco out of his beard.

It was tough on Laura Jean, her husband's free-thinking. Laura Jean liked things neat and tidy and nothing out of the ordinary, nothing for folks to notice. Freedom ran about town barefoot and unkempt, leaving in his wake a trail of disapproving glances. It shouldn't be, people said, not in these modern times, there was no need. When the boy gashed his toe on a broken bottle and spilled blood all along the sidewalk, a storekeeper, who didn't give his name, called up welfare and reported Freedom's shoeless roamings to the authorities.

The following week a stiff-backed, skinny young man appeared at Larry's door, dressed in a pale blue suit and black, shiny shoes. It was a hot spring morning. The young man's feet were damp and swollen. His shoes pinched. He was kept standing on the gravel path by the father while he related the complaint. He tried to see past the bearded, barefoot man picking his teeth with a penknife but Larry – if his feet weren't in motion – had the habit of swaying from side to side, and what with the heat, the glare and all, the welfare worker didn't get a chance to check out the interior.

– You folks down at county buildings, you think wildness and badness is the same thing, s'that what you're tellin me?

– Didn't say that, sir.

– Didn't say you did, boy. Just doing a little personal surmising.

– Going barefoot is a health hazard, Mr Myrtle, sir.

– Somebody say my boy sick?

– Said he'd cut his foot and been bleeding all over the joint.

The young man scratched the bristly back of his neck, looked down at his pointy-toed shoes.

– Guess you wanna see him.

– Guess I do, sir.

Larry turned on his heels and called on the boy who charged through the hall, butted his father in the gut, straightened up, grinned briefly and held out a grubby hand to the welfare worker.

– Howdy, said the boy, and shook the stranger's hand gravely.

Since he was tiny Freedom had never been keen on scissors anywhere near his hair so he'd got to grow it long, like a girl's, got to keep his tumble of blonde curls, even though Larry knew – he'd seen with his own eyes – what happened to faggots, hippies, niggers, newcomers and anyone else who didn't qualify, whose face didn't fit. It wasn't pretty but then not too much about the town was pretty, except the view of the ocean. But the boy was still young, there was time enough to cut his hair.

Freedom stood on the stoop. His eyes – the same fierce blue as his mother's – narrowed into glittering slits against the sunlight. He was wearing nothing but a pair of loose canvas shorts, streaked, like his legs, with dirt. His skin was brown as a peanut, his slight body hard and muscular, more like the build of a healthy adolescent than a six-year-old. His teeth were strong, white and even, his toes long and straight. The welfare worker could see no sign of a festering wound.

– Y'oughta give up them things, said the boy, pointing at the young man's shoes. Leastways when it's hot. Them things is pure wicked to toes.

He wiggled his own toes, making them tap out a rhythm on the planks, then sprung onto his hands, throwing his legs above his head.

The sun was beating down on the welfare worker's neck which was reddening above his collar. Nobody was inviting him into the shade of the porch. It must be near lunchtime. He was hungry. His schedule for the day was tight. It didn't look like he was going to get a damn thing settled here. He was ready to go. He'd put in a preliminary report and send out a letter.

Laura Jean came round the side of the house and picked her way across the gravel. She was wearing dark glasses, a skimpy white sun-dress and red, high-heeled sandals. She stopped on the driveway.

– Sellin somethin?

– No ma'am.

– Bible boy?

– Nope.

– Look like a bible boy to me.

Her mouth was smiling but the welfare worker couldn't see her eyes, couldn't see if they were smiling too. He wanted to see her eyes, wanted to know what her eyes were doing. He'd had a rough morning and this woman was a change from the lank-haired, slack-bodied, foul-mouthed mothers he'd called on earlier. She took a couple of steps towards him and he watched her hips sway, just a fraction, just enough.

The welfare worker pushed up the cuff of his jacket, pulling the shirt with it exposing the watch.

– Well, I guess, he said, raising his clipboard to his chest like a shield, Better be getting along now. Be seeing you, Mr Myrtle, sir.

– The hell you will, boy, said Larry, as the welfare worker crunched down the drive to his car.

Larry had lived in town all his life but apart from Laura Jean and the boy he paid it scant attention, took no part in its activities. The boat was what he gave his attention to. On the boat he felt real, whole, in control. He'd breathe in and feel the air hit the base of his lungs, taste the weather on his tongue, feel the heat or chill on his eyelids, the wind on the wings of his ears, on his spit-wet finger. He'd hunt the fish like someone possessed, dropping nets round the clock, go four, five, six nights without sleep, nothing to keep him going but strong sweet coffee, candy bars and Willie Nelson crooning and crackling. Without making mistakes. Sometimes his eyes closed at the wheel and sometimes he saw things that weren't really there but he and the ocean got along.

He and the ocean had a fine arrangement, as relationships go, plenty of variety, a fair-and-foul-weather romance. He loved her from his scalp to his toes, with their yellowed horny nails, toes which would stretch and spread on board and curl up on shore. Like his mind. His mind and his toes were very similar, if you were looking for connections; if you were the kind of person who needed to make connections. If you were like Larry Myrtle. When he was thinking, his toes responded. He could gauge the weather in his mind through his feet. It was a pity people didn't like him walking into bars and restaurants barefoot, but the God's honest truth was that his feet weren't so good to look at, and even though he always ordered the chef's special and tipped excessively, he was rarely made welcome.

It was the only real physical difference that he noticed, the curling and uncurling of his toes. Of course he rocked around like anyone else after a long sea trip and fell out of bed on his first night ashore, unless he slept out back in the hammock. Laura Jean had never taken kindly to this, in fact she got kinda cold and quiet and hard inside when he picked up his sleeping bag from the woodshed, kissed her cheek and wandered out to sleep under the stars, to be where he felt at home.

The house was confusing. It wasn't big – though room enough to satisfy Laura Jean – but it had too many doors. Sometimes he felt lost in his own home and called on Freedom to help him out. Mom's gone and changed things around again, one of them would say, although what was different wasn't easy to tell. Laura Jean kept the place like a showpiece in the mall. Unless she was mad at Larry and then she let it go right to hell. Thing was, only Laura Jean could give a damn about mess. The boy enjoyed the change of scenery, incorporated the household jumble into his games. Larry couldn't care less about the house. But he did care about Laura Jean, cared deeply and with an intensity which alarmed and saddened him.

They'd met up north. He'd been fishing off the New England coast for the summer. When the boat was docked – to unload the catch and stock up for the next trip – Larry and the rest of the crew slept on board and ate in town. After so much time cooped up together, the men liked to get off on their own. She'd been waitressing in a diner – Utility Lunch the place was called, a cheap, clean place which lived up to its name and didn't give itself no fancy airs. Larry's habit was never to eat at the same place twice but he broke it to sit and watch the tall, even-featured girl waiting on tables at Utility Lunch. It was the way she moved across the floor that he noticed first. Even when she was carrying a tray she walked straight and easy, unhurried, her feet noiselessly skimming the floor. Grace was what came to mind. Fluid grace.

It was soothing to watch her, like someone was massaging his eyelids, easing away the sting from too much looking at water and too little sleeping. Just sitting there was good, watching her moving back and forth. Better than hunting women in the bars. He drank more coffee than was good for him so he could hang out a bit longer, so he could hear her giggle lightly as the steam flushed up into her face, so he could smell her and look at her face up close. She smelled of honeysuckle and hamburger and coffee. Here eyes were bright and clear, her hair a downy blonde which looked natural. She didn't use much make-up, only a touch of pink on her lips, and a little dark stuff around the eyes, just enough to set off the blue of them.

Sometimes he still had the feeling that if he closed his eyes, if he stopped watching over Laura Jean, she'd vanish. They didn't make much sense as man and wife. Everything about Laura Jean was careful, refined, and smooth. She took great care of her appearance even though she didn't go anyplace much. She showered twice a day, waxed her legs religiously, pressed her clothes until they were sharp enough to stand up on their own. She might let the house go, but never herself.

Offshore, Larry caught more fish than any of the other local skippers and it was all for her and the boy, to make them more comfortable. At home, he never let himself go overboard on booze or drugs, fixed what needed fixing about the house and spent all his free time with the boy. But no way could he look smart. He hated a razor and a buttoned-up collar more than most things, more than the way people squinted at his toes and his long, pointed teeth, more than walking down the hot street in sunshine and hearing spurts of laughter at his back – dirty, filthy laughter, his wife's name spat amongst all that filth. But they were only bored boys with nothing better to do and maybe he'd been the same. He didn't remember. Didn't remember much from his boyhood, didn't remember much about then. He'd made himself forget it, scrubbed at the memory until it had come up clean and raw, like a deck, empty and chafing and ready for the next catch.

He was a good husband but he was never what Laura Jean would have wanted, if she'd really sat down and thought about it. He didn't look right. He didn't speak right and he didn't speak enough. Laura Jean liked company. He was away more than home and when he was home he didn't say a whole lot. But the worst of it was how much he loved her. He loved her so much he was in constant fear of losing her, of pushing her away by some wrong move, word, look. His love for her made him frightened to go near her. At sea he imagined them together in every which way but when it came to the real thing, to seeing her lying between crisp white sheets all grace and smoothness, the nearness, the scent of real warm flesh made him panic, clutch her roughly, press hard against her, inside her, fuck her in an ugly, terrified frenzy. Afterwards he felt like a criminal.

Laura Jean reapplied her lipstick, combed her hair, threw a light jacket over her sun-dress and picked up the car keys. Larry was sitting at the table, scratching out his list of supplies in his cramped, childish hand, the letters rocking and rolling across the page. His toes were in knots. A complete list was important. A simple omission, like salt or sugar or cigarettes, could make for serious problems. He'd never taken drink on board, not since Billy Boy went over the side and got sliced in two. Meals, sleep and porn were the only diversions available. A good dinner counted for a lot, was something to look forward to and something to keep you going. The porn was for the crew. Single boys, mostly. They got kinda restless.

Because of the time of year, late spring, he was heading up north again, staying as long as there were fish to catch, which might be most of the summer. Since he'd become a family man, since he had Laura Jean and the boy to miss, to pine for, the summer fishing was something he dreaded, something he worked himself to the bone to get over with as fast as possible.

Last year his entire crew walked out on him after only two trips. He just pushed them – and himself more than anyone – too damn hard, pushed the boys – and they were good boys too, that was the truth – pushed them to the point where they held out against him, told him to shove his catch, put his life on ice, told him he was turning into a crazy person, a Goddamn mad Ahab and they wouldn't work for no crazy person, wouldn't drive themselves to an early grave. Big enough bucks were made taking things a mite more easy. Larry knew it, knew he asked too much. But every day away from Laura Jean pained him so much he couldn't, wouldn't slow up for fear another day would be what did it, what took her from him.

– How many days now? said the boy, pulling on Larry's arm.
  – Three more breakfasts.
  – Wanna come, Dad.
  Larry looked up from his list and ran a rough, chapped hand through the boy's curls.
  – So who's gonna look after Laura Jean for Larry Myrtle if it ain't Freedom?
  – I guess. Guess I can take care of it.

As they drove downtown, Laura Jean began asking about the welfare worker. Mostly she was trying to figure out who had called him about the boy, like it would be better to know, to know where she stood, to know which stores to avoid. It wasn't so easy for Laura Jean to shut off from the talk. She had to live with it, after all. She was there living with it every day he wasn't around. He didn't know a whole lot about who she spent time with. She'd mention a few girlfriends, mothers she met for coffee or beer or cook-outs with the kids. But no men, she never mentioned men.

When Larry first met Laura Jean, she had a real low opinion of men. He couldn't quite figure it out but it seemed like he'd got her on his side because he'd been so hooked he'd asked for nothing, nothing at all. For sure that was how things worked out between them, when he asked for nothing. But now it was different, now he couldn't keep things clear in his head.

Out on the open water, he'd be standing at the wheel, watching the sway and swell of the waves, the sunlight leaping on the tips like flames. Fire on water. Flames which did not burn, did not consume. The ocean would not be consumed, would always be in motion. And constant motion was like a gentle hand against his face – smooth, light fingers stroking his eyelids.

It couldn't be enough for a girl like Laura Jean, on her own with the boy for weeks on end. The girl liked company and got precious little of it. He had the crew at least, day and night. Somebody to yell at across the deck. Didn't get down to much of a conversation but a few words here and there had always been enough for him. When the boy went to bed at night didn't Laura Jean feel lonesome? Didn't she ache to get out, to go running down the driveway in her high heels, in the dark, over the gravel, to something, somebody, somebody who didn't seize up at the sight of her and grip her arm on the street so hard his fingers left bruises? He couldn't see how she wasn't eaten up with restlessness, couldn't see how nobody wouldn't come by offering some personal consolation.

As usual, the days before sailing eased by in a flurry of preparations and leave-takings. Larry was about to try and fix some problem with the bathroom door that Laura Jean had just remembered about and couldn't wait all summer, when the phone rang. Laura Jean took the call. Larry was out in the shed picking up his tools. He went looking for Laura Jean to find out the exact problem and saw her talking on the phone, one foot resting against the wall.

Ten minutes later he came back again and found her still

talking. She had a glass of red wine in her hand, the receiver cradled against her ear, head thrown back so he could see her throat, see the wine going down and the laughter bubbling up. And it seemed to him that it was the first time he'd heard her laugh since way back when she poured him all those cups of coffee in Utility Lunch. She still smiled a lot, she had an easy, open smile; but laugh? It sounded strange, different from the light, girlish laugh he had been so taken by. It sounded dirty.

– Gonna be all night? he said. Laura Jean mouthed something and waved him away.

By the time they sat down to eat, the pie crust was charred and the vegetables were soggy. Freedom had taken himself off to bed after bullying a promise out of Larry that next summer or for damn sure the summer after, they'd rent a place in New England. Laura Jean and the boy would drive up and spend the summer in port. And fishing. Next summer or the one after for sure the boy would get to go fishing.

They ate without speaking. Larry looked up from his plate at Laura Jean. Laura Jean was looking out of the window. Her mouth was open slightly, her lips moist and stained purple from the wine. The clock on the dresser had a loud, angry tick. Had it always sounded like that? How come he'd never noticed it before? In a couple of hours he'd have to sleep, to put in some rest but now, now he had to get through to his wife, had to speak to her, to stop listening to the time ticking away, to his heart racing, had to get across the ocean of silence welling up between them...

– Laura Jean... Honey... Something happening out there?

Laura Jean turned away from the window.

– Couldn't you use a damn toothpick like any other person?

Larry put the knife down on the table.

– Who called on the phone?

– That welfare boy.

– I was telling Freedom we could rent a house up north next summer. You reckon?

Laura Jean looked down at her sandal dangling from her

tanned foot. Her toenails were scarlet.

– Honey...

– You know I hate that name, so why in God's name d'ya haveta keep on using it?

The clock again. The tick, the tap of Laura Jean's sandal against the table-leg, the clockhand turning one two three circles, a late bird twittering home to roost, the tightness in his chest, the scratching of his toenails against his ankle.

– Chrissakes Larry, d'ya haveta be such a goddamn peasant?

She looked straight at him, eyes flashing, no trace of a smile anywhere. She'd said these exact same words before, but with a smile, a kiss on the ear. Laura Jean had always preferred his ear to his mouth. His mouth was kinda hard to get near, buried in all that beard.

– Didn't never seem like it bothered you before.

– Maybe you just didn't notice, Maybe there's a whole lot you didn't notice.

– Like what?

– Like nothing.

Larry poured wine into Laura Jean's glass and then his own. He raised his glass to his mouth and drank. And drank. Laura Jean sipped and smoked and looked past him out of the window where the darkness was seeping across the glass.

– Bathroom door's all fixed. Gonna haveta tell Freedom to go easy on them fixtures.

– Tell him yourself. He don't pay me no heed. Boy's getting too big and wild for all this do-as-you-please, Larry.

– That what your welfare boy been saying?

– Maybe. Maybe I just figured it for myself.

Here in the house, with nothing moving except time, with the table solid and still, anchored between them, that was what it was, the lack of movement, that was all, if the house were rocking he'd know where he was, what to do, but he was always off-balance, always needing to right himself, to square himself up.

– So what's the story with the welfare boy?
    – What d'ya think? Shoes for Freedom. A haircut. Schoolin.
    – Took him a hell of a time to tell you that.
    – …
    – Got a hankering for him, have you?
    – Chrissakes, Larry. he was calling about *our son*.

Laura Jean stood up and began to clear the table. Larry watched as, with the old professional flair, she stacked the plates on her arm and moved to and fro between the sink and the table with the same fluid grace. But no smile. She splayed her fingers and scooped up the empty wine glasses. Larry caught hold of her, pulled her to him and pressed his face into the dark cloth of her blouse. He rocked against her, tried to picture her pouring coffee and smiling up at him through the steam. But he couldn't hold the picture in his mind, couldn't hold it against the sight of her talking on the phone to the welfare worker.

The first catch of the season swings up from the stern. The crammed, seething bag hangs over the deck while the gates are hooked. The line released, the net opened, the deck is knee-deep in the spoils of the sea. No matter how many times Larry goes hunting fish he's always disgusted by the first sight of the catch. Like something out of hell it was, an orgy of thrashing, flailing, gorging, a whole mess of sea life a-slipping and a-sliding every which way, eating, being eaten and all the while suffocating. Heads in mouths, tails in mouths, guts spilling through gills, eggs sacs bursting and being swallowed up by the nearest free set of jaws.

The boys are already busy with their staves, spearing trash fish and kicking them through the slips. Larry wades into the thick of the catch to check it out. Too many frigging skate. One has sunk its teeth into his boot – a big one, belly up. He hates skate. Their sleek, grey backs he could cope with but belly up there were like accusations: those pale undersides, the shocked, pink, throbbing mouths, the soft exposed genitals. The Goddamn deck is covered in pale kite-shaped skate, covered in accusations.

The wound where his stave went in is oozing dark blood but the fish won't let go its grip of his boot. With his free foot Larry kicks at its head. The skate slaps, twists, hangs on. Larry raises his stave and brings it down again, this time between the eyes. The jaw jerks open. He yanks his boot free, sluices through the blood and guts and slime, trying to fix his mind on cod and flounder but all he sees are splayed white bellies, pink mouths, soft, defenceless, skate. If he could just fix his mind on water, motion, the harmony of the waves, things might settle, he'd maybe get back his balance, the air could clear. But in his mind is fog and deep water and there's no way of telling.

Every day I count wasted in which
there has been no dancing.
Nietzche

A Day Without Dancing

THE COURTYARD HAS a way of catching voices and flinging them around, of magnifying every sound so, though it's a quiet place – some days as quiet as the village graveyard with its proliferation of glazed, everlasting flowers – if people are around, I know about it. Inside the L-shaped building where I wait for my night visitors, sounds roll down the wood-floored corridors; boot heels, keys scraping in locks, coughs. It's as well that the apartments have been modernised and the beds are plain, new creaky affairs from the IKEA outside Paris. I wouldn't want the history of this place crawling out of my mattress; better it skittles in from a corridor or drifts through the open window and its pale leaf-printed curtains, mirroring the garden.

All the occupied apartments and studios look inwards onto the courtyard, giving the impression that the artists prefer to huddle together, to look out at each other or down the long slim garden to the river and turn their backs on the sleepy village. But it would be unfair to say that the locale is of no interest to them; every day they make their forays into the outside world;

they shop for bread, meat, stamps, wine, and drop into the Hôtel de la Terrasse to drink coffee, cognac, pastis, to hear French spoken and put aside the tongues they have brought with them. And when the quaint delights of the village are exhausted, there are plenty of walks, most of which involve the river or the canal.

The roads are to be avoided; for such a rural place the traffic is heavy and hostile to pedestrians. This wasn't so when my night visitors were physically in residence. No cars and motorbikes then, no woodcutters with chain-saws tearing holes in tranquil afternoons, just horses clopping around and carriage wheels trundling over cobbles. Armed with notebooks and palettes, the writers recorded walks in the forest, the painters propped up easels all over the place and reinvented the river, the willows and washhouses, the mill, and – endlessly – each other.

Nowadays the artists might as well be on the moon; the landscape and those who inhabit it rarely feature in anybody's work. I'm aware that depicting the picturesque has been passé for several generations but to wilfully ignore one's surroundings, is it not wasteful? I try not to pry but sometimes I wonder what this lot do with their time. And my suggestions. I'm beginning to think they don't hear anything I say, or have decided to ignore me. I know this is nonsense, a muse must carry on for eternity, available to all comers, but I can't help hoping that I might be able to retire. Sometimes I forget that they are here at all, sometimes I imagine no living person is here, that I'm alone in the building with only my night visitors for company.

August (Mr Strindberg) is with me now. I need my wits about me when August appears. He was always hard work but now… He shows me a photograph, of Verlaine on his deathbed. The poet's body is propped up on pillows, face turned to the wall, a spray of flowers at the head and feet.

– You see the animal, big animal, on Verlaine's stomach?

August's eyes are glassy.

– What kind of animal?

– Ach! Questions! Animal, big animal, there. And there, on the floor, little... *djavül*...

The photograph is very old of course and faded. I hold it under my swan-necked IKEA bed light and look again; the floral wallpaper in the background looks dusty and indistinct, the pattern disappearing in places but there's no animal or *djavül*; August is hallucinating. Among other things, he has become infected by the fashion for dabbling in alchemy. If only he would turn his face to the sun instead of glowering into darkness all the time, he would have no need for such nonsense. He's clean, well dressed, attractive in an intense kind of way but so gloomy. I wish I knew some good jokes. Gloomy visitors have a way of making me feel too responsible for them, unlike cheery ones. August's gloom hangs over me like a punishment.

– Why don't you go up to Paris, I say. Enjoy yourself for a change.

– Paris! Temptations! Too many temptations!

Everything here smells of anise; the detergent, the washing up liquid, the furniture polish, the sweets in their pretty tins, the drink, the food. It's pleasant at first but overpowering, eclipsing everything else; a bit like August, who is at the window, smoking as always, looking out into the courtyard and scowling. Tonight the artists are sitting out on the patio, eating and drinking. It's a mild night; the spring breeze carries the tang of sap and bonhomie. The candles twitch faintly, faces around the table bloom as the yellow light flows over them.

– This sitting around, talking, this discussing, for what?

– They're having a party, August. Ramon's wife Ritta has just arrived from Spain.

– Madrid or Barcelona?

– I don't know. It's a welcome party.

– Welcome! For what she come?

– To be with Ramon, I suppose. To stop him being lonely.

– Nobody stop lonely. No wife, no husband stop lonely.

– Perhaps it's nicer being lonely together.

– Lonely always hell. Always, always hell.

August's line in conversation could wear down anyone's spirit, even that of a seasoned muse like myself. But even though he is glaring down at the welcome party for Ritta, he is interested all the same.

– Why he sit like stone? Why no dance?

– Nobody else is dancing.

– But his wife she come.

– Yes... Did you ever dance, August?

– In dreams only. My wife she dance. My wife make me lonely.

I expect August's wife has been making a bit too much of an impression. She's a striking woman who thrives on attention and – being an actress – knows how to get it. If August won't listen to me, a woman who keeps him on his toes is a good thing. And if she makes him greedy for her glances, too bad.

– Are you a good dancer in your dreams?

– I don't remember. But you see this little wife of Ramon, she is so happy, throwing her smile to everybody. But he, he look at his feet. You see, you see this?

– I see nothing from my bed.

– You get up. You look.

– I've seen her already, August. She seems nice.

– Nice. Nice! What is this nice?

August is right about the dancing. More dancing is what this place needs. Peace is an airy thing but the silence which hangs over the tiled patio and its primrose yellow coach lights is heavy, suffocating as smog. My night visitors have little time for silence. Of course they spend some of their time with no one but me whispering in their ears but otherwise they eat and drink and talk, suck the juices and chew the bones of each day as if it might be their last. And I am right about August; he's drawn to Ramon's wife exactly because – like his own wife – she doesn't save her personality for the conjugal bedroom.

Perhaps August sees himself in Ramon. Ramon has been on a ten-day bender. A friendly and philosophical drunk, he tacked in and out of the Hôtel de la Terrasse declaring that he'd solved the problem of existence, found the key to life in the swaying bright sail of alcohol. He sobered up only just in time for his wife's arrival. Everybody knew about Ramon's drinking; he stopped the others in the street to tell them about it. But now his wife is here and he's better; subdued, withdrawn, but better. As soon as Ritta arrived, they had sex, to reggae music. Accompanied by Toots and the Maytals a few moans of pleasure filtered into the courtyard. I expect they'll be at it again later, making up for lost time.

Edvard's wife isn't due to arrive for some weeks yet but Edvard is a more self-sufficient man, tidy as a well-tended allotment, amusing himself – and occasionally others – with esoteric jokes. Of them all, Edvard has most faith in me. In his quiet, meditative way he has been reducing the world to what he sees as its essentials: coloured rings in grey, blue and orange, the colour scheme of the centre. There is a part of Edvard's imagination which he conceals even from me, possibly the most interesting part. It is linked to an earlier period in his life, to the songs of Jacques Brel and Edith Piaf.

Jan is missing his wife badly. Though she writes every day, he moons about his room, agonising about whether his opera about the fall of the Berlin Wall will ever be completed. Self-doubt and the weight of the past press on Jan's rounded shoulders and if, during his inspirational walks, he must cross paths with any of the others, he becomes hunched and anxious as a fugitive. Like Ramon, I think he too may be more fond of the bottle than of me.

August is really more interested in the wider picture and is pleased to discover that in the village at least, things haven't changed much. The old washhouses on the riverbank are still there, though now they shelter small boats or have become weekend picnic huts for folk from the city. The villagers are still squat blocks of humanity who move slowly, talk fast and put on white shirts for Sunday. The café clientele lurches from one inebriated generation to another and the butcher's wife is still a pink, fleshy woman with muscular legs, dainty feet and a trilling, metallic *bonjour*. On the mediaeval bridge, in the afternoon sun, old men and children throw bread to the river birds and young men, caps pulled low over their eyes, pretend to fish. August wants to know if there are still coypu in the river. There are; at night they swim beneath the bridge, noiseless black blurs which barely ripple the water. Satisfied, August nods and departs.

Laughter rises from the patio. Edvard has told a joke which for once everybody understands. Even Ramon is laughing, his deep voice creaking like a wheelbarrow. The meal is finished and the cleaning up, or, as August has it, *the interminable toil of keeping life's dirt at bay*, has begun. There is a great deal of cleaning done here. Sweeping and soaping, sponging and mopping; in this the artists work as a team, a busy, efficient, wholehearted team. If only they could approach their art so clearly, cleanly.

– You are resting again, you lazy girl!

I always feel cheered up when Carl visits. (Carl Larsson, painter of landscapes and domestic interiors.) Those apple cheeks, straw-yellow hair, eyes like hard blue sweets. When I tell him about my difficulties with the new crowd, he chuckles like a cartoon Santa.

– You no tempt them anymore, sweetmeat? You no find some little hooks for to pull them out? Look, you can do like this, very easy...

With a bent pin, Carl coaxes a snail out of its shell and holds it up. For once the pungency of garlic outdoes the anise.

– You want?

– I don't eat anymore.

– Ahhh. So you think you can do when we cannot?

– Muses are a special case. Anyway, I don't like snails.

– Some chocolate maybe?

Carl pulls a bag of broken chocolate from the pocket of his smock.

– Save it for a rainy day, Carl.

– *Ja, ja*, says Carl, momentarily pensive.

Carl really doesn't need my nagging when the sun is out. He's up with the lark then, and out on the riverbank, throwing himself on his heaped palette like a ravenous man at a feast. Only in the rain when all the colour is drained from the landscape and the village becomes a daguerreotype of itself, he's restless and grumpy, clomping down the narrow corridor on thunderous clogs, slapping the walls with his broad, blunt hands. He knows that I can't control the climate. He knows too that there's plenty else for him to do indoors at the moment, like building a crib, for example. Carl is about to become a father, an event he's anticipating with glorious exuberance, but as yet he hasn't got around to much in the way of practical application. His wife Karin has almost reached term and Carl is still bellyaching about the rain. If only I could tell him that in time, rain and fatherhood will serve him well.

The candles have been blown out, the table cleared. Everyone has moved inside except Ramon who is attempting to plant a baguette in the middle of the garden. Dear oh dear, am I really here for this? Jan appears, carrying a neatly tied bag of rubbish to the wheelie bin in the courtyard. With this simple purpose in mind, he looks almost cheerful. On his return to the kitchen he stops politely to look at Ramon's bread plant. Jan would prefer to have wrapped up the baguette in cling film and put it in the fridge for breakfast but he smiles anyway.

While Ritta organises coffee and Calvados, Ramon wanders down to the river to commune with the drowned moon. Still sick from his last drinking binge and fighting the longing to joining the others in a nightcap, the seconds stretch to eternity. In this he has my sympathy; for me too, time is always a tormentor. Edvard is ceremoniously laying a tray with little glasses, plain but pleasing cups and saucers, a plate of dark chocolate. A distant, private smile crinkles his tidy face as he carries the tray through to the sitting room which, for too long, has only been the meeting place of ghosts. Orange light spills into the courtyard as Ritta pours coffee and Edvard, enjoying his role of the perfect waiter, hands round Calvados. I hear L's cough. (Louis, RLS, Stevenson, you'll know the name in some form.) It's deep tonight, like an axe splitting his ribs. Sometimes he changes his mind and doesn't call, just flits by the door and then I know things are bad. But tonight – I'm happy to say – he's visiting; pale, bright-eyed and shockingly slight. I pull out a chair for him, padding it with pillows from my bed. In spite of the sickness eating away at his body, L's mind is quicksilver. If the artists downstairs could see the dancing light in his eyes, his pitiful bird bones... And now he has met the American woman, he is a-flutter with love. Soon love and sickness will take him far from my not too comfortable armchair. I miss him already.

– You look well, I say, though he doesn't. He never does.

– I'm grand. On top of the world. This woman...

– I know.

– I can't describe the feeling, queanie, it's like something growing inside me, something sprouting and spreading ...

L looks down at his lap and laughs.

– Don't I do that for you anymore?

He laughs again, adjusts his muffler, shifts in his seat; he is never comfortable in one position for long.

– You know that without you, I'd be a nail lacking a hammer. But it's not quite the same.

I expect L to be too caught up with his own heart to be interested in my problems with the artists but no, he wants to know all about them and listens intently to my reports on everyone's lack of progress, pulling thoughtfully on his inconsequential moustache.

– I don't envy you, queanie. A deil o a trauchle they're gien ye.

L begins coughing again, his chest snapping to his knees at each expectoration. He covers his mouth with a snowy handkerchief. It's not long now before he'll begin to spit blood. He pulls himself out of the chair and slips away. I can hear him coughing long after he leaves. I forgot to ask him about August's hallucinations.

From the window at the top of the stairs I can see the street. Already the Hôtel de la Terrasse has closed its shutters though the same clutch of drinkers will still be inside. Directly above the boulangerie, the first-floor windows are wide open but the room is in darkness; I'm beginning to wonder whether L has been imagining things; his head is so full of stories that sometimes he confuses his internal life with the world outside.

I lean on the window ledge, breathing in the anise-scented floor polish. The staircase is original. On the top step of the broad, deeply-scored oak boards a crude star has been gouged out – August? The flooring in the upstairs corridor is new, carefully stained to blend in with the staircase. At the join, woodworm has eaten away part of the step leaving a gash of darkness between old wood and new.

Ramon and Ritta are talking quietly in their room, Edvard is listening to Piaf regretting nothing for the third time this evening. From Jan's room, as always, no sound escapes. It's now several nights since the welcome dinner for Ritta and life has returned to its original state of strained solitude. Still, something may have come from the get-together. Ramon has stopped shaking. The morning after the welcome dinner, Jan threw himself into an aria about disintegration, though, by dinnertime, it went in the wheelie bin along with the cigarette ends and the empties. Edvard has begun work on something which, he explained to me, represents a transitional state between need and desire. To my jaded eye, it looks like more coloured rings.

Above the boulangerie, lights are switched on and the small room leaps out into the darkness. Red and green spots beam inwards from the open window creating a suspended, open-air stage. A young voice begins to hum, there's some shuffling of feet and then he appears, just as L described him, a boy of eleven or twelve, stepping forward into the light, his serious eyes looking straight ahead into the darkness, silky black hair flashing red and green as he moves around behind the open window. One arm is buried up to the elbow in a red cotton devil complete with rubber horns and a long, coiling tail. On the other, a mermaid sways. The devil snakes towards the mermaid, the mermaid backs off, head bobbing, hair like bleached seaweed clinging to pearly breasts. As the devil moves into the green spot his grin turns luminous and lewd. The mermaid shimmies, blushes from head to fish tail. While he adjusts the lights, the boy drapes his puppets over the rusty, ornate railing. Still humming, his voice clear and sweet, he intensifies the red spot and removes a yellow filter, turning green back to blue. When he's satisfied with his alterations, he slips his hands back into the puppets and glances out into the darkness. I wave. A mermaid and a devil wave back. The boy takes up a new position, hums another melody. He barely looks at what he's doing; it's not his eyes which guide his movements but some inner compass. The devil writhes in a red hell. The mermaid floats in a pool of celestial blue. For the first time in a long, long while I feel inspired.

Some other books published by **Luath Press**

Lord of Illusions
Dilys Rose
1 84282 076 1 PB £7.99

Lord of Illusions is the fourth collection of short stories from award-winning Scottish writer Dilys Rose. Exploring the human condition in all its glory – and all its folly – *Lord of Illusions* treats both with humour and compassion.

Often wry, always thought-provoking, this new collection offers intriguing glimpses into the minds and desires of a diverse cast of characters; from jockey to masseuse, from pornographer to magician, from hesitant transvestite to far-from-home aid worker. Each of these finely crafted stories, with their subtle twists and turns, their changes of mood and tone, demonstrate the versatile appeal of the short story, for which Dilys Rose is deservedly celebrated.

Praise for Rose's other work:
A born professional
MURIEL SPARK

Although Dilys Rose makes writing look effortless, make no mistake, to do so takes talent, skill and effort.
THE HERALD

Rose is at her best – economical, moral and compassionate. THE GUARDIAN

Outlandish Affairs
Edited by Evan Rosenthal and Amanda Robinson
1 84282 055 9 PB £9.99

A plethora of bizarre and unusual questions arise when writers from both sides of the Atlantic – inspired by the multicultural nature of society – try to tackle the age old question of love.

When is a country singer gay and when is he straight?

Have you ever truly loved a seal?

Will *West Side Story* inspire the music of love to blossom?

Does an Icelandic strongman, semi-naked in a New York diner, do it for you?

Can Saddam Hussein be Prince Charming?

Have you ever dated anyone from another country, culture, world?

And if so, did sparks fly?

Discover in these stories what might happen when amorous encounters cross boundaries.

Details of these and other Luath Press titles are to be found at www.luath.co.uk

Luath Press Limited

committed to publishing well written books worth reading

LUATH PRESS takes its name from Robert Burns, whose little collie Luath (*Gael.*, swift or nimble) tripped up Jean Armour at a wedding and gave him the chance to speak to the woman who was to be his wife and the abiding love of his life. Burns called one of *The Twa Dogs* Luath after Cuchullin's hunting dog in *Ossian's Fingal*.
Luath Press was established in 1981 in the heart of Burns country, and is now based a few steps up the road from Burns' first lodgings on Edinburgh's Royal Mile. Luath offers you distinctive writing with a hint of unexpected pleasures.

Most bookshops in the UK, the US, Canada, Australia, New Zealand and parts of Europe, either carry our books in stock or can order them for you. To order direct from us, please send a £sterling cheque, postal order, international money order or your credit card details (number, address of cardholder and expiry date) to us at the address below. Please add post and packing as follows: UK – £1.00 per delivery address; overseas surface mail – £2.50 per delivery address; overseas airmail – £3.50 for the first book to each delivery address, plus £1.00 for each additional book by airmail to the same address. If your order is a gift, we will happily enclose your card or message at no extra charge.

Luath Press Limited
543/2 Castlehill
The Royal Mile
Edinburgh EH1 2ND
Scotland
Telephone: 0131 225 4326 (24 hours)
Fax: 0131 225 4324
email: gavin.macdougall@luath. co.uk
Website: www. luath.co.uk